SCANDAL'S SPLENDOR

Highland Heather Romancing a Scot: Castle Brides

Book Seven

Collette Cameron®

Attn: Permissions Coordinator
Blue Rose Romance® LLC
info@collettecameronbooks.com
eBook ISBN: 978-1-955259-99-6
Print Book ISBN: 978-1-955259-90-3
collettecameronbooks.com

FREE BOOK!

JOIN MY EXCLUSIVE MAILING LIST
Collette Cameron Newsletter

AND GET A FREE EBOOK!

https://collettecameronbooks.com/freegift

Plus Sneak Peeks, Giveaways, Contests, Exclusive Content, and More... P.S. I promise only good stuff ~ **no** spam!

CONTENTS

ONE

Scottish Highlands
A Miserable Stretch of Road

Early December 1818

G *od's bones!*
      "God above, save us."
"*Laird* have mercy on our souls."

Unlike the post chaise's other occupants, Seonaid Ferguson swallowed her alarmed yelp and wedging her back firmly into the corner, gripped the shabby seat with white-knuckled determination. Setting her jaw against the teeth-cracking ride, she took several measured breaths.

Stay calm.

The laboring coach tilted at an alarming angle before righting, once more ricocheting the four occupants about like billiard balls upon a felt tabletop.

More frightened shrieks and fervent petitions to the Almighty resounded within the closed confines as her timid mouse of a chaperon, Mrs. Thomasina Wetherby, clung to her with the tenacity of a barnacle on a rock.

This time, her pulse hammering in her ears, Seonaid, too, sent up a silent plea for protection.

Struggling to breathe, she commanded her heart to vacate her throat and return to its proper place at once. She didn't expect the palpitating organ to resume a regular rhythm while the chaise bucked and jerked like an unbroken stallion, but at least she could inhale a trifle easier.

Only when they reached the Hare's Foot Inn, would her pulse and breathing completely return to normal. *After a bracing cup of whisky-laced tea.* The chaise shuddered and groaned, and the wind shrieked furiously, doing its utmost to pummel the vehicle into tinder.

Perhaps two cups were in order.

More whisky than tea.

Face as white as the dense snow swirling about the sturdy coach and battering their courageous drivers, Mrs. Wetherby seized Seonaid's hand. Trembling, her button-sized pupils expanding in terror, the chaperone wept noisily and buried her face in Seonaid's shoulder.

Possessed with more fortitude, Una, Seonaid's abigail, clenched her hands and pressed her mouth into a thin, white-lipped line.

Arthur Fletcher, the dour-faced cleric sitting beside Una, clutched his prayer book and, eyes tightly shut, muttered unceasingly beneath his garlicky breath. A mixture of dirty wool, greasy hair, and worn, stinky leather wafted throughout the carriage's already musty interior each time he shifted the slightest.

Una scowled before angling her shoulder in his direction and deliberately pointing her nose in the opposite.

At the last stop, after Seonaid and her companions stretched their legs and ate a small repast, they'd prepared to board the chaise. Two passengers weren't continuing on to Craigcutty, and she'd quite anticipated a less crowded conveyance for the trip's remainder.

Until Reverend Fletcher dashed that hope.

Claiming he could only sit in the right, forward-facing seat lest he become ill, he proceeded to scramble into the vehicle first, practically shoving the women aside.

Once seated, a trio of critical gazes trained upon him, he fidgeted for a few awkward moments. Then, with an arrogant thrust of his weak chin, declared himself Craigcutty's new rector.

New rector?

Whatever happened to Reverend Wallace?

Seonaid's brother, Ewan McTavish, was *laird* of Craiglocky Keep and the surrounding lands and village, including Craigcutty. None of her family had mentioned anything about a new vicar in their letters. But then again, they'd no doubt believed her too occupied with enjoying her first Season to be interested in trivial matters from home.

Profoundly wrong.

On both accounts.

The Season had been an *experience* she'd prefer not repeat. Ever.

Shocked and saddened by the loss of Reverend Wallace, a beloved family friend, Seonaid had murmured a cursory greeting and quite forgot to mention her connection to the village.

A few minutes after the post chaise resumed its grueling journey, she'd been glad her manners had temporarily deserted her. Otherwise, she might've been obligated to attempt conversation with the terse cleric.

After he'd finally settled his gaunt frame into a corner and thoroughly scrutinized the women, he'd closed his eyes and either slept or prayed. The latter, aloud. Frequently and vehemently.

A ferocious wind gust rocked the coach, stealing Seonaid's breath and slamming her against the side. Her head smacked the window, and she winced as Mrs. Wetherby's ample girth rammed into her, pinning her against the holey padding.

Her companion's ongoing squeals muffled a crude noise that escaped the vicar and sounded suspiciously like a curse.

Gingerly touching her throbbing temple, Seonaid positioned herself more securely against the seat. Barring freezing first, bruises would cover her, head to hip.

The coach bounced again, and she flinched when a brick banged into her foot.

Make that bruised toes and ankles too.

Used for warming the passengers' feet, the bricks had long since grown cold. With the conveyance's labored movements, the bricks pelted back and forth, further scraping the scuffed floor and wreaking havoc on anything in their way.

How much farther to the posting house?

Would they reach the inn?

Not by coach, Seonaid feared, and walking in this snowstorm meant certain death. She rubbed the window's ice-covered glass, straining to see beyond the raging white.

Nature's wrath at her worst. And they were squarely in the middle of the blizzard. Too far along to turn 'round now, and God alone knew how much farther to their destination. Biting her lip, she closed her eyes for a moment against the panic squeezing her lungs.

This is what you get for being hasty and impulsive.

This was the first time she'd ever heaved good sense and caution aside, and look at the outcome. Surely the Hare's Foot must be nearby. Peering harder into the gloomy gray, she willed the posting house to appear amid the swirling, white dervish.

They'd traveled over three hours in this wretchedness. Though with her nerves stretched taut as a gossamer thread, Mrs. Wetherby's incessant whimpering, and the vicar's calamitous predictions, the duration seemed intolerably longer.

Pure folly to have traveled on after changing the team, but how could anyone have predicted the occasional pretty snowflake feathering from the sky would become a fierce winter storm, making the road virtually impassable?

Where was her bothersome *an dara shealladh* when she needed the second sight? Her fey or sight of a seer—whatever one wanted to call the prophetic episodes—plagued her frequently enough of late.

She had no control over the unsolicited visions, and more than once, she'd tried to stop an onset, to no avail. The images came without warning, whenever they chose, and often— though not always—portended something ominous.

Still, if she must endure the burden of the apparitions, as she had these past ten years, she would welcome helpful foretelling of horrid, blood-congealing snowstorms such as this.

Reverend Fletcher's gruff muttering drew her reluctant attention.

And warnings about smelly, uppish passengers too.

The chaise's rear wheels skidded, and outside, a harsh oath rent the weighty silence that accompanied heavy snowfall. How the drivers managed was beyond her. They must be near frozen through.

Accepting the Needhams' offer of their traveling chariot would've been wiser. The sleeker, cleaner conveyance made better time, and Seonaid could've avoided this inhospitable weather and Reverend Fletcher's trying company.

She hadn't wanted to inconvenience her hosts, though, and a fortnight without their main source of distance transportation would've been difficult. So, much to her regret, she'd declined their generous offer, hired a hack, and made arrangements to have her remaining possessions sent to Craiglocky later.

Another violent lurch toppled Reverend Fletcher's dilapidated Bible onto the floor. "Devil's work this frigid storm be, I tell ye."

Una grunted, and with a minute exasperated shake of her head, gathered her simple cloak tighter, aiming her irritated gaze ceiling-ward. Her periodic toe tapping revealed her nearly spent patience.

"Or an evil curse by one of Lucifer's handmaidens." Retrieving the cracked, leather-bound volume, the vicar's hooded, suspicion-filled hazel eyes focused on each woman in turn.

Coldness didn't cause the shudder puckering Seonaid's skin.

Fletcher certainly wasn't the jovial, kind Reverend Wallace. In fact, something peculiar lingered about the other clergyman—a mien she couldn't quite identify but made her leery, nonetheless.

Una's profuse auburn eyebrows vaulted skyward, and her full mouth jerked in incredulity at Fletcher's absurd declaration. Descended from Celts, she steadfastly observed many traditions and rituals the Kirk once considered pagan. A few Scots clerics still disapproved, although nowhere near the number as in England's Church.

To Seonaid's relief, her superstitious maid didn't scoff aloud. She just tapped her toes faster, pursed her lips, and exchanged a knowing glance with Seonaid. Observant and intelligent, Una had also elected to use discretion near the reverend.

If he learned of Seonaid's second sight, he'd not be the first to misinterpret it, or try to exploit her in the same manner as a gypsy fortune-teller or a parlor oddity.

Really, people could be utterly ignorant and ridiculous.

After one fey episode while in London, she'd received six invitations to entertain guests and perform readings the next day.

Readings, indeed. Claptrap.

Honestly, what did *le bon ton* think? She could glimpse inside their haughty heads, conjure a revelation, and recite it like a tidily penned eulogy or a snippet from a gossip rag?

"Why yes, Lady Clutterbuck.

"It's as obvious as those five wiry hairs protruding from your chin that you're a tenacious gossip who delights in spreading tattle with the same abandon as a farmer hurling slop to his hogs.

"And, my dear lady, given your propensity to stoutness, you really oughtn't to eat four maid of honor tarts whilst hiding in an alcove after you filled your plate three times during dinner."

Seonaid's parents would share the Needhams' outrage if they learned what Seonaid had been subjected to, and she supposed sympathy prompted the Needhams to yield to her decision to travel with only two female companions.

Mrs. Wetherby peeked from her lap robe's folds and squeaked, "Handmaidens, Vicar?"

Been ruminating on that mad assertion, had she? No doubt more bothersome dramatics would result.

"Aye, handmaidens, ye ken?" Caressing his Bible with his spindly glove-clad fingers, his reedy voice deepened eerily.

Wasn't there something in the Bible about daft fellows too?

"Sorceresses. Seers. Soothsayers. Witches. The good book"

—he pounded the Bible—"warns believers to beware of vile seductresses and their wicked wiles."

Yes. Definitely lacking in the upper works.

Harshness colored his last few strident words, and he stared intently at Seonaid.

At his denunciation, she arched a brow. Pray God no fey visions came upon her while in his company. In a blink, he'd have her tied to a stake and a blazing torch in his hand as he condemned her soul to hell.

"*Hmph*. And I believe it also says we're not to judge others, especially by their appearances or circumstances." Folding her arms across her substantial bosom, Una pinned him with a bland stare, despite the superior, darkling scowl he directed at her.

Ire flashed in Una's eyes, and she opened her mouth to speak again, but Seonaid gave a faint negative shake of her head.

For once, Una snapped her mouth shut without voicing her thoughts. Their situation was strained enough without a full-on argument in the confined space.

Reverend Fletcher's thin lips bent into a triumphant smirk.

Foolish man if he supposed his glare had silenced Una. She'd spared him a verbal lashing for Seonaid's sake. Given her mutinous expression, Una still longed to unleash her sharp tongue on him.

If he didn't cease, Seonaid might very well permit Una the privilege.

"I shall pray for our deliverance from this tempest." Bending his neck once more, he focused his reverent entreaties on calling God's wrath down upon Satan's daughters and condemning them to eternal hellfire and damnation.

He seemed unduly bloodthirsty for God's servant.

In what moldy crevice had Ewan found this man?

Seonaid promptly chastised herself for her unkind thoughts. The journey had been trying for everyone. Cold, hungry, and more than a touch anxious, no one within the carriage was at their best.

As the horizon acquired a deep pewter hue, the storm relentlessly pounded the coach. Although it was only afternoon, the sky appeared near gloaming outdoors.

Face pale as death, Mrs. Wetherby's grip tightened until Seonaid's fingers tingled, then grew as numb as her frozen feet had hours before. She wiggled her toes in her woolen stockings and serviceable half boots, grimacing when hundreds of needle-like pricks tormented her.

At least she could still feel her feet.

Despite her lined kerseymere pelisse, double layered mantle, three lap robes, and a fur muff, icy arrows prodded to the marrow of her bones.

The poor drivers, outrider, and horses must be suffering much worse from the cold, yet the coach daren't stop. In moments, the snow would encompass the vehicle and obstruct the roads. Their only hope was to push onward before the way became blocked.

A ferocious blast slammed into the chaise, rattling the windows and her taut nerves. Even Una blanched this time, and Reverend Fletcher squeaked like a terrified toddler.

"We're going to die. Freeze to death. Our bodies won't be found for days. *Weeks.*" Mrs. Wetherby dove deeper beneath the lap robes. In the grayish half-light blanketing the interior, a half-crazed glint shone in her eyes, and her panicked panting produced tiny puffs of frozen air. "Oh, whyever did I agree to accompany you, Miss Ferguson?"

Why, Mrs. Wetherby?

You begged to because you needed the money and travel accommodations to your sister's.

Mrs. Wetherby's head disappeared beneath the robes for a moment.

Taking another swig from the flask she stashed in her cloak's interior pocket, no doubt. *That* detail—the frequent libation of strong spirits—she'd forgone mentioning during her lengthy interview with Seonaid and the Needhams.

More muffled murmurs about dying emerged from the lap robes.

Die?

Absolutely not.

Seonaid refused to perish on this wretched stretch of Highland road in the company of a cursing rector and a whining sot. Forcing in a steadying breath, she patted Mrs. Wetherby's mittened hand. Though thirty years her senior, the woman trembled and sniveled like a wee bairn.

"We're not going to die," Seonaid said, using a comforting tone. "An inn lies a little farther along, and we'll seek lodgings there. A toasty fire to warm us, hot food in our stomachs, a comfortable bed to sleep in, and soon this will seem like a grand adventure." *Not likely, but the words sounded reassuring.* "Surely this storm will have abated by tomorrow."

A horse whinnied, and more yelling echoed from the drivers.

Leaning forward, Seonaid scraped at the window, vainly trying to dislodge the frozen coating.

A twinkling later, all movement stopped.

Two

S eonaid strained to see beyond the window and hear what caused the coach to stop.

Had they arrived? Or were they finally stuck?

God help them if the latter was the cause.

Muted voices called to one another, and a light appeared outside the door. A moment later, a man, so bundled only his merry blue eyes twinkled above his scarf, extended his hand.

"Let's get ye inside and warmed. I am Angus Kerrigan. My wife and I own the Hare's Foot. Hot mulled wine be awaitin' ye. And fresh tea and cock-a-leekie soup too. Come now."

Tension eased from Seonaid's shoulders, and relief swept her as she slumped against the seat, savoring her first deep breath in hours.

Reverend Fletcher clambered to exit the chaise first, roughly knocking Mrs. Wetherby onto her bottom and sending her flask skittering into a brick.

Sputtering and fussing, she righted herself and frowned. Jabbing a finger after his scurrying form, Mrs. Wetherby retrieved her flask. "He's no gentleman."

"Nae. He be an inconsiderate, selfish oaf." Una gestured

for Seonaid and Mrs. Wetherby to alight. "Get ye within. Ye both look nigh on to collapsin'."

Moments later, a blast of welcoming, fragrant warmth engulfed Seonaid. She sniffed the air. Wood smoke, fresh bread, meat of some kind, and if she wasn't mistaken, Scotch pies. She inhaled again. Oh, and praise the saints, shortbread.

Grumbling its displeasure, her stomach constricted, reminding her she hadn't eaten since dawn.

Mrs. Wetherby made straight for the soot-stained hearth, hovering so close to the heat her skirts were in danger of igniting. Still wearing mittens, she accepted a steaming cup of mulled wine and a roll from a cheerful maid. For the first time in hours, a hint of color touched the chaperone's plump cheeks as she happily munched and sipped.

She whispered something to the servant, and after a startled glance and a brief nod, the girl wove her way amongst the tables to speak to Mr. Kerrigan.

His grizzled brows danced in apparent surprise before he shrugged a beefy shoulder and produced a generous finger's worth of whisky.

The maid delivered the spirit to Mrs. Wetherby, who tossed back the umber liquid in a single gulp, and, afterward, peered longingly at the empty tumbler.

Well, at least she wouldn't be a nervous ninny all night, and if history repeated, she'd be foxed in an hour. And snoring loudly in two.

Facing the grinning, rosy-faced Mrs. Kerrigan, wiping her hands on her less than pristine apron, Seonaid smiled in genuine appreciation. As soon as she'd secured lodgings, she meant to dive into a hearty Scotch pie. "I shall need two rooms, please."

"I be sorry, Miss, but the vicar claimed the last empty chamber. He insisted, even though I suggested with two beds, ye ladies should have it." The look she speared the cleric would've charred a goose's rump feathers. Lifting her apologetic gaze, she fiddled with something in her apron's pocket. "He threatened to call down the Almighty's disfavor and curse me and my kin if'n I refused to let him have the room."

He would, the repugnant churl.

What kind of reverend exploited people's fears?

"Ye and the other ladies be welcome to sleep before the common room's hearth. We've plenty of extra pallets and blankets. Ye bein' a lady, I might be able to borrow a privacy screen from a chamber fer ye."

Untying her bonnet, Seonaid strove to curb the insults she yearned to toss at Reverend Fletcher's head. Nae, not toss. Pummel him with. As soon as she arrived home, a serious conversation with Ewan was in order. Fletcher simply couldn't take Reverend Wallace's place.

Divested of his greatcoat, Reverend Fletcher ate with gusto, taking hefty draughts from his tankard between huge bites. More than once, his mouth worked as his distrusting gaze darted from person to person, though the guilty boor studiously avoided looking in her direction.

Talking to himself or praying?

Queer one, he was.

Don't judge others, Seonaid, Mother's soft voice chastised.

Well, he *was* rather off-putting. And sometimes the unvarnished truth needed saying, whether it sounded judgmental or not.

Desperate to do something with her hands lest she clench them in anger or smack the vicar atop his weirdly parted, oily hair with one of her bulging valises, Seonaid removed her silk-lined, ermine-rimmed bonnet. The bag contained several medicinal journals and would pack a nice wallop. Maybe it would darken his daylights or knock some common decency into him.

Surely Fletcher comprehended the women would be

forced to sleep on the muddy, footprint-covered floor, and yet he'd still claimed the last chamber. So far, she hadn't observed a single godly virtue in the man. What had possessed Ewan to retain the toad for the parish?

Seonaid pursed her mouth and willed her disgruntled musings to cease.

As Mother often proclaimed, people weren't always what they claimed or seemed, and a wise person valued others for their character, not status or abilities.

Vicar Fletcher would do well to apply those concepts.

Seonaid raised her gaze to the dusty, roughly hewn, cobweb-strewn rafters and dragged in a deep breath.

Una and Mrs. Wetherby wouldn't take the sleeping arrangements well. Each suffered from sore bones, and the teeming taproom hinted others might also be without a room tonight. Mrs. Wetherby's fussing and grumbling already rang in Seonaid's ears.

Perhaps she ought to encourage Mrs. Wetherby to imbibe heavily tonight, if only to spare Seonaid her complaints.

A scraggly-toothed Highlander grinned at Seonaid before nudging his equally filthy, tartan-clad friend and whispering something. The pair broke into guffaws, earning them curious looks from those nearby and sending a shudder rippling along her shoulders.

Their size, long dirty hair, and orangey-red plaid identified them as Blackhalls. They were a pox amongst the Highlanders and since they'd abducted her sister, Isobel, the McTavishes' sworn enemy.

Sure as snow still sifted from the sky, Seonaid wouldn't close her eyes tonight. Weariness engulfed her, and she released a silent sigh. Lord, she couldn't remember when she'd been this exhausted, and that she'd, in part, brought the state upon herself—*fine, mostly been responsible for it*—vexed all the more.

Sleep had eluded her before her departure from London,

and a casket boasted a more comfortable sleeping surface than the thin straw mattresses she'd tossed and turned upon the past two nights. Not possessed of a complaining or peevish nature, the remnants of Seonaid's forbearance had disappeared with the last gust of wintery wind.

"Do you, perchance, have a private parlor I can rent instead of a boarding room?" At least a parlor would afford privacy, and perhaps it contained a settee or two for Una and Mrs. Wetherby to sleep upon.

Shaking her head, Mrs. Kerrigan gave Seonaid a remorseful smile. "It also be taken fer the night by two families travelin' together."

Ye gods. How many people sought shelter within this cramped inn?

Homesick, fatigued, tired of strangers and Mrs. Wetherby's whining, Seonaid longed to crawl into her downy bed at Craiglocky and sleep for a week.

"Very well. There's no help for it." Lifting a shoulder, she summoned a half-smile. "At least we shall be warm and fed."

"*Donnez à ces femmes* the vicar's chamber. He can share mine."

Seonaid stiffened.

That voice. Nae Jesus!

A slightly French-accented baritone she'd hoped to never have to hear again. One which had haunted her for months.

Reverend Fletcher's head snapped up so rapidly, he poked himself in the cheek with his forkful. Mouth plunging downward, he snatched his serviette, then angrily wiped away the gravy trickling a greasy path to his pointed chin.

Spine rigid, Seonaid schooled her face into unyielding angles. A string of oaths no refined lady had any business knowing whizzed across her mind in rapid succession.

Why must she continually run into Jacques, Monsieur le baron de Devaux-Rousset? Especially presently, when her reserves wouldn't half fill a child's thimble, and only supreme self-control kept her from shrilly telling him and the reverend to go bugger themselves.

Partially turning her head, she met Monsieur le baron's boldly amused gaze before his focus dropped to her mouth, and his lips inched upward. Had a woman besides her ever spurned his attention? Certainly none she'd witnessed while in France.

She barely managed to check her frown. Gads, she'd be a wrinkled crone by one-and-twenty if she encountered Monsieur de Devaux-Rousset regularly.

Raven brows swooped low over his hooded coffee bean-brown eyes, framed by impossibly thick eyelashes. His full mouth slid into its familiar sideways smirk above a chin a jot too strong to be classically handsome, but which suited him perfectly.

The half-inch white strip to the left of his mouth didn't detract from his devilish good looks either. *Blast it all.* In fact, the scar gave him a debonair, dashing buccaneer appearance.

From the confident glint in his eyes, he was all too aware of that fact.

Attired in buckskins, a deep russet hunting coat complemented by an ochre and claret striped waistcoat, and a nattily tied neckcloth from which winked a jasper pin, he exemplified peerage perfection. An unexpected, unexplainable, but delightfully naughty urge to see him with his shirt collar open and sleeves rolled to his elbows swept over her.

She blinked to clear her muddled—*disquieting*—thoughts and purposely redirected her suggestive ponderings.

Did his mustache hide more scarring?

How had he come by the mark?

That question arose each time they met, and still, she'd never acquired the gumption to ask him. Not only wasn't she forward, but polite conversation between them wasn't their forte. They usually ignored or avoided one another.

Or bickered like scolding squirrels.

As unwelcome as fresh horse droppings in the salon, recollections of their meetings beset her memory. Every time Seonaid encountered Monsieur le Baron, he brought out her worst traits. Characteristics she didn't know she carried and sequestered deep within, and she didn't like herself afterward.

That was what came from the odious man presuming she was the courtesan he'd arranged a clandestine *tête-à-tête* with at the last play she'd attended in Paris.

Before meeting him, she'd always prided herself on her kindness and mellow temperament.

People expected her benevolence.

She expected it of herself.

She closed her eyes for a fraction, humiliation's heat bathing from her chest to her hairline, no doubt leaving her cheeks glowing like hot coals. The scene in Paris taunted her still, as did his clean, manly scent. Slightly spicy, but also musky with a hint of fresh linen.

Though her family assumed homesickness compelled her early return from France, truth be told, *he* was the reason for her swift departure. Hopefully, they'd never learn of the nearly ruinous scandal.

"We meet yet again, Mademoiselle Ferguson." His amused tone grated, immediately sparking exasperation. "I suspect Fate must have a hand in our encounters, *non?*"

No. Definitely not.

Even Fate wasn't that perverse or cruel.

Seonaid reluctantly opened her eyes, angling her head in the merest greeting. "Monsieur. I thought"—*prayed*—"I'd seen the last of you in London."

～

"Ah, I'm delighted that isn't the case, *ma petite*. Dare I hope you feel the same, *oui*?" Jacques chuckled at the startled expression upon Mademoiselle Ferguson's face. Or perhaps piqued better described the look.

As intended, he'd miffed her.

She quickly tried to hide her emotions with her typical demure composure, but the minutest jut of her dainty chin betrayed her agitation.

He couldn't say he wasn't pleased to see her, even if the feeling wasn't mutual. She provided a splendid visual feast.

Still, he oughtn't to tease her. A gentleman wouldn't.

Attired in a cherry-red mantle, which accented her toasty-brown chestnut locks and satiny-white skin to perfection, she was, as always, exquisite. And fagged to death, if he read her correctly.

It could be, seeing him caused her haggard expression. However, he preferred to believe her harrowing journey in this storm triggered her upset and not the sight of him. The last notion rather bruised his manly pride.

Many a man, and woman, had lost his or her life in a raging winter tempest such as the one currently pummeling the Scottish Highlands. He'd been half-frozen himself by the time he made the Hare's Foot Inn.

At first, when her melodious speech carried to him in his secluded corner, he believed the two Scotches he'd downed to warm himself had him half foxed already. Or his nighttime imaginings were now manifesting in the daylight.

No other woman owned such a soothing, musical voice, and when Jacques glimpsed her, he'd gulped his third Scotch to prevent himself from throttling the vicar for his unchivalrous behavior.

Taking the last remaining chamber.

Forcing elderly women and a lady of quality to sleep on the filthy floor.

What sort of a selfish, uncharitable knave did that?

The solution to Mademoiselle Ferguson's dilemma was simple enough, but would she accept Jacques's offer, or would obstinacy choose for her? She'd made it emphatically clear she couldn't abide him, and instinct told him she'd not take kindly to being in his debt.

Her older traveling companion slumped into a chair and closed her eyes, causing Mademoiselle Ferguson's winged brows to tweak together. Concern pinching her face, she fidgeted with her bonnet's crimson ribbons as her astute regard slid to the other woman she'd entered with, now dozing near the fire.

Here was his chance to entice.

Like the serpent in the Garden of Eden, his conscience chastised.

"Your companions are weary, *non?*" He flicked his forefinger toward the snoozing women. The servant's head bobbed as she tried to keep a watchful eye on her ward, and the older woman's chin rested upon her chest, her sonorous snores reverberating off the rafters. Not a whole lot of chaperoning going on there, by any measure.

Mademoiselle Ferguson worried her lower lip with her neat, white teeth, and a wavy tendril escaped her upswept hair, brushing her cheek.

That night in Paris, her beauty had befuddled him, and he'd stolen a highly satisfying taste of those sweet lips, earning him a stinging slap for his audacity. It had been worth it. Would be worth it again, truth to tell.

As she stood in the entrance, shoulders drooping and barely able to keep her head up, an irresistible desire to protect her overwhelmed him. He stared, stupefied, for an extended moment.

Dangerous, that.

Half lowering his eyelids to block the tantalizing view, he collected his scattered wits.

He couldn't permit himself feelings. If his share in Oakberry Quarry, a Scottish silver mine, didn't prove a profitable venture—a *very* profitable venture since he'd invested the last of his funds and borrowed against his property—he would have no recourse but to marry an heiress in order to save *le Manoir des Jardins.*

Perhaps a cossetted American keen for a title but who would expect nothing from her husband in the way of affection. If she preferred to remain in America, all the better.

Unlike many other French aristocrats, his lands weren't entailed, nor had they been seized during the revolt and restored to him afterward. Six generations of Devaux-Roussets had been born, lived, and died in the *château.* Not doing everything within his power to save the manor and lands didn't bear contemplating.

The blood of his ancestors—his sister's, brother-in-law's, and nephew's too—had been spilled defending *le manoir.* By God, he'd do whatever necessary, short of selling, to preserve her splendor.

His family deserved that much.

So, he'd ventured to Scotland and had three months to determine whether his mining gamble paid off. His creditors —and *Père's* creditors as well—wouldn't wait much longer.

Mortgaged to her glorious spires and turrets, the mansion had fallen into decay. Her war-ravaged lands produced scant more than a handful of scraggy garden patches, more weed than vegetables, and a few scrawny sheep.

With a promise of payment in full in three months, he'd barely staved the creditors from confiscating anything not nailed down.

Resisting the urge to tuck the silky curl teasing

Mademoiselle Ferguson's cheek behind her ear, he entwined his hands at his lower back.

Consternation bracketing her mouth, she twisted her lips back and forth. Was she aware she did that when nervous or thinking?

Capturing those lips beneath mine again would still that tantalizing motion.

"Well, Mademoiselle? What say you?" Smoothing his mustache, he concealed a smile at her transparent reluctance.

If it weren't for the other women, she'd deny the need for protection and, no doubt, his gallantry as well. Though she was not overlarge in stature, she'd nonetheless clobbered him soundly after their short but sweet kiss. He'd borne the bruise for a week.

His battered senses had suffered far longer.

"Such distinguished *dames* shouldn't sleep upon the floor, *non*?" Tempting her with the obvious, he pressed his advantage. "And the vicar doesn't require two beds."

Her gentle gaze flicked to each middling-aged woman in turn, then remained on Reverend Fletcher briefly. A steely glint flashed in her large, expressive eyes, deepening their color to a warm treacle before she rapidly concealed the look.

She regally tipped her head in acquiescence. "Thank you, Monsieur de Devaux-Rousset. I gratefully accept on behalf of my aged companions."

A snort nearly choked him.

On behalf of her companions?

He didn't doubt for an instant she would've plopped her delightfully tight *derrière* onto the dirty slats lining the floor for the night if it hadn't been for the other *dames*.

Mademoiselle Ferguson strove to conceal her more volatile side.

So much so, in fact, that Jacques doubted few others had been the target of her heated outrage. Or even suspected she had a fiery streak simmering inside. He rather liked her lack of control around him.

He smoothed his mustache again, hiding his appreciative smile. "I'll need a pallet brought to my chamber—"

"Nae, ye winna." Reverend Fletcher stood, scraping his chair backward and throwing his napkin onto the table. He stalked to the counter, his thin face lined with aggravation.

Several patrons watched his progress, and conversation in the common room petered.

"I be a *mon* of God." He slapped the countertop, contempt thickening his tinny tone. "And I be refusin' to share a room with a *heathen*."

A harsh sound, half gasp, half hiss, escaped Mademoiselle Ferguson as she bristled in outrage. "How dare you refer to the Monsieur as a heathen?"

Appreciation infused Jacques at her unexpected defense.

She straightened to her full height and stabbed Fletcher with a blistering glare. "You, *sir*, are the one sorely lacking in social graces and common courtesy, else you'd not subject three travel-weary women to sleeping upon the floor while you enjoy a comfortable bed and another goes unused."

Bravo, ma petite.

A sinister gleam shone fleetingly in Fletcher's eyes before he dismissed her with a reproachful scowl. Speaking to the anxious innkeeper, he bent his lanky form over the counter and thrust his thumb toward Jacques. "I nae be sharin' a room with a filthy Frenchie."

THREE

Eyeing the rector, Jacques's nostrils twitched, as did Mademoiselle Ferguson's. He checked the laugh welling in his throat.

"*Zut.* Given the aroma you're emitting, Monsieur, I dare say I see the inside of a bathtub far more frequently than you, and I'm certain my clothes are laundered more regularly as well."

A few guests laughed or tittered, and the innkeeper hid a toothy smile behind her hand.

"*Je ne pense pas qu'on lui ait dit que la pureté de l'âme passe d'abord par celle du corps,*" Jacques murmured from the side of his mouth.

Mademoiselle Ferguson's lips quivered, but she admirably brought them under control. The twinkle in her eye remained unrestrained, though. "*C'est précisément cela.*"

Exactly so.

Warmth permeated him at the intimate humor they shared.

"What did ye say in that devil's tongue?" Fletcher glowered and levered upright.

"Monsieur de Devaux-Rousset simply made a reference to an adage about cleanliness and Godliness." Her agreeable smile widened when Fletcher choked on an irate oath.

Impudent minx.

"Nonetheless, Vicar, I'm willing to share my chamber with you so the *dames* might have a bed." Jacques cocked his head. How prideful was Fletcher? "I'll sleep on the pallet."

Downwind or with my head out the window.

"Nae. I paid fer the room and be meanin' to sleep in it. By myself." Reverend Fletcher surveyed the now silent taproom, disapproval etched on many travelers' countenances.

A flicker of unease flitted over his craggy features before he puffed out his chest and elevated his head proudly. Looking down his reedy nose that supercilious way, he bore a rather distinct resemblance to the cranes wandering Craiglocky's loch.

The look didn't favor him.

"I be Craigcutty's temporary rector, and I be sure Laird McTavish nae have a wish fer his new cleric to associate with ungodly Frenchmen."

Acting as if excrement filled his mouth, he spat the last word.

Tried and convicted by a hypocrite.

Fletcher wrongly assumed Jacques was Catholic. What would the fellow do if he knew Jacques aided in Napoleon's defeat and capture?

One finger at a time, Mademoiselle Ferguson removed her gloves, a placid smile hovering about her pink, bowed mouth. "I rather believed that was a rector's primary duty. To win others to the Lord with kindness, love, and acceptance. Yes?"

Geniality grappled with accusation in her direct gaze.

"*Dinna* be tellin' me the *Laird's* ways, lassie." Narrowing his eyes to cunning slits, Reverend Fletcher gave her an inflexible stare. "Where did ye say ye be travelin' to?"

Dropping her gloves within her bonnet's silk lining, she shrugged. "I didn't."

Jacques chuckled delightedly again. *Merde*, she had an adorable, precocious bent.

"Surely, you're aware whom you've shared a post chaise with, Vicar, *non*?" Canting his head, Jacques met Fletcher's indolent stare head on. "She's—"

"Please, allow me." Smiling, Mademoiselle Ferguson laid her delicate hand on Jacques's forearm. "I confess, I shall quite enjoy the...*surprise*."

A scorching jolt swept upward from her touch, and he instinctively almost jerked his arm away. *Mon Dieu*. The first time she'd voluntarily touched him, and he acted like a man besotted. She'd never smiled at him directly before either, and her genuine amusement's potency nearly knocked him flat on his arse.

For an instant, confusion knitted her smooth forehead and wrinkled her nose, but as usual, she adeptly masked her puzzlement. Such skill took repeated practice.

Fascinating.

She hid her true emotions.

If only he had the time to discover why.

Grinning, Jacques winked and bent into a mocking half-bow. "By all means. I'm positive I shall relish the telling immensely."

More than once, he'd been a recipient of her tongue flaying. In the most modulated of tones, she verbally separated meat from bone as expertly as a seasoned butcher wielding a knife.

Mademoiselle Ferguson's stern-faced, six-foot maid tramped toward them, her bearing both protective and challenging. She raked the men with her unyielding, mossy gaze before her expression softened, and she addressed her mistress.

"What be happenin' here, Miss Seonaid?"

"Oh, nothing of import, Una. I was about to inform Vicar Fletcher that Laird McTavish, also known as the Viscount Sethwick, is..." A saucy smile pulling her mouth's edges upward, she paused to draw in a strategic breath.

Adorable tease.

"My brother."

Fletcher's jaw sagged to his scrawny chest, and he blinked like an owl blinded by afternoon sunlight. "Brother? I didna ken." Eyebrows and mouth swooping downward, his visage took on a shrewd edge. "Why be a young lass like ye travelin' alone, and why dinnae ye have a brogue?"

"Och, she be returnin' from a London Season, not that it be yer business. And ye can see she nae be travelin' alone." Spearing him a quelling frown, Una crossed her thick arms and stepped slightly in front of Mademoiselle Ferguson.

In a contest of strength between Una and Fletcher, the abigail would thrash the cleric soundly.

Swallowing and tugging at his neckcloth, Fletcher retreated a reflexive step.

Le poltron.

The cleric might be a coward, but even Jacques wouldn't want to cross that she-bear while protecting her charge.

"As for my lack of a heavy brogue," Mademoiselle Ferguson's clipped speech conveyed her disdain for the vicar, "an overly zealous governess determined that my sisters and I should speak the King's English as well as a British subject. I assure ye, I ken how to speak Scots."

The last lyrical sentence rolled off her tongue.

Facing the anxious proprietor, Jacques offered his most disarming smile and slid her a few coins. "Please give the *dames* the vicar's room, *oui*? And he may have mine. I'm happy to sleep upon a pallet somewhere in this fine establishment."

Mrs. Kerrigan's freckled face broke into a wide grin. "Aye,

a perfect solution, m'laird. Thank ye. Vicar Fletcher, give me yer key, please, and I be havin' yer things moved at once." She glanced at his unfinished dinner. "Have yerself a seat, and a hot, fresh meal will be brought to ye. I've clootie dumpling for dessert too."

A clever way to pacify a disgruntled guest.

With a mutinous glare, Fletcher relinquished his key and accepted one for Jacques's room before stomping back to his table. As he passed, guests swiftly presented their backs in condemnation. His ears glowing, Fletcher's features settled into angry furrows.

Hounds' teeth, what a surly chap. He'd certainly chosen the wrong profession. Did *anyone* attend the services he preached? That question would soon be answered since Jacques planned on staying in the area.

What a horrid notion—listening to a sermon by Fletcher.

"Let's get ye registered, lass," Mrs. Kerrigan said. "It be a third-floor room, but I can get a laddie to help with yer luggage."

"There's no need. I've just my valises."

Where was the remainder of her luggage?

A London Season required trunks of clothing and fallalls. What about her companions? Did they travel as lightly too?

A few moments later, Mademoiselle Ferguson dropped the key into her reticule.

"Thank you again, Monsieur de Devaux-Rousset." Her composed mien shrouded her once more.

"My pleasure, but please drop the Rousset. It's quite too much to manage in one mouthful." He sketched a brief bow. "Excuse me, *s'il vous plaît*. I must remove my things from my former chamber." He smiled at Mrs. Kerrigan. "I'll return the key as soon as I've finished."

"Monsieur le baron, where will you sleep?" Mademoiselle Ferguson's gaze roved the assembled guests, lingering a moment on a few seedier patrons. Her jaw's subtle tightening gave her discomfit away.

There'd been no question of sleeping with the likes of them nearby. If she'd refused the offer of Jacques's room, he'd have slept below too. With a loaded pistol and his knife tucked in his Hessians.

"Oh, there's no shortage of cozy nooks where one might stow a pallet." He gave another swaggering wink. "I shall be fine. I've slept in far harsher conditions, I assure you."

Three years of espionage had exposed him to hellish sleeping environs many times.

"Well, I thank you again." After giving a brief nod, she faced Una. "I'd prefer to eat in our chamber. Would you please collect Mrs. Wetherby and ask that bathing water be sent to our room as soon as convenient?"

"*Aye*, lass. And a hot tea toddy too, I be thinkin'." Eager to complete her mistress's bidding, Una bustled off.

A tippler dared fondle her rear as she passed, and Una clouted him in the ear. "I have more respect fer myself than to dally with vermin like ye."

Elbows resting atop the countertop, Jacques perused the room in search of an acceptable spot to stow his belongings. Maybe the alcove near the stairs.

The four ruffians hovering at a table near the window raised the hairs on his nape, and that revealed much. He'd stake his barony that the grimy quartet were robbers or pad borrowers forced to seek shelter here. As an English spy during the war, he wasn't a stranger to lowlifes and horse thieves.

Memories briefly assailed him, but he stifled the pain and regret.

France meant nothing.

He owed his homeland even less, and still, he couldn't bring himself to abandon *le Manoir des Jardins*. How could he when his entire family lay buried in the once elegant gardens the *château* was named after?

"Mademoiselle Ferguson, may I escort you to your room? I'm not comfortable with you venturing there alone. While most customers here are stranded travelers like ourselves, there's also an unsavory element present."

And that was why he'd sleep outside her door. And why he'd either insist she and her companions complete the journey in his hired coach, or he'd exchange places with the rector.

That ought to set the self-righteous tosspot into a sputtering dudgeon again.

Moreover, Jacques owed McTavish a debt of gratitude, and after seeing his sister home, the debt would be paid.

Well, that wasn't Jacques's singular motivation.

This woman had entangled his thoughts for months. But every time he approached her or attempted conversation, she retreated with a racehorse's alacrity and a badger's ferocity.

"Yes, I appreciate the offer. A few men here do make me uncomfortable." She gathered her belongings. Weariness was carved across her fine features, shadowing her gentle eyes. "I'm truly grateful for your generosity. I'm sure you aren't looking forward to an uncomfortable night on the floor after traveling all day."

Likely several nights sprawled on the floor, given the storm's savagery.

And that created other worries.

Did the inn have sufficient supplies to last several days? Hungry, bored, and confined men habitually drank too much, and the belligerent ones either started fights or demanded women for their more primal urges.

Too bad Jacques traveled alone, but he'd disbanded his smuggling and informant system after buying into Oakberry, and a valet was a luxury he couldn't afford.

Not many of the patrons hunkered over their tankards, food, or cards appeared capable of defending themselves against anything more aggressive than a horsefly. Dragging his attention back to Mademoiselle Ferguson, her mesmerizing eyes ensnared him.

Toast brown irises ringed by deep jade glittered with citrine flecks and, if he wasn't mistaken, true concern for his comfort. Her half-French heritage was evident in her small straight nose and her face's delicate angles and high cheekbones. An intense desire to sample her lips' softness again assailed him.

Christ, *quell salaud*. He was a *bâtard*, envisioning her in an intimate embrace when she practically slept on her feet.

"You didn't explain what brought you to Scotland again, Monsieur." Several steps ahead, she pitched the question over her shoulder.

A wicked smile splitting his face, he hurried to relieve her of her valises. "I might move here."

Four

A red squirrel could've built a sizable nest in Seonaid's gaping mouth. Only plowing into a small trunk left near the stairs by a careless servant—or perhaps a guest eager for a stiff peck or the fire's warmth—roused her from her flabbergasted daze.

She rubbed her sore knee. Another bruise, no doubt.

Move to Scotland?

Monsieur de Devaux held a French title. Surely, he but teased.

"You're fatigued, *ma petite*. Let me assist you." Brazenly, he gripped her elbow, steadying her.

At his touch, a sensation much like heavy, warm velvet encompassed her. Comforting yet sensual too. And alarming in its intensity.

Gently, and without meeting his astute gaze, she extracted her arm on the pretense of lifting her gown for the risers. Stones weighted her eyelids, and she swallowed an unladylike yawn. He, on the other hand, never looked more dashing and virile. Utterly unfair.

Climbing the narrow stairs, she tried to keep her hips from swaying, much too aware he followed close behind.

"Why isn't your family journeying with you?" An innocent enough question, except a note of true concern, or perhaps censure, tinted Monsieur's words.

"I left London rather abruptly and didn't want to wait until someone could be sent from Craiglocky to accompany me. Besides, Mrs. Wetherby was anxious to find a traveling companion and gladly served as my chaperone."

A bit of an exaggeration, there. Mrs. Wetherby had been paid handsomely to speedily depart London.

"It's not typical and can be dangerous, *non*?" His deep, accented baritone caressed her.

How could a man's voice be so deliciously pleasant? And bother it all, why did Seonaid notice? Especially Jacques's? A man who piqued her to no end most of the time, and she didn't vex easily.

She shook her head. "No, it's not commonly done, but I felt that, under the circumstances, and with my maid and a chaperone, it was acceptable."

Barely.

Undoubtedly, her parents' chastisement awaited her upon her arrival, and probably Ewan's too. He respected his stepfather Hugh Ferguson immensely. Regardless, as *laird*, Ewan would likely feel it his duty to reprimand her.

Truthfully, she expected it. Deserved it.

Fiercely loyal and dedicated to the clan, members were obliged to consider how their actions affected the tribe, and single lasses gallivanting from England to Scotland in the dead of winter, even with a pair of middling-aged women, bordered on scandalous.

A splendid sort of scandal, because for a few brief days, Seonaid was completely in charge of her life.

Freedom's taste proved intoxicating and addicting.

Her family's admonishments would be naught compared to what she'd endured in London. What she'd continue to withstand as her visions grew stronger and occurred more frequently, as seemed the case lately.

Dread hitched her breath, momentarily making her dizzy, and she placed a palm against the coarse planks lining the stairway. Why did people have to turn her God-given gift into a circus attraction or fair exhibit?

Over her shoulder, Monsieur de Devaux regarded her intently.

How could she explain she couldn't bear being a spectacle any longer?

Her second sight wasn't a secret to him, though he'd not been present during a prior onset. Nonetheless, he hadn't a notion what a cumbersome yoke her fey had become.

No one did. Not even her family. They believed her special and blessed, that she treasured the anomaly. People also overestimated how much she actually saw in advance.

Their ignorance exposed how little they knew her.

From the beginning, she'd detested the revelations. As a ten-year-old child, her first one had foretold her grandmother's death after a prolonged illness. Seonaid had blamed herself for months afterward.

More than once, she'd feigned ignorance of an ominous event's revelation. How could she be the bearer of sorrowful tidings? To her knowledge, naught could be done to change the vision's outcome, so wasn't it better to let people go about their lives until the tragedy occurred?

Most people endured the occasional bad or terrifying dreams. But imagine your worst fears played out while wide awake, and escaping them was impossible.

Except, perhaps, by losing my virginity.

Una had whispered that last helpful tidbit when, after an especially disturbing vision in which Seonaid's dear cousin

Gregor had been wounded, she'd collapsed in her chamber, overcome by tears.

She sighed, sadness replacing her unpleasant musings. What was to become of her? True, her sex restricted her options, but the second sight, more so.

"You're an uncommonly brave woman, I think, Mademoiselle Ferguson."

Ridiculously pleased at Monsieur de Devaux's compliment, although she shouldn't be, she permitted a tiny smile. Not as much brave as desperate, but she couldn't tell him that.

"I don't fear much when in Una's company. She's immensely proud of her Viking heritage and knows how to wield a knife. I too have been trained in weaponry, as has every female in my family."

"Yes, but a man should be with you for added protection." His boots pounded rhythmically behind her. "Your family knows you're coming, *non*? I should think this weather has them worried."

They'd attained the second-floor landing and turned the corner to ascend to the third story. She tramped up the last few stairs, her heavy pelisse, the lengthy climb, and exhaustion's shroud taking their toll.

"I did send a letter." *The day before we departed.* "So my parents do know approximately when to expect me—" An unbidden yawn interrupted her, and covering her mouth, she blinked sleepily. "Excuse me. But yes, they're also aware Highland travel this time of year can be a trifle unpredictable."

She yawned again. Perhaps she'd skip eating altogether and seek her bed.

God forbid they should become snowed in.

The unpleasant notion nearly stopped her upward trek. The longer the delay in her arrival, the more frantic her family would become. Mother would demand Father, Ewan, and half the clan immediately set out to find her.

One night in a modest lodging might be excused, but several with the riffraff below? Seonaid nibbled her lower lip. Surely her reputation wouldn't suffer, especially with Una and Mrs. Wetherby sleeping within the same chamber. Another swell of gratitude swept her for Monsieur de Devaux's interference.

Perhaps he wasn't a complete toad after all.

Conceding that her abrupt departure from London mightn't have been the best plan pricked her pride. But she would've had to wait for her parents' letter to be delivered, and then for whomever they designated to fetch her from London to arrive. At least three weeks of waiting. Probably longer.

No. She had had quite enough of Polite Society after they treated her like a curiosity. Other than closeting herself in her chamber for nigh on a month or more, she'd done what she needed to, and, frankly, she relished the control for once.

She'd never wanted the second sight but tried to accept her *gift* and hoped God intended it for good. Truthfully, in recent years, *an dara shealladh* had become more of a curse, and she dreaded a vision's onset. If she never had another, that suited her perfectly.

Grandmother ceased having hers when she married, and with all her heart, Seonaid secretly hoped the same would happen to her. Except, in general, men hadn't shown her much interest.

Intrigue and perverse fascination about her visions and foresight brought a few 'round, but her gift intimidated most males, including the brawny Highlanders.

She hardly blamed them.

Who wanted a wife able to foretell your death or other disagreeable things Providence might send your way? Or, perhaps, a wife who might distinguish your indiscretions, your innermost secrets, or if you'd lied to her?

After nearly ten years, she still didn't understand what

caused an onset, so she couldn't assure a spouse she mightn't learn something unpleasant.

As much as she'd missed home, apprehension coiled inside her, knotting her belly. Her sisters had married, and Dugall, her beloved younger brother, was off to university soon. Who would keep her company besides her menagerie?

Oh, she'd plenty of acquaintances and a few friends in the village, but, with the exception of Mother, no female confidants. She didn't know what her role was at Craiglocky anymore other than a healer of animals and, occasionally, of people too.

Wearily stepping to the door of her chamber, Seonaid fished in her reticule for the key. If she'd known Monsieur le baron intended to play the gentleman and carry her valises, she'd have held the key instead. Finding the metal length at last, she offered him an apologetic smile.

With a slight scrape, the key slid home, and the reluctant lock gave way. Dusk, encouraged by the unrelenting storm, had claimed her due early, and long shadows hid the room's modest contents.

Monsieur de Devaux made quick work of lighting the candle sitting atop a bedside table, and then two more on a wall sconce. Hands upon his narrow hips, he surveyed the simple chamber. "Not as well-appointed as you're accustomed to, I dare say, but it appears clean, *non*?"

Tossing her possessions onto the closest bed, she shook her head. "You're mistaken if you think I require fripperies and fancy furnishings. While I can appreciate beauty and finery, I prefer simplicity in all things."

"I'm not surprised, *ma petite*." Appreciation warmed his dark eyes.

"Oh?" Calling her *ma petite* was much too forward. She should have reprimanded him the first time below, but quite frankly, she'd been too tired.

He arced his lips into a charming smile, one he'd used regularly given the fine lines near his eyes' outer corners and framing his handsome mouth, as he retrieved her valises from where he'd left them by the doorway. "Some things are completely exquisite and memorable as they are. Adornment and embellishment detract from their splendor."

Another compliment?

Heady delight wrestled with logic's warning.

The mesmerizing spark in his lovely, pewter-flecked jet eyes, and the way he blended his vowels, made each word a sensual caress that reverberated to her toes and sent heat coursing along her veins.

By all that was holy, Monsieur de Devaux was a practiced rogue if he caused her—an intelligent, insightful woman immune to his charms and good looks—to react thusly.

You're no more immune, Seonaid Célestine Heather Ferguson, than he's Scots and cows cluck.

She *was* too immune.

After all, she wasn't a green girl fresh from the schoolroom. No, indeed. Why, she'd experienced a London Season with fine gentlemen galore, and Craiglocky had many handsome men coming and going. Plus, she'd spent three months amongst France's High Society.

She knew about men.

Except, none other than Monsieur de Devaux ever looked at her with a heated, alluring gaze. Or said the outrageous things he dared. Why did he continue to pay her marked attention? Perhaps all Frenchmen were equally obtuse and overly confident of their maleness.

Yes. That must be it. She should've recalled as much from her botched stint in Paris. Frenchmen were an arrogant, cocky bunch.

Placing her leather valises onto the bed, he examined the

powdery white drifting from the sky beyond the window. "We might be here for a few days."

"I was afraid of that." Nodding, she tugged one bag atop the colorful quilt toward her, then patted the case's sides. "I've plenty of reading material, embroidery, and playing cards."

"No dagger or dueling pistol?" He tapped the top with a long, well-manicured finger, yet his hand showed signs of toil as well.

At her inquisitive look, he chuckled.

"You mentioned you're trained in weaponry. That's a Scottish tradition, *non?*"

"Not really. More of a Ferguson one. I'm most skilled with a short sword." She unlatched the satchel's top and after opening it, withdrew a delicately carved silver stiletto sheath. "And I do have a blade with me. I shall sleep with it beneath my pillow."

Stepping nearer, he took her hand, which still clenched the knife far harder than necessary. Spicy muskiness wafted upward as he bent, and her nostrils quivered in remembrance. His supple mouth grazed her knuckles, and, this time, not only did her silly knees threaten to buckle, something came loose in her stomach and flopped about.

Hunger? Fatigue? Tension?

Not attraction. Not to *him*. She wouldn't allow it.

The day's events had weakened her defenses. Tomorrow, after a good night's rest, common sense would return full on.

I hope.

"You have no need to fear, mademoiselle. I shall act as your protector while we're here."

But who will protect me from you?

A short, disbelieving laugh escaped Seonaid, more from nerves than humor. "And how do you intend to do that, Monsieur de Devaux? Lay your pallet outside my chamber door each night?"

Head tilted, the curly, slightly too-long hair at his nape teased his russet collar, and he slanted his ebony brows over eyes the hue of twilight fog. "*Exactement.*"

"You cannot be serious." How would she sleep, knowing he was a few feet away? The man had her in a dither, and she loathed it.

"Your door will be barred from within." He pointed at a sturdy bolt. "And I shall simply be a deterrent to any sot who oversteps the bounds, *oui*?"

"No." She shook her head but stopped at once when pain pinched between her eyes. A common occurrence when she became overly fatigued. "I don't want you to act as my protect—"

"You may thank me suitably later, *ma petite*." Winking, he sketched a bow. Then with a flash of white teeth, and while whistling a haunting melody, he and his masculine glory took their leave.

Seonaid still gaped at the door when Una and Mrs. Wetherby lumbered in a few moments later, breathing heavily from their labored climb.

"What are ye starin' at the door fer?" Una peered into the hallway and scratched her head. Brow knitted, she shifted her puzzled gaze to Seonaid. "Well?"

"Nothing of import."

"*Hmph*," Una huffed, unfastening her cloak. "And that be why ye be standin' there lookin' confounded?"

Sliding her dagger beneath her pillow, Seonaid lifted a shoulder. "Monsieur de Devaux's humor is somewhat peculiar."

Smelling suspiciously of spirits, Mrs. Wetherby wobbled straight to the other bed, and after letting her cloak drop to the floor, lay down without removing her shoes. "Something's afoot below," she mumbled sleepily—*or halfway to bosky*—as she dragged the quilt to her chins.

"What d'ye mean?" Hands splayed upon her generous hips, Una gave the pickled chaperone a gimlet stare.

Evidently, her patience with Mrs. Wetherby had grown as sparse as Seonaid's.

"Ye drank so freely, I be surprised if'n ye can recall yer name." Disapproval creased her forehead.

"On m'way back from th' necessary, I overheard whispered arguing in th' kitchen. Th' innkeepers fear thieves or highwayman be amongst us." Mrs. Wetherby sighed and shut her eyes, then snuggled further into her pillow. "Might be robbed, ravished, or murdered in m'sleep."

Una shut the door, drew the pin home with a comforting clink, and leaned against the wood, her forehead furrowed into deep ridges. "Truth in that. A rough lot be under this roof. Best plan on sleepin' with yer blade in hand, Miss Seonaid. I ken I shall."

FIVE

Jacques stood as Mademoiselle Ferguson, followed by her ever-watchful towering maid, entered the common room. He'd hoped she would choose to eat below rather than dine in her chamber as she had last evening.

Unable to retire and take up his self-appointed station outside her door until the others had sought their third-story rooms, he'd been forced to endure a yawn-inspiring, boring-as-death evening in the taproom.

A minuscule grin tugged his mouth upward.

Not entirely tedious, perhaps.

Mrs. Kerrigan, wielding a broom and swearing in Gaelic as she chased her husband from the kitchen, had proven quite entertaining. So had the Highlander toppling off his chair in a drunken stupor. Unfortunately, his tartan snagged on the way down, exposing his hairy arse.

That Jacques hadn't needed to see.

Up at dawn, he'd made use of the kitchen to shave and cleanse his teeth before venturing to the stables and checking on his horseflesh to determine the feasibility of leaving. Despite their cramped quarters, the horses fared well. Still, no one but a fool would leave today. Nearly eighteen inches of snow carpeted the road.

Hesitating at the common room's entrance, Mademoiselle Ferguson perused the guests before speaking over her shoulder to her maid. Seonaid's beauty stood out starkly in the room, much like a delicate, pink rose tossed atop a fly-ridden dung heap.

His lips twitched at the image. The other patrons mightn't appreciate the comparison.

Mrs. Wetherby remained conspicuously absent, but after the copious amount of whisky she'd downed before Una hauled her upstairs, if the woman roused before noon, he'd be astounded.

Not the best choice of an attendant, and all the more reason he'd assigned himself the role of Seonaid's guardian until they reached Craiglocky Keep. That detail she needn't discover since based on her adamant refusal of his protection last night, she'd probably raise a fuss and refuse his escort.

Reverend Fletcher had yet to make an appearance this morning too. Last night, once he'd finished eating, he'd scowled at the other guests, and muttering about the trials of contending with unholy rabble, shambled upstairs.

Perchance circumstances or birth forced him into service in the church rather than his own choice. That would certainly account for his gruff behavior. Just as well he was absent this morning since most of the tables were full, save Jacques's, nestled below a window in a corner next to the fire-place. Besides, unless the rector offered him a fortune vast enough to save *le Manoir des Jardins*, Jacques wasn't eating with the surly vicar.

Indicating the vacant chairs surrounding his table—chairs he'd politely refused others in anticipation of Seonaid's imminent appearance—he gestured and invited her to join him in breaking her fast. He'd waited to eat as well, despite his stomach's adamant, loud, and increasingly frequent protests.

The night had passed uneventfully, more likely due to the footpads' inability to pike off once they'd robbed their victims, rather than lack of plotting to steal from them.

Even now, the scurrilous chaps lounged upon their benches, scrutinizing the guests and exchanging a calculated whisper every few minutes. Their attention hovered on Seonaid's graceful advance toward his table. Emerald earrings dangled from her delicate ears and a matching brooch was pinned to her fichu.

Better have a word with her about wearing jewels while we're stranded here.

Truth to tell, she'd be wise to put them in his care. His coach contained a concealed drawer.

Jacques arched a contemptuous brow and, issuing a silent dare across the short distance, gave the gawkers a quashing scowl. Few men could best him with a blade. In fact, only one had ever.

Seonaid's brother, Laird McTavish.

To a slovenly man, the *crétins* glowered and curled their lips, exposing yellowed or missing teeth. But as spineless poltroons do, their attention skittered away from his unspoken challenge. Their kind didn't fight if they could avoid it. *Non*, they skulked about in the dark with the other vermin.

During the night, the snow had ceased falling. Given the vivid sunlight streaming through and heating the dust-covered, irregular windowpanes, the pristine white blanketing the Highlands mightn't last long. A day or two of warmer temperatures could have them on the road by week's end.

It was bittersweet knowledge. He would, at last, be able to inspect his mining venture, and pray God that it proved lucrative. Otherwise...

Stuffing the dismal thought into an appropriately dingy corner of his mind, he focused on Seonaid elegantly wending her way amongst the tables, her hips' gentle sway tempting far more than they should. A most welcome distraction from his rueful reverie.

A sudden image invaded his ponderings.

Seonaid lying gloriously nude across his bed's burgundy and gold coverlet. Her silky hair fanning the pillows, and her slender arms reaching for him.

Merde.

Hunger must have addled his brain. Or he'd gone *fou*, mad. As delicious as the vision was, he promptly quelled it.

McTavish would gut him in a flash if he ever suspected Jacques's wayward musings. They were puzzling contemplations given his restricted circumstances. He was practical if naught else, and entertaining fanciful thoughts about Seonaid perpetuated unadulterated madness indeed.

Although, he rather liked their forced company. Being snowbound gave him an opportunity to unwrap the protective layers she swathed herself in. Perhaps he could, at last, unravel how she'd managed to snarl his thoughts and reasoning while setting his blood afire.

No good could come of it, though.

He'd nothing to offer, and simply because she'd been forced to accept his generosity last night and again this morning didn't mean her feelings toward him had changed an iota.

In Paris, he *had* behaved abominably, and she hadn't forgiven him yet. Mightn't ever, truth be told. Nevertheless, he could make amends.

Hands full of dirty dishes, Mrs. Kerrigan spoke to Seonaid in passing, and a kind smile lit Seonaid's face as she responded. Whatever she murmured caused the innkeeper to beam.

Most ill-fated that Seonaid sought respite in the same

theater alcove he had arranged to meet a female smuggling contact. And more unfortunate, Jean-Louis de Carnot had seen him slip into the niche.

Sloppy on Jacques's part, that.

Or perchance, Gabrielle de Ludres, his informant for three years, had indeed betrayed him. The aging courtesan retired shortly thereafter, leaving France for good, word had it.

Fortuitous? Possibly.

Carnot's presence? Entirely too convenient.

The blackguard's lands marched parallel to Jacques's, and Carnot had coveted *le Manoir des Jardins's château* and superior acreage for years.

Too damned coincidental that while Jacques had been away on a mission, the house had been ransacked, and his sister, her husband, and their four-year-old son died in the *mêlée,* along with several servants. More than one survivor claimed they recognized Carnot's hirelings dressed as British soldiers during the attack.

As an agent, Jacques could scarcely complain about the English raiding his ancestral home. France and England were at war, after all. In any event, that auspicious night in Paris, he'd no choice but to provide Carnot an eyeful and act the womanizing rakehell—a role Jacques had carefully cultivated. Too many of his contacts' lives still depended upon their identities as well as their loyalties remaining hidden.

Entranced from the moment his lips had grazed Seonaid's, he momentarily lost himself in the passionate kiss. Whether paralyzed by shock or outrage, she'd not protested at first. He'd like to think she'd enjoyed the stolen kiss as much as he.

"Good morrow, Monsieur." Her pleasant greeting in her unusual, soothing voice quashed his reverie.

Wearing a black and emerald gown that enhanced her dewy skin and vibrant eyes, Seonaid appeared much refreshed from her night's rest. Offering a sympathetic smile to a mother holding a squirming toddler, she slipped onto a chair.

Spirals of steam whirled upward from the wooden oat porridge bowls Kerrigan set upon the marred tabletop. Thick slices of dark bread, cheese, milk, and tea followed. A ruckus clamored from beyond the kitchen, and casting a frenzied glance behind him, the innkeeper heaved a hefty sigh. "Can I get ye anythin' else?"

"I'm fine, thank you." Spreading her serviette in her lap, Seonaid tilted her head graciously.

Taking his seat, Jacques slipped the overworked man a coin. "As am I, *merci*."

"Thank ye, sir." With a small, upward pull of his mouth, Kerrigan hurried to the kitchen.

Hopefully, his wife didn't await him with her broom again.

"Miss Seonaid," Una said, "if'n ye dinnae mind, I be makin' myself useful in the kitchen." Turning her somewhat intimidating regard on Jacques, she canted her head. "Ye can see me from here if'n ye need me, and I be sure his monsieur-shipness wouldn't mind my absence."

Checking a grin, Jacques flicked his fingers. "Monsieur will do."

Though partially hidden from the entry, their table was visible from the kitchen. Likely, given the crowd, Una felt it safe to leave her ward's side.

Seonaid's attention flitted between Una and Jacques, her fine sable brows drawn together and her nose crinkling the endearing way it did when she was puzzled. "All right, Una. The proprietors are rather harried, and I don't doubt they'd be grateful. Thank you for offering."

"Aye." With a brusque tilt of her gray-threaded orangey head, Una strode to the kitchen.

His conscience twinging, Jacques scooted an extra chair to

the wiggling girl's table. "Here. This might help with *l'enfant.*"

Smiling her appreciation, the mother slid her daughter onto the chair. The curly-haired toddler promptly stood and, grinning, stomped her feet in a childish jig, her mop of ginger ringlets pirouetting with each clumsy step.

"That was kind of you. The poor woman couldn't eat a bite with her daughter practically turning flips in her lap. She certainly is a spirited child. She reminds me of my sister, Adaira." Seonaid smiled and lifted the teapot. "Tea, Monsieur?"

"Please, and will you call me Jacques?" Pouring fresh milk onto his porridge, he winked. "At least when we're alone?"

Instead of immediately denying his request, her solemn gaze probed his for a protracted moment before she suddenly smiled, that dazzling flash of joy that had him blinking like an inebriated buffoon again.

"Since I don't foresee us being alone too terribly much, I suppose it cannot hurt. Even if it isn't quite the thing." Scooping a spoonful of porridge, she slid him an indirect glance. "And yes, you may call me Seonaid. Only when we cannot be overheard, however."

Zut. She'd read his mind. Chance, surely.

"Adaira?" he asked. "She's the, ah, adventurous sister?"

Abducted an earl, if he recalled correctly. The other sister —what was her name?

Isabelle?

Non, Isobel.

She wasn't a stranger to escapades either. She'd been the one captured by rogue Scots. The sisters were all spirited Scotswomen, though the one beside him did her utmost to mask the trait.

"Yes, Addy's been called that. And more." Releasing a

musical chuckle, merriment lit Seonaid's eyes. "You mentioned you're contemplating a move to Scotland?"

She took a neat bite of bread and chewing, awaited his response.

Jacques had never considered eating a sensual act before. But when her dainty pink tongue flicked out to catch a stray crumb from her lower lip, an assortment of creative ways the appendage might otherwise be employed flooded his mind.

His groin tightened uncomfortably.

Inhaling a lengthy, deliberate breath, he scrounged around in his mind, seeking the question she'd asked.

Ah, yes, his fabricated move to Scotland.

"I but teased, *ma petite*. I shall be here for a mite over three months, overseeing my investment in a mining operation not too distant from Craigcutty."

He'd wait to tell her McTavish invited him to stay at the keep for the duration of his visit. She mightn't take the news well, and they'd entered an unspoken truce. A frosty, silent carriage ride to Craiglocky didn't appeal. So, unless the need arose, he'd keep mute about the matter. Let McTavish or his lady deliver the news when they arrived.

Teacup at her pert mouth, Seonaid blew upon the steaming liquid.

A team of oxen couldn't have pried Jacques's gaze from her pursed lips.

She hadn't a notion of how enticing she was.

"Why would you invest in Scotland, Monsieur, rather than your homeland?"

Keen intelligence shone in her umber-hued eyes. No russet sparks spewed from them, as was typical when in his presence, just warm, curious regard.

A man could get used to those doe-like eyes peering at him.

He gave himself a severe mental shake. He wouldn't—*couldn't*—be that man.

Taking a dainty sip, she studied him above the cup's rim. "Excuse my ignorance, but aren't there profitable mines in France? I should think that would be far more convenient than journeying to Scotland's Highlands. Especially in December."

Fingering his fork's handle, he lifted a shoulder. What would she say if he told her he'd invested in the Scottish quarry because he wanted to see her on occasion?

Fine, as often as I can contrive.

"Other than my estate, I'd prefer not to have further ties to France. When I visited here last, McTavish made mention of a possible investment opportunity too fortuitous to pass up."

More precisely, Jacques's last chance, other than an arranged marriage.

"Ah."

He gave her a bland glance.

What did *Ah* mean?

"Please accept my condolences on your mother's passing. Ewan mentioned the tragedy. You have my deepest sympathies. She was most gracious to me the times we met." A slight huskiness tinged Seonaid's voice, and moisture glistened in her eyes.

Her compassion penetrated the protective shell he'd built around his heart, and he didn't much like the vulnerability lancing him.

"I'm sure it's been difficult for you, Jacques."

Jacques wasn't going to dredge up that horridness again. However, he rested easier with the knowledge his murdering stepfather hadn't escaped justice.

"*Merci*. It has been. My entire family, including my sister, her husband, and her son, now rest together in *le Manoir des Jardins's* cemetery."

In the midst of pouring more tea, Seonaid paused, her eyes

wide and mouth parted. "Your sister *too*? How awful. You're entirely alone then?"

"*Oui*, which is another reason I must restore my estate. For my family and to preserve the home they cherished." And because he'd vowed to *Maman* he would do so. Even if he had avoided the place since she married that conniving, cheating sot, Pierre Renault.

"Yet, you're here." She indicated the common room with a lifted finger.

Curiosity fairly screamed from Seonaid, but etiquette prevented her from probing. She twisted her mouth in that delightful way she did when thinking, and he relinquished.

"I inherited an estate in deplorable condition, and I've essentially wagered my future in Oakberry Quarry in hopes that she'll enable me to return *le Manoir des Jardins* to her former splendor."

"And if the mine disappoints?" True concern glinted in Seonaid eyes. "What will you do?"

Draft horses couldn't have dragged the truth from his mouth. And why he should be reticent to tell her he must marry for gain confounded more than a little.

Jacques shrugged and made a noncommittal noise in the back of his throat. "I shall come up with something."

Head slanted, she contemplated him for an extended, rather disquieting, moment.

"Why do I get the sense your acquaintance with Ewan is more than either of you admits? It's no secret he worked as an agent for England's War Office during the war." She leaned forward, excitement and intensity in her gaze, and lowered her voice. After casting a furtive glance around, she whispered, "Perhaps *you* did the same?"

Merde. She was too damned astute by far.

"I'm afraid my life isn't as exciting as your brother's." Jacques cut a piece of cheese for her, then one for himself. "I'll own, you have quite a creative imagination. Another benefit of your gift?"

Instantly, her comportment changed, and her open expression and friendly gaze retreated behind the impenetrable, aloof fortress she usually presented. He could see her erecting the fortified bastillions around herself. Before her eyes shuttered completely, several emotions—fear, betrayal, pain, rejection, and finally resignation—flickered in their wounded depths.

Wounded?

Mon Dieu. He'd committed a horrendous blunder by mentioning the second sight. Her family spoke openly of her visions, and she'd never responded thus. What had changed to cause such a reaction? Did she not discuss her revelations in public?

A hunch niggled. "Is that why you left London in a rush? With scarcely any luggage? Did something happen regarding your...*gift?*"

"I prefer not to speak about *that.*" After sweeping a guarded peek 'round the noisy room, she notched her chin upward, her cool and dense-as-winter-fog-gaze resting upon him. "Please excuse me."

She set her serviette beside her plate and made to scoot her chair away.

Pressing his hand atop hers, Jacques stilled her. "No, wait, *ma petite.* I beg your pardon. I'm not sure how I've offended you, but it wasn't my intent. I can see you're deeply troubled—"

To his utter horror, Seonaid's lower lip quivered. Pulling her hand from beneath his, she dropped her gaze to her lap.

"*Ma chère?*"

A solitary crystalline teardrop glided down her ivory cheek, and she swiftly averted her face, surreptitiously wiping the corner of her eye with her bent forefinger.

Jacques edged his chair closer, angling his back toward the other diners, shielding her. This secluded nook proved most providential. "Tell me what troubles you so, *s'il vous plaît*. Is it your gift?"

"I assure you, Monsieur de Devaux, it's *no* gift." Her concentration fixed outdoors, she bent her pretty mouth upward the merest bit. The soulful eyes brimming with despair that she leveled upon him pierced his heart. "I grow weary of knowing what is to come and of being an oddity that some people want to exploit and others curse."

"That's why you left London, *non*? News of your..." Not wanting to offend her further, Jacques scrambled for the right word. "*Uniqueness* became known?"

Her moist eyes rounded slightly, and she dipped her head.

"Some *le bon ton* members wanted me to call forth revelations and do readings, like a gypsy fortune-teller or soothsayer practicing forbidden arts." She sniffed and swiped away another fat droplet. "I'm not like that. I could never be like that."

Jacques touched her arm. "You've told your family how they treated you, *non*?"

Torment glistened in her beautiful eyes. Considerable consternation too. God, how frightening it must be for her. And how alone she must feel.

Switching her attention outdoors once more, Seonaid gave a short shake of her head. "No. Only you know."

She'd trusted him with something so intimate?

An unnamed emotion welled in him, coursing through his veins, warming his blood and heart. And made him want to take her away and keep her safe. Always.

"Where be the innkeepers?" Reverend Fletcher stomped into the common room, his head swinging back and forth like a rat seeking dinner.

At his infuriated demand, conversations paused, and every

head in the common room jerked in his direction. The toddler scampered onto her mother's lap. Whimpering, she buried her curly head in her mother's shoulder.

Children shouldn't respond with terror when a rector entered the room. Not since the Inquisition, leastways.

Jacques tapped his fingertips atop the table, disliking Fletcher even more this morning than last night.

Discreetly drying her eyes, Seonaid exchanged a skeptical look with Jacques. "He's a mite off his head, I think."

"More than a little." He thrust his chin toward the door. "His soul's blacker than the Earl of Hell's waistcoat."

She chuckled again, this time her tear-clogged throat producing a low, husky purr. "Quotin' Scots adages, are ye?"

Kerrigan hurried to the disgruntled rector. "How can I help ye, Vicar?"

"Hag-ridden I be all night." Accusation accented each harsh word. "I dinnae sleep a wink."

"Hag-ridden?" Jacques rubbed an eyebrow. Even a hag wouldn't want to ride that fetid, scrawny frame. "I don't understand."

"It means ridden by hags or witches during one's sleep. Sometimes it refers to frightful dreams or even the inability to move." Slanting Jacques a sideways look, Seonaid sipped her tea. "Apparently, he's quite obsessed with that sort of paranatural thing."

Raising a bony finger, Reverend Fletcher shook it, glowering 'round the room. "Somebody's practicin' the devil's craft, I tell ye."

Several patrons gasped nervously while others openly scoffed. Sobbing in earnest, the small girl let out a petrified wail.

"*Jacques*?" Seonaid's alarmed tone and her hand clasping at his arm alerted him.

He whipped 'round to face her.

Chalk pale, she stared vacantly out the window, her brows drawn together into a tense vee.

Mon Dieu, a vision right now?

With the damned hell-fired rector lurking across the room and stirring everyone's qualms?

Only one sensible thing a man could do when faced with a situation like this.

Leaning forward, Jacques cupped Seonaid's face. Framing her delicate jaw with his forefinger and thumb, he stared into the vacant pool of her eyes. Her lids slowly lowered and then, ever so lightly, he brushed his lips over hers.

Six

One instant, Seonaid saw Father tumbling from the stable's burning roof, and the next, a sweet yet tantalizing comfort unlike anything she'd ever known overcame her. She never wanted the peaceful serenity to end. Maybe if she kept her eyes shut, it wouldn't.

"Seonaid?" A calloused hand brushed her cheek, and that same wonderful deep voice, his breath hot against her skin, whispered, "Open your eyes, *chérie*."

"No." She pressed her nose against his wonderful smelling face. Manly, a mite spicy, and crisp like soap. "I dreamed I was being kissed, and it was splendid."

Ah, there again, his marvelous mouth settled atop hers—a feathery wisp, no more, but causing the most delightful sensations to awaken elsewhere.

His mustache rasped against her, both prickly and silky soft.

These types of episodes, she'd gladly welcome.

"You must, *ma petite*." He kissed her nose. "Yonder pinch-faced troll watches us."

It took a moment to comprehend the soft, warm lips tenderly pressing against hers had been real, and not a dream or another type of vision.

Seonaid's eyelids flew open, and she stared into inky black irises brimming with tenderness.

Jacques.

She'd never had a vision interrupted before. They played out from start to end. Hope and despair simultaneously ensnared her. Her second sight *could* be changed, or at least be manipulated.

By a kiss.

But Father...

"I must get home. There's been a fire. Father's hurt." Tears blurred her eyes and frustration choked her. *Damnation.* They couldn't leave. Not until the snow melted from the roads.

How badly hurt was Hugh Ferguson? What had caused the fire?

Straightening to peer outside, Jacques shook his dark head. Two hostlers, each leading a pair of horses, trudged through knee-high snow.

"I suspect it will be at least two days, mayhap longer, before the roads are travelable by chaise or coach." Jacques touched her hand. "I think it wiser if you finish the journey in my carriage."

He hadn't made a request, but she'd no desire to argue the point. She far preferred Jacques's company to Reverend Fletcher's. His smell too.

She nearly smiled. A day ago, she'd have believed herself off her head for entertaining a harebrained notion like welcoming Jacques's presence. She'd have assumed she'd gone mad even addressing him by his given name.

And today. After his kiss...

Be sensible, Seonaid.

One minuscule—all right, two sense-warping kisses—didn't alter what a scoundrel he'd been. Surely, the emotional upset about Father caused her momentary lapse in judgment and good sense.

"I'd journey by horseback, except neither Una nor Mrs. Wetherby rides." Sighing, she balanced her elbows atop the blemished table and cradled her chin in her hands. "We're good and stuck then." She peeked sideways. "I'm worried, Jacques. I'm rarely wrong about these things."

Resting his cheek upon his knuckles, he angled his head, his ebony eyes mildly probing. What did he seek? "That must be—"

A pungent odor assaulted her nose, even as a caustic voice grated behind her. "I be tellin' yer brother of yer harlot's conduct."

Seonaid nearly jumped from her skin.

Had Reverend Fletcher heard them?

She spun to face him, then wrinkled her nose. Did the man have an aversion to soap and water? He positively reeked.

"Kissin' a Frenchie in public, and ye not wed to him. Pure, sinful wickedness." Shaking his finger with a grime-caked nail in her face, he sneered. "Yer brother be needin' to find ye a husband afore he be disgraced. If'n any man will have such an immoral wench to wife."

Vile scunner.

"You cross the mark, Vicar. Rest assured, my brother *will* be informed of *exactly* what has taken place." Seonaid sent Jacques a meaningful glance, and folding her arms, gave Reverend Fletcher a falsely congenial smile. "By the by, precisely how long are we blessed with *your* presence in Craigcutty?"

"Dinnae try to flatter me." Jabbing his thumbs into his stained lapels, Fletcher peered down his nose. "I'm sure Laird

McTavish be appreciatin' how seriously I am watchin' over my appointed flock. Ye'll be doin' penance fer yer ungodly behavior. Mark my words."

Penance? Truly daft as a Bedlam boarder.

Fully at ease, Jacques rested an elbow along the back of his chair and hooked an ankle across his knee. "I suggest you not interfere when you aren't acquainted with the entire circumstances. Mademoiselle Ferguson and I met in Paris months ago, and I've made numerous trips to Scotland to further our acquaintance. Her brother's aware of my intentions to court her."

At his colossal lie, Seonaid managed to keep her jaw from becoming unhinged. Just.

"*Ye* mean to marry the lass?"

Utterly absurd.

Waves of disapproval pulsating from him, Reverend Fletcher squinted at Jacques. He gave a slight disbelieving shake of his head. "I canna believe Laird McTavish be pleased. She should be marryin' her own kind, not a *foreigner*." He could barely get the word past his pursed lips. "A man who'd firmly rein in her scandalous ways instead of encouragin' them."

"So you say." Cutting mockery slanted Jacques's mouth.

"Mr. Fletcher," Seonaid said, yearning to wipe the superior expression from his face. "My mother is French, and my brother, the laird, is half French, as am I."

Fletcher blanched, but she dug the verbal knife deeper.

"I strongly suggest you refrain from disparaging the French further lest you rouse my brother's legendary temper." Seonaid drew in a fortifying breath. If the man had redeeming qualities, she'd yet to see a single one.

Jacques elevated a brow in approval.

Una bustled to their table, carrying a laden tray. "Vicar

Fletcher, I be sure ye must be starved after yer unrestful night. Have a seat, and I be servin' ye right up."

Extremely intuitive, had Una detected Seonaid's episode and sought to distract the reverend? Probably. Few people knew Seonaid better than Una.

She jerked her sturdy chin toward the entrance. "Miss Seonaid, Mr. Kerrigan offered ye and the baron the private parlor on the other side of the stairway if'n ye've a mind to use it. The other guests have decided to stay in the common room. There be a fireplace, books, and a chess set in there. I assured him ye'd pay verra well for the privilege."

"*I* should be provided the parlor's use." Reverend Fletcher's envious gaze flew to the closed door.

Why? Because you've such a pious opinion of yourself?

Folding her hands in her lap, Seonaid returned his expectant stare. Chances were, he didn't have coin to rent the private room, and neither she nor Jacques would volunteer a shilling.

His demeanor lofty, he puffed out his skinny chest. "I be needin' the solitude fer my prayers."

"Well then..." Jacques veered his attention from the smallish, chafed spot he'd been examining on his thumb. "Might I suggest you return upstairs and make use of your private chamber where, I'm sure, you can pray in complete solitude?"

Seonaid bit her tongue against a naughty chuckle.

Anger and humiliation snapping in his eyes, Reverend Fletcher flushed.

"I suppose this table be fine." Easing his lanky form into the sturdy chair Jacques vacated, he waved his hand at Una. "This guid woman be knowin' how to treat a man of the cloth with the respect he deserves."

"Och, indeed I do." With a brazen wink at Seonaid over the back of Reverend Fletcher's head, she stumbled and deposited the tray's contents onto his lap.

His outraged shriek shook the snow from the trees and sent the toddler to caterwauling louder as the other guests hooted and guffawed.

"Maybe now ye'll bathe and wash yer clothes, ye reekin' sot." Una tossed a towel at him before marching back to the kitchen.

Seonaid's lips trembled with restrained amusement, and the reverend caught the slight movement.

"Ye'd best take care, woman," he said slowly through gritted teeth. Fist clenched tight, a muscle in his jaw jumped spasmodically as he speared her with a hate-filled glare.

Except for the child's sniffles, the taproom grew still.

"I nae be toleratin' rebelliousness in me flock," Fletcher said, spittle forming at the corners of his mouth. He stabbed a finger at her. "I deal harshly with insurrection and heretics."

So great was his fury, Seonaid wouldn't have been altogether taken aback if fire had spewed from his eyes and mouth.

Everyone's attention remained riveted on their argument, even the ringlet-haloed toddler, her thumb jammed into her mouth, and her cheek resting against her mother's bosom.

"It's most fortunate it's not *your* flock, then, isn't it?" Seonaid rose, burning to slap his sanctimonious face. "And it will *never* be."

Marshaling her composure, she sailed past him.

~

THREE DAYS LATER

Despite being squished between Una and Mrs. Wetherby, the rhythm of Jacques's bumping and swaying chaise lulled Seonaid into a fitful doze. Every few moments, she started awake and found him and Reverend Fletcher watching her.

One with warm regard, and the other with...

Well, she hadn't quite discerned the vicar's expression, but whatever the sentiment was, warning bells clanged unceasingly between her ears.

At times, a gleam disturbingly close to longing—*or lust*—shadowed his unexceptional hazel eyes. At others, judgment and condemnation so intense that her skin prickled caused her to edge farther behind Una's broad back.

Smelling much better after Una's *accident* had required the laundering of his clothes, which Seonaid volunteered to pay for, he'd sunken into a foul-tempered, silent sulk, keeping his distance from her and the other guests.

She didn't regret his absence at all.

Seonaid couldn't shake the suspicion that ill-disposed to start, he either blamed her for Una's antics, or presumed she'd encouraged it and now considered them foes. As if they'd ever been, or would ever be, cozy.

Over the course of the past three days, Jacques's courteous attention, quick wit, and fanciful stories had kept her anxiety about Father somewhat at bay. Worry simmered in her mind's recesses, but with no recourse other than to wait until the roads thawed, she welcomed the diversion.

Reverting to his prior formal politesse, Jacques hadn't attempted any more kisses. Not that she'd have permitted another, no matter how splendid the fleeting experience.

It simply wouldn't do to develop a *tendre* for him. He'd return to France shortly, and she had no desire to venture there again. No small wonder Mother, though French-born herself, had stayed in Scotland after her first husband died. The French and Scots were as different as frogs and squirrels.

Marrying someone other than a Scot was possible, but Seonaid didn't want to leave Scotland. That rather complicated things since everyone within two hundred miles of Craigcutty had no doubt heard rumors of her *an dara shealladh.*

An outsider or a Sassenach then, but one who didn't object to living in Scotland. Perhaps Ewan was acquainted with someone. He certainly had connections enough and a substantial sphere of influence as well.

Yes, indeed. Why hadn't the idea occurred to Seonaid before?

Eyes half-closed, she examined Jacques through her eyelashes. His dark slate greatcoat accented his blue-black hair and sinfully dark eyelashes. Next to him, Reverend Fletcher appeared a rather dowdy, rumpled sparrow.

No one could've convinced her she'd not only tolerate Jacques's company, but enjoy it, even look forward to it. To her consternation, she'd miss him once she was home. He'd been a pleasant distraction from her troubles, and since his nerve-tingling kiss, she had no more visions.

Not altogether unusual.

Weeks or months often passed between them. Wiggling her fingers within her muff, she closed her eyes and relived the brush of Jacques's lips upon hers.

Utterly wicked. And marvelous. And not to be repeated.

She wouldn't have believed a man's kiss could cause a flush of excitement days later, or that if she concentrated hard, she might yet taste him.

Seonaid dared a tiny lick of her lower lip.

"I count us fortunate the thieves merely stole horses and didn't rob us or worse." Nestled in her corner, poking Seonaid in the rib with a pudgy elbow, Mrs. Wetherby gave a drowsy affirmation. "I knew from the moment we arrived that they were a sorry, untrustworthy lot."

Last night, after cracking the ill-fated hostler tending the Hare's Foot stables over the head, the pad borrowers had made off with a dozen horses.

"*Aye.* Good thin' the commotion awakened the monsieur and the other men, or who *kens* how many animals might have been stolen." Adjusting her cramped position, Una flicked Reverend Fletcher a dispassionate glance.

He couldn't be counted among the bolder men who'd torn after the horse thieves. In fact, though his room faced the stables and only someone deaf or dead could've failed to hear the ruckus below, he'd not poked his haughty nose from his chamber until morning.

Of its own volition, Seonaid's gaze dropped to Jacques's bandaged sword hand. During the scuffle, a thief's knife had grazed his palm, and though the cut wasn't deep, she fretted about infection. To speed healing and fight the dirty blade's putridity, she'd treated the wound with a mixture of mallow and chamomile.

This morning, Reverend Fletcher had watched her ministrations with keen interest but kept his thoughts to himself. Attempting polite conversation, Seonaid had explained how she and Gregor, Ewan's cousin, frequently tended the keep's and village's ill or injured with herbal concoctions or tinctures.

He'd answered with noncommittal grunts until she'd given up and fallen silent.

When they stopped next, she needed to change Jacques's bandage. Thank goodness, she generally traveled with small samples of healing herbs. One never knew when they might be useful.

More pleasant weather had enabled the guests to depart, but the shortage of horseflesh required the passengers to squeeze into fewer carriages.

Only a fool would believe it coincidental that every other coach, chaise, and carriage quickly filled to bursting, and no one provided the vicar a seat. Since their party traveled to Craigcutty, they'd been obligated to offer him a place in Jacques's chaise.

However, more than one uncharitable thought pealed about in Seonaid's head. That proved bothersome too. Since when had she become shrewish and unamiable? Unkind in her musings even? Matters were complex enough with her second sight's unpredictability, but the absence of her easygoing and compassionate nature troubled her as much.

The carriage jolted, and Mrs. Wetherby's elbow gouged Seonaid deeper.

Wincing, Seonaid gently pushed the offending arm away and, giving Una a contrite smile, edged an inch closer to her.

Worry about Father chafed worse than riding bum-naked, bareback all day. How badly had he been hurt? Perhaps he hadn't been. He was strong and agile for a man his age.

Seonaid sagged against the seat and permitted her mouth a tiny, pessimistic twist.

Nae. He *was* injured.

In the depths of her being, she felt it. Knew it to be true. Why then, wasn't she allowed to know what happened? That proved nearly as frustrating as the vision itself.

In the crowded, stuffy chaise, the miles dragged by, each seemingly longer than the last. She'd have preferred traveling by horseback. Riding fast, she and Jacques could've made Craiglocky by mid-afternoon.

At her reputation's expense.

Though she hadn't a riding habit, and it spelled certain ruination, she'd still been tempted, until Jacques firmly quashed the notion.

"*Ma petite*, I'll not have your good name in tatters." He'd taken her hand and given it a gentle squeeze. "You must be patient."

Patient?

She'd spent a lifetime being patient and biddable, and she feared she'd soon come to scorn the trait.

"When do you suppose we'll stop? I'm quite famished." Mrs. Wetherby leaned forward to examine the scenery.

Did she expect an inn would suddenly appear beside

them? More likely, she needed a quaff or two of spirits, and with Reverend Fletcher's hawkish gaze noting their every blink and breath, she didn't dare sneak a sip from her flask.

Flicking a disinterested look to the window, Jacques tapped his muscled thigh with his uninjured fingertips. "Soon, Madame. The team tires, I think, *non*?"

Resting her head against the plush velvet squab, Seonaid willed herself to sleep. Both men disturbed her in ways she couldn't quite distinguish, and other than staring at the floor, or craning her neck to peer past her stout seatmates, her choice of view was limited.

A short while later, she woke abruptly.

She yawned delicately. She'd been dreaming one of those erratic, nonsensical dreams that occurred when she half-dozed, somewhere between deep sleep and true wakefulness.

Pistols drawn, highwaymen had surrounded the chaise and were demanding the passengers' money and valuables. When Jacques refused, they'd pointed a gun at his and Fletcher's heads.

True to his cowardly character, the rector had blurted that Jacques kept a gold pocket watch in his waistcoat, Seonaid's luggage contained jewels, and Mrs. Wetherby's cumbersome cloak hid a heavy purse.

In the dream, Mrs. Wetherby had fainted straightaway, and when a robber grabbed Seonaid, Una jumped to her protection and had been clubbed in the cheek.

A most disconcerting, true to reality dream.

Blinking sleepily, and still disturbed by the recollection, Seonaid tried to collect her bearings. Waking up and feeling the intense emotion was like...

God. No!

She lurched to the center of the coach. Planting a hand against the ceiling for balance, Seonaid looked out one window before pivoting and scrambling to peer out the other.

Lord, save us.

Una touched her back. "Miss Seonaid? Be somethin' amiss?"

"What in the Lord's blessed name be ye doin' flittin' amuck like a chicken afeared of the cook pot?" Fletcher snapped.

Yes, just ahead. The road narrowed between high, boulder-lined ridges. Exactly like her dream. No help for it. They must prepare themselves for the inevitable.

Seonaid whirled toward Jacques. "We're going to be set upon by highwaymen."

A shrill shriek escaped Mrs. Wetherby as she wilted against the seat, mopping her eyes.

"*Wheesht.* Enough of yer blasted hysterics." Giving the chaperone a stern look, Una reached under her gown. A moment later, she produced an impressive knife, which she'd concealed in her cloak's folds.

Seonaid withdrew her dagger from her boot.

His eyes protruding, Reverend Fletcher's mouth worked as inarticulate sounds emerged. At last he managed a stuttering, "H... how can ye p... possibly ken such a th... thin'?"

Seonaid had no intention of revealing how she'd come by the knowledge. Better to pretend she hadn't heard him.

"And why do ye women have knives?" Undoubtedly, he yearned to spout drivel about knives and the devil.

"Una, you watch out that window." Seonaid jerked her head toward the small rectangle nearest her maid. "I'll watch out this one. Mrs. Wetherby, scoot to the middle."

The older woman remained rooted in her seat, her eyes wide and stricken.

"Now, if you please." Seonaid essentially dragged her from the corner. Settling onto the seat's edge, Seonaid perused the Scots pine for movement as she deftly removed her gloves.

Jacques didn't question her but immediately slid open a

secret compartment under his seat. He glanced up, his gaze calm but intense. "How soon?"

Seonaid lifted a shoulder, her scarlet mantle's folds rippling with the action. "I don't know."

"Ye don't believe such hobgoblin twaddle?" Despite his protestation of disbelief, Reverend Fletcher wheezed and hugged his prayer book, terror etched upon his thin features.

Jacques extracted an impressive wooden dueling pistol case from within the cubicle, and after setting the guns upon the seat between him and the vicar—who still gaped and gasped like a bass freshly delivered from a pond—proceeded to load first one gun, then the other. "Can you hazard a guess?"

"What be this devilishness?" His suspicious gaze vacillating between Jacques and Seonaid, distrust creased Reverend Fletcher's contorted face.

Una rounded on him. "Shut yer mouth, ye jabberin' crow."

"Seonaid?" Jacques prompted softly.

She shut her eyes. "Soon."

Even as Seonaid answered, shouts reverberated outside, and the chaise slowed.

A crooked smile tipped Jacques's mouth. "I'd say now."

Hands folded and eyes squeezed tight, Reverend Fletcher ducked his head. Prayer certainly couldn't hurt, even if from the likes of him.

Releasing a stifled squeak, Mrs. Wetherby toppled behind Seonaid into a dead swoon. Just as well. They'd not have to soothe her or listen to her histrionics.

"Fletcher, have you any experience shooting?" Jacques held up an ivory-handled pistol.

Fervidly shaking his head, the rector's Adam's apple scuttled up and down like a terrified mouse scampering along a branch. "I be a *mon* of God. I have nae need for a weapon other than this."

Hand trembling, he lifted his Bible.

"While I appreciate and admire your faith, that won't impress the knights of the road who've stopped us." Jacques tucked the gun into his waistband, then arranged his jacket and greatcoat, concealing the butt.

A muffled shout rang out.

"Stand and deliver."

SEVEN

"Let me do the talking, *oui*?" Jacques met the eyes of everyone except the insensate Madame Wetherby. "No one else is to speak unless spoken to, and then say minimal. You understand, *non*?"

Keep things as calm as possible, and no one gets hurt.

Except a thief or two. If his plan played out.

"Aye." Reverend Fletcher gave a nervous twitch. "I shall pray."

At Jacques's stern glance, he mumbled, "Silently."

"Ladies, keep your weapons hidden. Don't use them unless you're set upon." Jacques waited for their consent. "Pull up your hoods, and keep your heads lowered."

Peering out the window, he swore inwardly. Four highwaymen. Maybe more hidden in the trees, like giant, unyielding sentinels, paralleling the road.

"Mademoiselle Ferguson, remove Madame Wetherby's jewelry and other valuables on her person." He glanced at Fletcher, then Una. "They usually want easily accessible valuables, so give me whatever jewels and money you have on you."

Face drawn but her bearing composed, Seonaid swiftly

complied. She passed him her reticule as well. Her jewels lay secured in the hidden compartment where they'd been since the day she'd worn them at the Hare's Foot Inn.

He stuffed everything into Madame Wetherby's larger, black velvet bag.

Pray God the bandits only sought plunder, not to ransom the passengers or ravish the women. Rage heavily dosed with dread twisted Jacques's gut. Even he couldn't stave off four armed curs.

Beautiful, young, and wealthy, Seonaid was most at risk.

The highwaymen had lain in wait for them—had known precisely where to stop the chaise, which meant they made a regular habit of this activity in this vicinity.

Seven kinds of fool was he for not anticipating something like this. But these knights of the road were bloody brazen, robbing a coach in broad daylight on a well-traveled road.

He chanced a peek out the window.

Cloths covered the lower parts of their faces, but he recognized two thieves' boots. They curs had been at the inn. His years as a spy taught him to note footwear. To escape detection, people changed their clothing but regularly forgot to switch their shoes or boots.

If that pair had been at the Hare's Foot Inn, the other robbers likely completed the foursome. He'd been right about the scurrilous *bâtards*.

And these pilferers had seen Seonaid's emeralds that first day. Would they remember them, or would they be content with snatching the heavy purse and picking through their stolen treasures later?

His countenance rebellious, Fletcher stuffed a smallish silver cross behind his collar. "It nae is valuable."

"Valuable or not, you don't want them to find that," Jacques said, pointing at the vicar's neck. *Idiot.* The token would get his throat slit. "Trust me. These robbers were at the inn. They might have seen you with the cross there."

Thrusting his chin at a stubborn angle, Fletcher opened his mouth to argue.

Mrs. Wetherby moaned and pressed a hand to her forehead.

Seonaid bent to reassure her. "Relax and take a few deep breaths. Monsieur de Devaux has things well in hand."

"Vicar, you do understand they're in a hurry, *non*? Knights of the road have been known to cut off fingers when a passenger doesn't remove a ring quickly enough to suit them." Jacques extended his hand and eyed his fingers. "Imagine what they might do to get to the trinket around your neck."

He squelched a laugh at Fletcher's audible gulp. Scant seconds passed before the vicar slapped the cross in Jacques's hand.

"Oh, dear." Seonaid met Jacques's questioning gaze. "Mrs. Wetherby fainted again, and I haven't any salts."

"Inside the coach," a gravelly voice called as the door was violently yanked open. It slammed against the chaise's bright yellow side. "Get out."

"We'll have to leave her here. I'll go first." After giving Seonaid a reassuring smile, Jacques exited the conveyance.

Hanging high in the cloud-dotted sky, the sun peeked through the trees, causing an occasional blinding glare where it reflected off the remaining snow mounds. A bird called a warning from the treetops. A moment later, another answered, followed by an alarmed squirrel's raucous scolding.

"Over there, guvna." Jerking his pistol's barrel toward two other highwaymen, the thief gave Jacques a rough shove in their direction. His disdainful, miry brown eyes glared at Jacques above the soiled cloth.

Same chap from the inn, all right.

The driver and outrider lay spread eagle, face down on the

road. No shots had been fired, and neither appeared injured, but from this distance, Jacques couldn't be positive. Did they still have their weapons? He required his men to carry arms at all times.

A surreptitious glance around answered his question.

Merde.

Two pistols lay near the chaise's front wheel.

Slowly looking from thief to thief, Jacques seized the opportunity to scrutinize the highwaymen and his surroundings.

Good, just the foursome.

They'd probably contrived this scheme the first day they'd been stranded at the inn.

A hefty fallen tree blocked the way, and snow-smattered, steep embankments along the sides of the narrow road prevented the chaise from going around the obstruction. Various-sized boulders, many as massive as the coach, marred the landscape and towered over the muddy route.

"A woman has fainted in the chaise," Jacques said. "I have her jewels and reticule."

Madame Wetherby would rouse soon. Hopefully, she'd have the good sense to stay put.

"We be searchin' her, just the same." The thief who'd ordered them from the coach spoke.

Though his lower face remained covered, Jacques didn't doubt a lewd grin skewed his mouth. Hopefully, Madame Wetherby would remain unconscious and wouldn't remember the indignity.

"Who's in charge?" Jacques displayed the small bulging bag.

"I be takin' the bonnie baubles, guv." A hefty fellow, possibly the ringleader, detached himself from the coach's shadow.

Poised to shoot if resistance came from inside the carriage?

A few moments later, the passengers, except Madame Wetherby, hovered on the road's sludgy edge. As Jacques had directed, the women kept their heads lowered, and Fletcher, a sickly shade somewhere between pond scum green and death gray, clutched his Bible and appeared about to cast up his oat cakes.

A pair of highwaymen trained guns on them while the other two sorted through their takings.

"Where be the bonnie lass's green gems?" Eyes squinted into an angry scowl, the largest brute strode toward Seonaid.

Jacques slipped his hand over her ice-cold fingers and flinched when she squeezed his hand tightly. She was utterly terrified, but you'd never detect it from her stoic composure. Damn, but that took extreme self-discipline. He'd known men who'd crumpled under less pressure.

Double damn that the bandits were determined to have all the loot. This wasn't quite to plan. No quick robbery and escape as Jacques had anticipated.

Best let them have the rest, and hopefully, the highwaymen would be on their way. They risked discovery the longer they waylaid the coach, and with each passing moment, the threat increased for everyone. Panicked and desperate footpads made stupid, impulsive decisions.

Deadly ones.

The hairs on his nape rose. He didn't like the way they eyed Seonaid either.

One thief's tethered horse shifted her weight uneasily and nickered. Another mount jerked his head and snorted. Grazing his jaw with his fingertips, Jacques lifted his eyes to the treetops. The birds and squirrels had grown silent.

Una had noticed the knights of the roads' unsavory regard and had positioned herself partially in front of her charge while Fletcher, hugging his prayer book and trembling like a tree leaf in a gale, answered questions put to him by another robber.

Pray God he possessed a whit of common sense and revealed nothing of import.

Again, the band's leader demanded, "Where be the rest of her pretties?"

"Tell him, Jacques." Though barely audible, Seonaid's voice was steady.

"There's a secret compartment beneath the coach's boot." Jacques motioned to the area. "I'll show you. You'll not be able to find it alone."

As promised, he produced the rest of their valuables, including the last of his funds and his father's gold pocket watch. The latter stung the worst. He'd nothing—*not a damn thing*—left of his family's legacy, save *le Manoir des Jardins*.

Snickering, the road agent roughly snatched Jacques's pin from the folds of his cravat.

"That's everything, *gentlemen*, I assure you. We've nothing else of worth." Boldly crossing to the women huddled together, he took Seonaid's elbow. "We shall be on our way then."

How, with a tree blocking the road?

"Nae so fast." The apparent leader shook his shaggy head and pointed at Seonaid. "She be quality. Might be she could bring a handsome ransom."

Merde.

What they'd do to Seonaid in the meanwhile didn't bear contemplating.

Inhaling sharply, she stiffened and adjusted her stance, her hidden blade at the ready. Desperation simmered in the glance she hurled to Jacques and cramped his lungs.

Given her set jaw and squared shoulders, Una, too, was prepared to fight.

Itching to snatch his pistol from his waistband, Jacques

calculated the odds. His men couldn't get to their weapons in time to help. He had one shot on him and another in the coach. Useless, the latter. Too far away. He bore a knife as well, but could Una or Seonaid each fend off an attacker?

Fletcher?

Jacques spared the reverend a fleeting glance.

No help there. He wasn't likely to whack them with his Bible. Tucking his forked tail between his knobby knees and trotting away on cloven hooves was more his nature.

Jacques counted it a bloody miracle Fletcher remained upright this long. A skirmish would have him toppling face-first into the mire. Swearing inwardly again, he searched the lane. The most traveled road to Craigcutty, and not a single, bloody rider or carriage had come upon them.

"The lass be stayin' with us." His voice belligerent, the biggest brute's lascivious gaze rested upon Seonaid.

"Och, she isnae. She be nobody but a governess dismissed from her position and returnin' to her village." Una grabbed Seonaid's arm and propelled her to the chaise. "Ye'd git nae ransom from her pauper family."

The thief laughed, a humorless guttural rumble. "Nae accordin' to the gabby vicar. She be Laird McTavish's kin."

Hands fisted, Jacques spun to face Fletcher. Would he suffer eternal damnation for corking a reverend? Even a craven, hypocritical, judgmental fraud?

"Ye canna hold her," Fletcher croaked. Posture rigid, he sliced Jacques a guilt-ridden peek and shook his head. "McTavish will be furious. I told ye so ye'd ken the foolishness of yer ways, darin' to waylay the laird's sister and his new rector."

Imbécile.

"*Wheesht.*" Snarling, another robber gave Fletcher a vicious shove. "Quit flappin' yer lips."

"*Non,* you boasted about your insignificant position, you

pompous, self-seeking *fils de—*" Barely preventing the foul oaths tapping against his teeth, Jacques strode to Seonaid. "I'll not leave her."

If he killed the leader, would the others flee?

"He be a French nobleman, and he be courtin' the *laird's* sister." Fletcher dared to step forward and point his Bible at Jacques. "Maybe ye can ransom him too. Let me go, and I'll take the ransom note to Laird McTavish myself."

A low hiss escaped Seonaid, and she impaled Fletcher with a glare of such utter abhorrence, he flinched. "So help me God, you'll rue the day you ever agreed to shepherd Craigcutty's parishioners."

"Be ye cursin' me?" The planes of his face settled into sinister creases, self-righteous ire radiating from every pore. "Och, ye better take care yerself, else people may start to question yer strange ways. Ye never explained how ye ken about the highwaymen stoppin' us. Awful peculiar, if'n ye ask me."

A threat if Jacques ever heard one. He'd also apprise McTavish of Fletcher's strangeness. The man was dangerous and demented too.

One knight of the road scratched his craggy cheek. "Heard tell McTavish has a sister with the second sight."

Una wrapped a protective arm around Seonaid. "Och, yer aff yer heid. Complete flummery. I've ken the lass since birth, and she nae more sees such rubbish than the reverend here sees demons and fairies." She angled forward, peering at Fletcher, and in *sotto voce* asked, "Tell me, Vicar, do ye see wee folk?"

"Dinnae be absurd." His perpetual scowl deepened into harsh grooves. "There nae be such thin's."

Una's brows peaked skeptically. *"Ach,* but there be devil's handmaidens?"

Fletcher sputtered, and Jacques choked on a laugh.

An unexpected glint in the woods caught his eye. Then

another. He casually perused the area past the chaise. An answering flicker glittered beyond a tree.

They had company. Lots of it.

A bird's trill rent the stillness, and Seonaid slowly lifted her head, her clever gaze honed and focused.

He nearly missed the almost indiscernible, pleased twitch of her mouth.

Mon Dieu.

Jacques scoured the trees.

McTavish was here.

EIGHT

When the bird tweeted again, and another familiar chirrup immediately echoed, Seonaid nearly shouted in glee.

Yes!

As a child, she had been taught the clan's signal.

Ewan and the others lurked in the forest.

Neck bent, she peeked toward the towering pines and bit her lower lip to prevent her instinctive smile.

Aha. There behind a tree trunk, a familiar maroon tartan.

Dugall? Duncan?

She relaxed the grip on her dagger. Better dead than repeatedly violated, which, as sure as horses neigh, would've been her fate.

Raucous shouts exploded around them.

Jacques shoved her and Una to the ground. "Get down. If you can, crawl underneath the coach and stay put until the skirmish ends."

"I can fight too." Seonaid brandished her dagger.

"*Non.* You cannot. You'd distract me, *chérie.* Go." He

brushed her cheek with his fingertips, then spun to attack an enraged robber.

Her ire evaporated.

How was she supposed to respond to that?

Una shook Seonaid's shoulder. "Lass, close yer hangin' jaw and move yer wee bum." She prodded her again. "Now."

As Seonaid scurried to the coach, her clan stormed the road in a flashing jumble of plaids, trews, buckskins, and blades.

The fray lasted mere moments. Three highwaymen lay dead, and Alasdair and Duncan McTavish, Ewan's cousin and uncle, held the fourth struggling bandit between them.

Ewan, unrumpled and scarcely breathing heavily, spun in a slow circle, his hand resting upon his sword. "Seonaid?"

Dugall, her far too handsome and giant younger brother, spotted her crouched underneath the coach and gave her a cocky smile. "There she be, Ewan."

"Here, Ewan. I'm here." Dropping her blade, and with tears streaming down her cheeks, she bolted into his open arms. "I cannot believe you're here. Please, tell me. How is Father?"

Gripping her upper arms, he leaned back, searching her face. "Ye ken?"

"Aye." She gave a shaky nod, mindful of Fletcher hovering nearby, his ears practically twisting in an effort to overhear them. Turning her back, she spoke quietly. "Three days ago. Is...he?" She swallowed and clasped his forearm. "How badly hurt is he?"

Ewan's astute regard swerved to Reverend Fletcher before gravitating to her again. Cupping her elbow, he steered her to a more private area a few feet away.

Dugall joined them, and after giving her a bone-crushing hug, chucked her chin. "Lass, you gave us quite a fright. Dinna be surprised if Mother is miffed with you for a wee mite. You're her last daughter, you know."

Of course, she knew.

Gone was the precocious lad usually into mischief, and in his place was a polite, self-assured gentleman. Since when had he ceased speaking with his usual heavy brogue? Did he think it necessary for university? Sadness bathed her, adding to despondency. Even Dugall was different. So much change.

For everyone but her.

Offering a budding smile, Seonaid half-shrugged. "I'm truly remorseful, but I had to leave London. My *an dara shealladh* became an issue." She slid Fletcher a covert glance. "I'd rather not discuss it now however, especially with Fletcher around."

She didn't miss the peevish turn of the vicar's mouth.

Did he truly think he should be privy to their reunion and private conversation? Where had he been during the scuffle? Cowering under a bush? Up a tree? Behind a boulder. Or mayhap using a baby squirrel for a shield?

Brushing several tendrils off her face, Seonaid lowered her voice. "There's something troubling and off-putting about him. I'm not sure what exactly, but he unnerves me in a way I've not experienced before."

"He does, does he?" Mouth tipped in amusement, Dugall wiggled his big fingers at the gawping reverend while whispering out the side of his mouth. "Och, do ye want me to pummel him fer ye, lass?"

There was the familiar Dugall.

"Nae, ye big oaf." A grin teased her mouth. Actually, she'd like to see Fletcher get his comeuppance. "Please, how does Father fare?"

"Hugh's leg is broken, and he has a few bruised ribs." Grinning, Ewan scratched his nose. "My stepfather is a rather horrid patient. Mother threatened to chain him to the bed if he left it once more before Doctor Paterson gave his permission."

"Sounds like my bullheaded father, all right." A watery chuckle escaped Seonaid as she dabbed at her eyes. "What happened? What caused the fire?"

"We can't be certain, but Duncan suspects arson." Consternation crinkled Ewan's forehead and the corners of his eyes. "Why are you traveling alone, Seonaid, and in December too? When your letter arrived yesterday, Mother was frantic with worry and insisted we leave at once to intercept you."

"Circumstances became intolerable, Ewan, and I was desperate to leave London." Casting her attention to her mud-splattered half-boots and pelisse's hem, she breathed out a poignant sigh.

How could she make him understand her dread?

Her fear of the future with her fey?

Without it too?

Squaring her shoulders, she met his concerned gaze directly. "I'll explain once we're home, but I hesitate to reveal too much with the vicar nearby."

Ewan speared the cleric a contemplative glance and made a sound in the back of his throat.

Wending his way to the coach—from which a completely befuddled Mrs. Wetherby poked her head, her bonnet hanging askew—Reverend Fletcher talked to himself once more.

Ewan raked a hand through his hair. "Very well. We'll discuss *everything* at Craiglocky. We can be there by nightfall if the weather holds." His eyes widened, and a crooked, boyish grin skewed his mouth. "Devaux."

His hand extended, Jacques strode in their direction. "McTavish." After clasping palms with Ewan and Dugall, Jacques speared a swift glance to the dead highwaymen sprawled over the horses.

"I think I'll introduce myself to the vicar. Or mayhap save

him from Una. She looks ready to slay the man," Dugall said with mischief shading his words. He pecked Seonaid's cheek before striding to the coach.

Reverend Fletcher dove into the coach with a vermin's timidity and speed.

Probably trying to hide in the seat's secret compartment.

Roaring with laughter, Dugall threw back his head but didn't slow his pace.

"How came you to be traveling with my sister? I'll admit to being rather shocked." Buttoning his coat, humor glinted in Ewan's turquoise eyes. "Forgive me, but you weren't exactly on the most genial of terms when you last met."

"*Oui*, well, *mon ami*, when I realized Mademoiselle Ferguson and I were stranded at the same posting house, and that she journeyed with only female companions, I felt it my duty to assign myself her protector and deliver her home safely."

Duty? Was that truly all the past three days had been?

What about the kisses?

Perchance he'd merely been chivalrously offering her comfort, and she'd imagined it as something more. Her first kiss, from him of all men, and the experience meant nothing.

Well, naturally, it hadn't.

It couldn't.

Foolish to expect it would. And Seonaid was not a fool.

While other women might be led by their hearts, she'd learned to rely upon logic, despite her unwanted visions. Love was well and good, and her family had been uncommonly blessed with love matches, but her reasons for marrying had nothing to do with sentimental claptrap. Eliminating her second sight motivated her.

Furthermore, if she married and her *an dara shealladh* remained, she might have to become a recluse. And if she loved her husband, how could she leave him?

"I didn't anticipate highwaymen waylaying us, although I'll admit that was shortsighted of me." Smoothing his mustache with his uninjured hand, Jacques lifted a shoulder and swept his enigmatic dark gaze over Seonaid.

Anything else you want to say? Why don't you tell Ewan you kissed me? Again.

Why she was piqued, Seonaid couldn't say and didn't truly want to examine. The sooner she reached Craiglocky, the sooner she could seriously plan the most practical means of acquiring a husband.

And he couldn't ever be Monsieur le baron.

Ewan regarded Jacques's bandaged hand. "Did that happen just now?"

"*Non*, last night when thieves decided they'd taken a liking to the horseflesh at our inn." Lifting his hand, he flashed her one of those smiles that caused her stomach to go wobbly. "Mademoiselle Ferguson's quite an accomplished nurse."

"Aye, she's always had uncommon healing skills. With animals too. Even wild creatures allow her to treat their wounds." Admiration shone in Ewan's eyes.

Her visions, on the other hand, he didn't understand entirely. No one did. How could they? The second sight wasn't that unusual in Scotland or unheard of in their family. Nonetheless, the anomaly fell far beyond what most people, even the Kirk, considered ordinary.

"*Zut*, I'm most grateful for your timely arrival, McTavish. The highwaymen intended to ransom your sister. Thanks to Fletcher blabbing the mademoiselle's identity." Jacques's handsome face folded in contempt. "He offered to deliver the ransom note himself. A magnanimous chap, *non*?"

"The devil he did." The scorching look Ewan shot the coach promised the matter was far from settled. "I presume he's Reverend Wallace's replacement until the good rector returns?"

"You didn't select Fletcher?" Seonaid asked.

Thank God. Maybe he could be given his *congé*. How did things of that nature work within the Kirk? Seonaid twisted her loose hair before securing the strand with a pin. "Attempting to garner preferential treatment, he used your name and position rather loosely."

Ewan frowned. "Vicar Wallace's mother is dying, and he asked to take a prolonged leave. He assured me he'd written the bishop and asked him to send a worthy man in his stay."

"*Non*, worthy isn't a word we'd use to describe Fletcher, eh *ma petite*?" Jacques gave Seonaid a devilish wink, and like an imbecile, she basked in his esteem.

Ewan's eyes narrowed a degree.

"Certainly not. His sort blackens honorable clerics' names and the profession as a whole." After retying her bonnet ribbons, she shivered and searched her pelisse's pockets for her gloves. Though sunbeams streamed through the gathering clouds, the air had cooled dramatically.

Given the horizon's pinkish-grey tint, more snow portended. They'd best get on the road. No more posting houses with snug fires and warm toddies awaited them before reaching Craiglocky.

Reverend Fletcher stuck his head out the coach door, reminding Seonaid of a wary mouse. After a moment's hesitation, he jumped to the ground. His conversation with Dugall had been strikingly short, and afterward, guardedness had replaced Dugall's usual jovial countenance.

She must ask him what had transpired.

Taking a moment to smooth his bedraggled coat and adjust his equally crumpled hat, Fletcher's calculating gaze flitted between Ewan, Jacques, and Seonaid. Marching across the distance, he studiously avoided meeting Dugall's and the other Highlanders' curious scrutiny.

One foot sank into a mud hole, and, arms flailing, Fletcher nearly toppled onto his face before regaining his balance.

Seonaid swore he choked off a vulgar curse. He continued to mutter as he scowled and attempted to scrape the mud from his boot by dragging the sole in a spot of grass bordering the road.

What was his tale?

What caused him to become bitter and suspicious? Or was his attitude an ingrained character flaw? Whyever had he chosen the Kirk as his profession then?

Perhaps he had no choice.

If so, Seonaid understood his position slightly better, his frustration and anger too. She'd absolutely no choice regarding her visions, and the older she grew, the more they molded her future.

Except that she'd had enough of them controlling her life. Either she speedily found a husband, or she'd take herself off to a quiet, remote cottage where, at least, she'd not have witnesses to her episodes.

Well, she *could* toss morals and good sense to the foaming sea and be freed of her virginity. The right herbs would prevent pregnancy, but how many couplings might it take to determine if the fey had stopped?

One, two, a dozen? More?

And how did she choose the man?

Rather awkward, that.

You see, my good fellow, I require you to lie with me until I'm rid of my second sight. Are you at all interested? The process might take some time and repetition.

What if she took the risk and her gamble didn't pay off? She still possessed the sight of a seer. Then where would she be?

Traipsing off to a dank mountain cave to live out her days in disgrace with the bats? Feared by many who didn't understand the nature of her gift? Perhaps even hated? Moments such as these, the dual yokes of anger and resentment overcame her, and she was hard-pressed not to rail her frustration.

Except until now, Seonaid hadn't railed. Hadn't complained. She'd meekly accepted her fate, mistakenly thinking she had no other option.

Nudging Ewan, she notched her chin. "The vicar comes this way. Please permit me to ride rather than endure his company in the coach the remainder of the journey."

"*Non*, he should ride, although I'm not sure he can sit a saddle." Jacques's dry observation earned him a conspiratorially raised brow from Ewan.

"Aye, I confess, the same thought crossed my mind." One hand resting on his hip, the other at his nape, Ewan considered the horses. "That mare might do, but honestly, with the weather turning bitter again, I don't think we can afford to have a plodding rider."

Fletcher stopped before Ewan and bowed his head differentially. "I presume I be havin' the honor of addressin' Laird McTavish himself?"

At Ewan's casual, affirming lift of his chin, the reverend swallowed and cut Seonaid an indecipherable glance.

Opening her eyes wide, she arched a mocking brow.
Well?

"Yer lairdship, my godly duty compels me to tell ye that Miss Ferguson engaged in public affection with this Frenchman. I saw her kiss him. Twice."

Rotten, *missish, tattlemongering frig pig.*

Seonaid clamped her jaw else she tell Fletcher to toss off, and then have to explain to Ewan how she'd come by such an uncouth expression.

Above their strong noses, Jacques's and Ewan's midnight brows collided at the same moment. Their identical flabbergasted expressions might have been comical another time.

If Fletcher had lied and claimed she'd danced naked as a robin atop the tables at the Hare's Foot, she didn't think they'd be any more astounded. Right now, however, she yearned for a parasol to smack the rector.

Twice.

Hard.

"*Non,* Vicar, you're gravely mistaken." Jacques's gaze, inflexible and dark as jet, bored into the gulping rector. "You saw me consoling a distraught, homesick woman, upset because she was stranded and compelled to wait out the storm. And as I told you then, I was previously acquainted with Mademoiselle Ferguson."

An innocent sounding partial truth. Wise to have left off

that courting balderdash. It was an outlandish thing to have contrived in the first place. Ewan mightn't understand, and given the reverend's penchant for dramatics, he'd demand a wedding ceremony as soon as they reached Craigcutty.

Or mayhap, one this instant.

They were in Scotland after all, where marrying proved easier than learning to properly pour tea. No banns. No licenses. One didn't need a cleric either, truth to tell. Agreeing to enter a union before witnesses sufficed.

Marry Jacques, indeed. A more ludicrous notion never occurred to Seonaid. Oh fine, a few had, but she'd not admit to the ideas. His kisses might devastate her composure, but until a few days ago, she couldn't abide the man.

Is that the real truth?

Yes.

No.

I don't know!

Honestly, that kiss in Paris had seared clear to her satin slippers too. As well it should. After all, he was an experienced libertine, no doubt highly practiced in the art of kissing.

She firmly stamped her maddening thoughts beneath her mental heel.

At Ewan's penetrating, expectant stare, Seonaid sighed. "Nothing untoward occurred, Ewan."

Another partial truth. She'd not deem the kiss something vile or ugly. Improper, yes, but she wouldn't regret it. Jacques had introduced her to something wondrous, given her a glimpse of hope.

His arms crossed, everything in Jacques's bearing dared the rector to contradict either of them.

"I ken what I saw, and it be more than comfortin' goin' on, I tell ye. She be actin' mighty fast, even if Devaux be courtin' her."

Ach, the gossipy knave.

"Courting her? Ah, it's come to that, has it?" A mixture of disbelief and amusement tipped Ewan's mouth.

Fletcher couldn't have seen what transpired between her and Jacques from his position. Unless he could stretch his neck several feet, or he'd tiptoed across the room to catch them unawares. The latter she wouldn't put past the crafty cull.

He sidled closer to Ewan. "And she kens thin's afore they happen. That no' be godly, ye have to admit."

Ewan's expression hardened, as rigid and inflexible as granite.

But Fletcher, seemingly oblivious, prattled on, reveling in his tale-bearing like gossipy Lady Clutterbuck. "I've seen the likes afore, I have." Eyes narrowed to triumphant slits, Reverend Fletcher moistened his already wet lower lip. "Though there be ways of purifyin' *her* kind."

A fierce, revulsion-borne shudder shook Seonaid, so intense that Ewan wrapped a protective arm around her shoulders, and Jacques took a threatening step forward.

"*Misérable tas de merde.*"

Miserable piece of excrement, indeed.

Either Ewan would call Jacques out for compromising her or cork the cleric for disparaging her.

She'd cheer the latter.

"Ewan." Duncan, wrapping his gray and vermilion knitted scarf more snugly about his neck as his long strides ate up the ground, pointed to the formidable horizon. "We'd best be movin' if we be outpacin' that."

Searching the horizon, Ewan took Seonaid's elbow. "Devaux and Fletcher, you will both ride and expect to ride hard. Those clouds carry another angry winter storm, and there's no shelter between here and Craigcutty."

Shuffling his feet, the vicar noisily cleared his throat and rubbed his hands on the front of his shabby coat. "I prefer the chaise if'n ye dinna—"

"But I *do* mind. Very much." Ewan towered above the quaking rector. "After what you dared imply about my sister, count yourself fortunate I don't plant you a facer. Or worse— man of God or not. That I even permit you to continue on with us is only due to my immense respect for Reverend Wallace."

Lethal with a blade, Ewan's tongue punctured equally sharp when his temper was aroused.

Seonaid could've no more prevented her lips from arcing than have stopped the storm bearing down upon them.

Jacques laughed outright, a delicious mirthful timbre deep in his chest, earning him a loathing-filled glower from the gloriously mute rector.

After pivoting her to face the chaise, Ewan gave a slight shove. "Go and tell the other women to brace themselves for a jarring journey. If they need a moment's privacy, this is the time to take it. We shan't be stopping."

A repeat of a few days ago. Splendid. Seonaid had best sit on the chaise's opposite side so she could sport bruises evenly on her person.

Pulling her pelisse aside, she hurried across the soggy ground. Halfway to the conveyance, Reverend Fletcher's furious words pulled her up short.

"*Laird*, I intend to write the bishop myself and inform him of yer sister's heretic ways. It be my duty. I'm sure he'll be verra interested in why Wallace kept her soothsayin' and sorcery a secret—"

His voice ended on a strangled gasp.

"You do that, Fletcher, and it will be *my* duty to run you through, *oui*?"

Rustling, followed by a stifled squawk, filled the unnerving quietness.

Her heart beating somewhere in her wobbly knees' vicinity, Seonaid slowly pivoted.

Jacques's large hand encircled Fletcher's skinny throat.

"I would think as a man of the cloth, you would've learned when to speak and when to hold your tongue, *non*? And that it's never, and I do mean *never*, acceptable for you to speak of Mademoiselle Ferguson with such irreverence and contempt."

Ewan made no move to intervene but simply observed dispassionately as the rector, his face radish-red and eyes bulging like a toad caught in a predator's mouth, clawed in vain at Jacques's hand.

Stupid, stupid simpleton.

Only a complete beef-wit threatened men of Jacques's and Ewan's ilk. If, as Seonaid suspected, Jacques had been in the same line of service as Ewan during the war, he had killed. Undoubtedly, more than once.

"If I weren't certain you'd perish, I'd demand we leave your sorry arse here. Only my displaced sense of decency compels me to allow you to continue on." Jacques flung the rector away from him with the force and distaste of a man holding a gyrating viper.

Jacques was as dangerous as Ewan. Foolish for the rector to make him an enemy.

You once considered him thus.

Nearly falling, Fletcher stumbled backward a few steps before regaining his balance. His wary gaze traveled around the stretch of road, and he raised a shaky hand to his throat.

Jacques's taut stance, steely eyes, and flexing jaw betrayed a man in rigid control of his temper.

Seonaid didn't doubt one iota that his respect for the women and reverence for the cleric's position, if not the man himself, kept Reverend Fletcher from a sound thrashing.

"Rest assured. I shall be writing the bishop as well." Pulling his plaid tam o' shanter onto his head, Ewan stabbed the seemingly contrite cleric a dark glower. "I'd rather Craigcutty hadn't a rector until Wallace's return than allow you to stay in my village. You do the Kirk a disservice, and I intend to see you stripped of your position."

"Ye widnae dare," Fletcher stammered, nearly foaming with fear-induced fury. "Ye risk the Almighty's wrath."

Ewan shoved past him. "And you, sir, risk mine."

Ten

Craiglocky Keep

Early the next morning, before Jacques broke his fast or the chickens poked their speckled heads from their coops, Jacques strode Craiglocky's dim, chilly corridor on his way to McTavish's equally gloomy study.

Damnation. Summoned before I'd yet risen.

That didn't bode well.

Had McTavish spoken with Seonaid already?

Not unless he'd done so after Jacques retired last evening.

Conceivable but doubtful.

Like the other weary travelers, she'd gone to her chamber straightaway, and a tray had been sent to her room. If hers was anything like his drafty chamber, she probably still slept snuggled beneath a pile of warm bedcovers.

Except for a few servants silently scurrying about, the castle remained eerily quiet given the sixty-plus souls who slept beneath the barrel vaults gracing her roof.

After depositing a saddle-sore and half-frozen cantankerous Fletcher at the parsonage—temporarily, McTavish insisted—and Mrs. Wetherby at the Rose and Thistle Inn where her sister would retrieve her, the remainder of their exhausted entourage hadn't lumbered across the keep's drawbridge until late evening.

Heavy snowfall hampered their progress the last several miles, and they scarcely stayed ahead of the impending storm, now blowing a blinding white tumult outside.

Merde. Highland weather changed swifter than a popular courtesan's patrons.

Head wooly from several sleep-deprived nights, Jacques craved a cup—*non*, an entire pot—of his favorite coffee. Weak and tepid, the English brews he'd sampled this visit didn't compare to the dark, rich Arabian beans he preferred. In that regard, Jacques reluctantly conceded, the French's *café* surpassed the British's.

His footsteps, a hollow, echoing cadence on time-trodden stones, accompanied his pulse's slightly irregular rhythmic beat.

A prelude of what was to come?

His stomach pitched like a ship plunging towering waves.

Nerves? Me?

Fascinating. And most uncharacteristic.

Why the edginess?

The question begged answering, but Jacques wasn't treading that contorted path. He had one objective, one purpose for being here. Nothing—*no one, not even a sloe-eyed temptress*—could distract him from his goal.

Quirking his mouth to one side, he saluted a somber bust stationed atop a heavy, ornate carved table.

Fearsome lot, these Scots.

Not all.

A delicious-smelling, softly curved, velvety-lipped woman with impossibly expressive eyes framed by sooty lashes had been stamped upon his senses. His memory. Perhaps even more.

Seonaid had saved his life that night in Paris, for there were still those, including Carnot, who would gladly slit Jacques's throat for his part during the war if the truth were ever outed.

That she'd nearly succeeded in having him called out by her French cousin rankled. A great deal, truth to tell, since Jacques had been deemed a coward for flouting the challenge. Months later, direct cuts and barbed taunts still flew his way, and more than one High Society door had been closed to him. Not that he cared a damn what France's elites believed.

A nugatory crowd, the lot, and more affirmation he'd chosen well when he'd sided with the British. Perchance his maternal grandmother's English blood ran stronger than his French. Then why couldn't he turn his back on *le Manoir des Jardins* and sell the place? Or simply abandon her as many other stately homes had been deserted in recent years?

Carnot would snatch the coveted estate in a blink. And grandly restore her too.

Unthinkable.

That *meurtrier* wouldn't know the pleasure or honor as long as Jacques drew a breath.

If he didn't have an estate to restore, if necessity didn't require him to acquire funds by one means or another, if he hadn't offended Seonaid mightily in Paris... Perchance he'd explore the enigmatic, relentless stirrings she'd triggered and which now permeated the deepest part of his soul.

Stop woolgathering, man, and concentrate on the task at hand.

He needed McTavish's endorsement, and entertaining sensual musings about his sister wouldn't further Jacques's cause. He had much to lose. Everything, in fact, if McTavish withdrew his support.

A bourgeoning sneer skewed Jacques's mouth. Returning

to France, pockets to let, and brazenly seeking a rich-as-Croesus wife didn't sit well with his pride. Not that he was particularly prideful, but in his estimation, fortune hunters ranked slightly better than resurrectionists, toshers, or mudlarks.

He shook his head in disgust.

From their gilded frames, decades of grim-faced, piercing-eyed McTavish ancestors watched his progress.

Skirting a suit of armor standing at attention and wielding a wicked, mammoth ax—*mon Dieu, had a giant worn that chainmail and carried that weapon?*—Jacques considered where he'd stay if McTavish gave him the boot. Without abundant coin or another acquaintance nearby, his prospects proved humiliatingly dismal.

Three months.

That was the longest his creditors would wait. Nonetheless, he couldn't leave Scotland. Not before determining Oakberry Quarry's worth. And excavating in the dead of winter? He snorted. Bloody insane. He needed a damned miracle. At least the mine operated in the wintertime, unlike open pit quarries. A small reprieve, that.

Perhaps the camp had extra living quarters, or mayhap a miner would rent him a corner in his room. Even a humble shack would do. Jacques hadn't blunt to spare to let anything finer.

Another cynical smile twisted his mouth as he marched along.

Him—a baron with the blood of royalty flowing in his veins, owner of nearly a thousand acres boasting one of the most coveted *châteaux* in France—reduced to hanging upon the coat sleeves of a friend, his future dependent on stripping the Earth of her treasures.

A plump, fresh-faced maid in a starched apron and cap scooted by, offering him a shy smile. "*Guid* mornin' to ye, sir."

"I bid you good day as well," Jacques said, a trifle perfunctorily.

In all honesty, the tersely worded note delivered thirty minutes ago hadn't been unforeseen, and he hadn't expected to altogether escape an interrogation by McTavish. If someone reported a chap publicly kissing Jacques's sister, he would be as troubled.

Non, he'd be raising his sword in an affair of honor.

Known for his volatile temperament, McTavish hadn't demanded satisfaction yesterday while standing in the muck, and that gave Jacques a smattering of confidence.

Nevertheless, McTavish wasn't stupid, and though he'd directed the full force of his ire at the wily rector, he would demand accountability for each vile allegation against Jacques today.

Mentally preparing for the forthcoming dance of words, Jacques vacillated. Why not save McTavish both time and trouble? Tell him everything. Certainly, in a slightly different, more favorable light than the dotty cleric had, and pray fortune favored him.

He'd kissed Seonaid to stop her vision.

And because he couldn't forget her mouth's unequaled taste and exquisite suppleness.

The latter, McTavish need never know.

Rapping sharply on the stout door, Jacques examined the imposing arch overhead. How many generations had the McTavishes or their kin lived in this medieval monstrosity?

As long as his family at *le Manoir des Jardins*? Impressive and rustic, Craiglocky Keep possessed *un charme d'antan*, wholly different from the brightly gilded, ornate chambers and hallways of his home. Nevertheless, he didn't doubt the McTavishes cherished the place's bucolic charm as much as he treasured his home.

He lifted his hand to knock again when McTavish at last gruffly called, "Enter."

Oui, Jacques would spare McTavish the trouble and speak candidly.

The study remained exactly as he remembered from a meeting here a few months ago. Stately, dark, and *dismal*. Ancient, barbaric weaponry and crest-engraved shields graced two stone walls and another suit of much smaller, tarnished armor stared sightlessly at him from a corner's half-light.

Must they keep those rusty novelties about? Rather unnerved a fellow.

"Sit." Indicating the high-backed leather chairs before his cumbersome walnut desk with a curt angling of his head, McTavish scratched away at the foolscap before him.

After sitting, Jacques hooked an ankle over his knee and smiled. "I'll admit I'm surprised you waited until this morning to have a go at me."

Go on the offensive. Another skill he'd learned as an agent. But one McTavish possessed as well.

"Were you aware your sister fears her visions? Dreads what others say about them?" Flipping two fingers upward, Jacques arched a knowing brow. "That she left London because the *haut ton* tried to exploit her gift like a cheap gypsy fortune-teller?"

Hand poised in replacing his quill in its holder, McTavish froze. His mouth and brows descended, and he carefully laid the creamy plume in its appointed place. "To my knowledge, Seonaid hasn't ever expressed anything of that nature to anyone."

"Well, she told me, and the rector is a perfect example of why she wants to keep her fey hidden. He essentially accused her of witchcraft." *Mais quel fils de pute*! Witch hunter indeed. "She's bloody terrified, especially since she cannot control their occurrences."

The air left McTavish in a rasping whoosh as he slumped into his chair. Drumming his fingers upon his chair's arms, he gauged Jacques.

They'd worked together under life and death situations, had forged a relationship founded on trust and dependence. Based on their history, McTavish had no reason to doubt him, so he waited uncomplainingly as the Scot's brilliant mind processed what Jacques had revealed.

A firming of McTavish's lips and the merest slant of his mouth confirmed his acquiescence. "Explain the kiss then."

"While breakfasting in the common room, she saw Sir Hugh's fall. Fletcher's presence required I shock her out of the episode before he realized what occurred. That sod already suggested something untoward went on with her."

"That doesn't justify kissing her." Impatience weighted McTavish's words, tightening his lean features. His caustic gaze scraped over Jacques, leaving stinging condemnation in its wake. "Devaux, I'm trying hard not to jump to conclusions, but I honestly cannot conceive of a logical reason for your actions."

"There wasn't time to cajole her out of the vision or remove her from the room." Shrugging, Jacques switched his attention to the powdery white blurring the view outside the towering, mullioned window. Impossible to visit Oakberry today—for several days, perhaps. His gaze gravitated to his staid host. "Simply put, I didn't dare let Fletcher see her in the midst of a vision."

"Why? Because of that soothsayer and sorcery gibberish, he spouted?" McTavish shook his head. "Those types of nonsensical beliefs, and the persecution accompanying them, ceased years ago."

"Mostly true, but the church still burns witches in South America, and there've been sporadic killings of witches in Europe in recent times." Fletcher's insinuations and their possible ramifications sent dread tiptoeing along Jacques's spine.

McTavish exhaled a vulgar noise—half snort, half curse. "Primitive hogwash. Scotland's Kirk is far more civilized."

"You heard him say there are ways of dealing with 'her kind.' What do you think Fletcher referred to? A polite cozy in the grand parlor?" McTavish must understand the urgency. If ever a man was *fou*, completely mad, Fletcher fit the description. "Overzealous holy men have accused, condemned, and murdered innocents for years, McTavish. Sometimes their entire families too. I'm convinced Fletcher presents a danger to Seonaid."

"Seonaid?" McTavish's brows soared to his hairline, then hung there suspended. "You dare such familiarity?"

Damnation. Stupid, careless slip.

"Forgive me. I overstepped the bounds, but we Frenchmen are passionate about such matters, *oui*?"

Mon Dieu, quel imbécile je suis. Passionate?

"Indeed." A cynical brow notched upward farther. McTavish's deceptively casual mien didn't fool Jacques. He wanted the truth. Would have the truth. All of it.

"Let me worry about Fletcher, Devaux. I haven't a qualm about tossing his skinny arse in my dungeon if he as much as utters another syllable against my sister." A shrewd glint entered McTavish's eyes, though a hint of humor shone there as well. "Tell me, what did Vicar Fletcher mean when he said you courted her?"

Remembered that tidbit, had he?

"It was the only acceptable, quick explanation I could come up with for kissing her and far less harmful than him disparaging her reputation, *non*?"

"And that be yer singular motivation?" McTavish leaned forward. After placing his forearms onto the burnished desktop, he laced his fingers. His brogue had thickened, and something more troublesome than doubt tempered his voice.

"Precisely what happened between you two in Paris? I'm not blind. I've seen how Seonaid reacts to you. And her response isn't at all typical for my sister."

Ah, he comes to the actual point.

"*Mon ami*, you've been itching to ask me that question for months, *non*?"

McTavish's expression relaxed a fraction, and he grinned. "Aye."

Uncrossing his legs, Jacques weighed his options. Lie and risk McTavish uncovering the truth later—which was guaranteed to make him an enemy. Or explain he'd had no choice but to kiss Seonaid that time too.

Doubtful McTavish would believe him. Though the truth, the explanation sounded preposterous and farfetched even to Jacques.

Once, he wanted to kiss Seonaid out of desire, not because one of them needed protecting.

Better set aside that dream, old chap.

He sighed.

Out with it, then.

Sitting back in his chair, he extended his legs before him and closed his eyes. *Mon Dieu,* he was tired. Mentally and physically. He yearned for the contentment his friend radiated.

McTavish, Viscount Sethwick in their *espionage* days, had been a far different man than this serene fellow sitting on the desk's other side. Well, given his current line of questioning, perhaps not wholly serene.

"Well? What have you to say?" A man accustomed to others obeying him straightaway, McTavish regarded Jacques expectantly.

"I arranged to meet a contact at the *Salle Richelieu* theatre. However, she failed to show, and my position was compromised. Mademoiselle Ferguson"—*a mite late for formality at this juncture*—"happened to be in the appointed alcove. To prevent detection, I kissed her." Jacques's cynical chuckle held no amusement. "Surely, even you can understand the need to protect my sources, *non*?"

Once a dedicated spy himself, McTavish couldn't argue against that logic. He'd have done the same in Jacques's position, and he damned well knew it.

"Yes, though it maddens me to admit you're right." Conceding a grudging nod, McTavish cast his attention to the window, a frown pulling his mouth downward farther. "What are your intentions toward Seonaid? She's not one of your trifling playthings."

Even he didn't know Jacques's reputation as a womanizing rakehell was an affected front. Jacques's conscience poked him.

Not entirely contrived.

The information he'd gleaned from women eager to share his bed had been quite useful. Except he usually contrived an excuse for why he couldn't accept their eager offers, which made them all the more desperate, it seemed.

Tragic and pitiful.

"You understand the direness of my circumstance, McTavish. Why I'm here, *non*? If Oakberry doesn't produce as anticipated, I shall return to France hardly more than an aristocratic pauper in a few weeks."

Nearly penniless nobles weren't permitted the privilege, or the extravagance, of love.

"If I'm to save and restore my estate, I shall have no recourse but to find a woman as hungry for a title as I am a sizable fortune."

On cue, as if in agreement or wanting to remind him of his reduced circumstances, his stomach complained noisily.

"Or food, at the moment." McTavish's attempt at levity fell short. "I'm saddened that you would settle for a loveless marriage, even if it's not altogether uncommon, and were I in your shoes, I cannot say I wouldn't do the same to save Craiglocky." He rubbed his chin, regarding Jacques intently. "You're essentially selling yourself."

A wry smile, perhaps more self-loathing than actual irony, tipped Jacques's lips. "A fair exchange, I suppose, *non*?"

Before uttering a single vow, Jacques would insist upon candidness between his bride and himself. His baroness would have no false illusions. Theirs would be a marriage of convenience, each gaining something the other wanted and provided.

All the more reason he couldn't permit his heart to become engaged. Such a union would be trial enough without his mooning over another woman.

What about an heir?

That delicacy he'd deal with when he must. Or perhaps, he'd permit the line to terminate, so his sons and grandsons wouldn't be encumbered with the burden that forced him to choose between his happiness and responsibilities.

"I could extend you funds." It was not the first time McTavish had offered.

"*Non, mon ami*, but I thank you. Unless Oakberry proves as prosperous as I pray she is, I've no way to repay your generosity." Lifting one shoulder a couple of inches, Jacques gave a rueful tilt of his mouth. "I've my pride if nothing else, and I won't be further indebted to you."

Shuffling through a pile of papers atop his desk, McTavish glanced up. "I shall permit you to stay on, at least until you've had an opportunity to visit the quarry yourself and speak with Newton, the mine's overseer." He waved distractedly behind his shoulder at the window edged in miniature snow mounds. "I can hardly turn you out in this weather in any event."

"Most considerate of you."

Except for a brief, sharp look, McTavish didn't respond to Jacques's sarcasm.

"Damn, I need to hire a secretary. Corrigan retired, and I've been fumbling along for months." Making an exasperated noise, he ruffled through a few more papers, then slanted Jacques an indirect look. "In the meanwhile, I would ask that you keep your distance from Seonaid. I also intend to speak with her about the incident at the inn."

"Naturally." Except for meals, Jacques and Seonaid needn't see one another. He could take a tray in his room part of the time too, or simply arrange to be absent during meals.

Finding the documents he sought, McTavish set it aside. He lifted an envelope. "This came for you two days ago."

He slid a missive across the desk.

Jacques lifted the neatly folded rectangle. The taupe-colored wax was imprinted with his man of business's seal. Likely it didn't bear cheerful tidings if Faucher determined the contents urgent enough they couldn't wait for his return to France.

After McTavish tucked the paper he'd located into his interior pocket, he proceeded to straighten the stack he'd rifled through.

"Seonaid's young and is an extremely sensitive soul. I won't have her hurt. Unlike our other sisters, she's fragile, gentle, and doesn't possess a strong spirit." His regard became grave. "Don't do anything to encourage her affections."

A distinct warning resonated in his last words.

Jacques stood and, after pulling his jacket into place, trod to the exit. Clasping the door handle, he paused.

"You're wrong, I'm happy to say. Seonaid's the strongest of the lot, *mon ami*, and I mean to prove it to you"—*and her*—"before I leave Scotland."

ELEVEN

Fighting tears, Seonaid kissed her father's broad cheek while sitting alongside him atop her parents' oversized bed.

"You're looking well, Father. I wanted to come to you straightaway last night, but we arrived quite late, and I assumed you'd be abed already."

Except for his bandaged leg, a vicious scrape marring his left cheek, and another across his hand, he'd appeared the epitome of health.

He'd fared far better than the stable, to be sure. Nothing but its charred skeleton remained. Thank God, no livestock had been lost, and the other barns hadn't been damaged. Only the nearest one's north end was slightly singed.

Grinning, Father tugged a lock of her hair. "Lass, I'm pleased to see ye, though I canna say I be happy about ye gallivantin' around Scotland on yer own."

"*Oui*, you worried a year from my life, *ma chérie*." Placing Father's breakfast tray atop his lap, Mother smiled, her brilliant turquoise eyes sparkling. "Whatever possessed you to do such a thing? Impulsiveness isn't like you."

Running her fingers across the soft, buttery-colored coverlet, Seonaid offered a contrite smile. "I'm sorry you were concerned."

Satisfied Father wouldn't dump the tray's contents onto their bed, Mother shifted her attention to Seonaid. "I'd expect such behavior of Adaira, or even Isobel, but you've naught given us cause to fret."

Biddable, boring, obedient Seonaid.

As Mother fussed over Father, Seonaid slipped from the bed. "I promise to explain why, and when I do, I believe you'll understand and forgive my rashness."

Mother bent near to arrange a serviette atop Father's chest, and he stole a quick kiss. Blushing like a young maid, she swatted him.

Married over two decades and still in love.

Sadness pinched Seonaid's heart.

Love. A luxury she must deny herself.

He snatched another peck, and Mother giggled.

"Hugh, behave yourself. Seonaid—"

"Och, nae harm in the lass seein' her parents kiss. She'll be married soon enough herself."

Sooner than they could've possibly anticipated.

Taking a seat at a small table placed on the bed's other side, Seonaid lifted the silver dome from her breakfast.

"*Umm*, I'd hoped Sorcha would make scones and tatties." Splitting the warm pastry, she inhaled the familiar aroma. Adding a generous dollop of creamy butter and marmalade to each half, she smiled. "I believe next to my family and pets, I missed Sorcha's marmalade most of all."

Chewing the delicious pastry, she nearly sighed in pleasure. No one, absolutely no one, made scones as tasty as Sorcha.

A moment later, her mother joined her and, once seated, poured them tea. She patted Seonaid's hand. "I'm glad you're home. Except for Yvette, I've been surrounded by men." Her mouth bent into a teasing smile, she angled her dark head toward the bed and slid Father an indirect gaze. "Some rather obstinate."

"*Hmph*, ye try havin' to stay abed fer days on end. I'll grow fat as a hog and weak as a lamb in nae time." Father's playful wink belied his complaining. "Yvette brings Broderick to visit daily. The laddie helps relieve my boredom."

"I haven't seen her yet, but Ewan mentioned she's increasing again." Scone at her mouth, Seonaid chuckled. "Actually, he boasted, prouder than a cock strutting in the bailey."

Her sister-in-law and brother were also desperately in love. Should she tell her parents she'd had another vision upon waking this morning, this one involving Yvette's pregnancy?

Ewan and Yvette would welcome two *bairn* girls, and though tiny and weeks early, the twins would be perfectly healthy. However, as a result of complications brought on by a difficult birth, Yvette would lose a great deal of blood and be barren afterward.

How could Seonaid reveal such awful news?

Imagine the terror her sweet sister-in-law would live with for months. Ewan and the rest of the family too.

Like a sharp pebble in her slipper, indecision niggled.

What if telling prepared them for the wee babes' arrival and helped save Yvette's life?

What if Seonaid was wrong and caused them to fret for naught? Though rarely, she had been mistaken before.

For instance, the time she'd seen Midwife McCready lying lifeless upon her cottage floor. Dutifully riding to the village, Father discovered her in a stupor after nipping her medicinal store of whisky a speck too generously.

Not dead. Just foxed to her plumpish, ruddy cheeks.

And two summers ago, when Seonaid had a vision of the

keep under attack by a band of rogue Scots. Again, her family accepted her fey's accuracy, and Ewan doubled the guards and patrols for six months. Nothing ever came of it.

Or that vision in Paris after meeting Jacques. She nearly snorted aloud. That one had been *wholly* inaccurate.

To see someone's future, having to decide whether to share the knowledge. God alone possessed that right, not a mere mortal.

Why she'd been given the capacity, Seonaid might never know. Some would call her ungrateful for disdaining her ability, but others, like Reverend Fletcher, deemed her visions unholy.

That was why she'd come to a firm conclusion before leaving her chamber. She must wed and lose her virginity as soon as possible. Three visions in less than a week—in four days, to be precise.

The increase in frequency alarmed her no end. How could she endure the foreboding? Keeping secret what she'd seen, or continually being the bearer of ill tidings might drive her to madness.

Anger flared, surging through her veins, scorching and unrelenting.

She didn't want the cursed *an dara shealladh* anymore, didn't want to be branded a soothsayer. Never had, truth to tell, and she feared that was her destiny unless she deliberately took measures to change the course.

No, she couldn't bear to tell Ewan and Yvette what their future held. Yet. For now, she'd keep that dreary knowledge to herself.

Forking a bite of egg, Seonaid gauged how long she could safely postpone the telling. "Yvette's expecting in April?"

Taking a dainty sip of tea, anticipation lit Mother's face. "*Oui*, and I think they're hoping for a girl this time."

They'd get their wish.

Seonaid could keep her secret until at least February then.

Chewing a good-sized bite of sausage, Father pointed his knife at her. "Ye'll be findin' yerself a *mon* soon enough, I'll wager." He wiggled his heavy brows. "Did any of those fine *Sassenachs* take yer fancy?"

No Englishman had. However, a certain Frenchman...

Never mind.

Jacques required a fortune, and though she possessed a generous dowry, it wouldn't restore an estate in deplorable condition. Moreover, she'd no desire to return to France or to leave Scotland to make a home elsewhere.

Unlike Isobel, who yearned for adventure and travel, Seonaid was content to remain home with her books, plants, and pets.

With the right man, you'd go anywhere.

Mother had.

She'd left France at seventeen, first married to Ewan's father, Liam McTavish, and then had stayed in Scotland to later marry Father.

Seonaid almost laughed at the image of her burly father sitting upon the dainty French furniture popular in the French homes she'd visited. He'd been as out of place there as she'd felt.

Yvette, Isobel, and Adaira had made the sacrifice as well.

Why was it only women who left their homelands for the men they loved? *Enough.* Why humor these ridiculous mental ramblings? Less than a week ago, Seonaid and Jacques couldn't be in the same room without quarreling.

"Nae, Father. I can honestly say no Englishman stole my heart."

"Hugh, *ma chére,* our Seonaid wouldn't likely have hustled to Craiglocky if that were the case, *non*?" An indulgent smile bent Mother's mouth. "She is young, and she's only returned home. There's plenty of time to contemplate marriage, *ma chéri, oui*?"

No time like the present.

"Well, Mother, Father." Seonaid directed her consideration from one doting parent to the other and took a fortifying breath. "Since you mentioned it. I wish to marry as soon as you can find a suitable man who also meets your approval."

Father's startled oath as he dropped hot tatties onto his chest muffled the clanking of Mother's fork, first hitting her plate, then bouncing onto the stone floor.

"*Mon Dieu*, why?" Mother breathed, blinking in confusion. Pressing a shaky hand to her throat, she cast Father a stunned, rather desperate, glance.

"Be that why ye fled London?" Father's deep brown eyes, so like Seonaid's, sank to her belly. "Are ye with child?" He sat up straighter, alert and suspicious. "Does the clan need to pay a *Sassenach* a visit?"

Seonaid's mouth fell open, and burning heat enveloped her cheeks. She should have expected that assumption. "Of course not! It's nothing of that nature, I assure you."

"*Chérie*, I don't understand. Your brother and sisters married for love, but you would have us choose your husband?" First confusion, then speculation crinkled the corners of Mother's eyes. "Precisely what happened in London?"

Mother was far too insightful.

Releasing a long, controlled breath, Seonaid laid her serviette beside her plate. "My visions are occurring much more frequently. Three in the past four days. In London, I was treated like a soothsayer, and yesterday, Craigcutty's temporary rector—Reverend Fletcher, a horrid maggot of a man you haven't met as yet—accused me of sorcery."

A sound much like an enraged growl rumbled from Father, his russet eyes spewing wrathful sparks. Clumsily plopping his tray beside him, and then grabbing a thick corner post, he made to leave the bed.

"Hugh Ferguson, stop this instant! If you reinjure your leg, you'll be stuck in bed that much longer. You'd be utterly unbearable then, *non*?" Mother pointed to the bed, her tone and demeanor formidable. "Be sensible and lie down, or I swear I shall tie you to the posts."

At Mother's firm command, he grudgingly complied. "I'll have the trow dragged from the village by his bollo—er throat. How dare he accuse my daughter of such evilness? And he a holy man, at that."

"Ewan already said as much to Fletcher." Clasping her hands in her lap to still their sudden shaking, Seonaid lifted her chin. "I want to rid myself of the second sight."

Puzzlement creased her mother's forehead, pleating the outer corner of her eyes. "What have your visions to do with a hasty marriage? *Ma chére*, if you choose the wrong man, you might be miserable for the rest of your life."

"I'm miserable now."

Stark, painful silence met her words, and similar shocked expressions etched her parents' faces.

Rot, she hadn't meant to blurt that.

"Lass, why didna ye say anythin' before?" Father's gentleness nearly unraveled Seonaid.

Swallowing the lump climbing her throat, she blinked away the fierce stinging behind her eyelids. The raw anguish etching their faces pierced her core, and rather than burst into tears, she focused her attention on the fluffy flakes drifting beyond the beveled diamond-shaped panes.

"Everyone has been fascinated by my second sight, and I suppose you assumed I was content with the unusual gift. But the truth is, I loathe being an oddity. I don't want to see and sense events before they happen. I'm weary of being the bearer of dire warnings or awful tidings."

A tear leaked from her eye, but she dashed it away. She didn't want pity. None of this was her parents' or her sibling's fault nor their doing. Nevertheless, she wanted to be done with the *an dara shealladh* once and for all.

What if I lose my innocence and still—

No.

Seonaid checked the wayward thought before it had a chance to finish forming. It must work. It simply must.

Mother gathered her near and gave her a ferocious hug. "I wish you'd mentioned something earlier, though I don't know how we can change anything."

"I've heard..." Seonaid cleared her throat. Rather awkward with Father sitting there, eagerness engraved on his rugged face. "Grandmother had the gift too, *erm*, until she married."

"Ach, that be the direction yer mind be takin'." Father rubbed his chin. "Aye, it might work."

"But, Hugh, married to a stranger. A man who doesn't love her to eliminate the fey?" Shaking her head, silver peeking from the raven strands, Mother's mouth swooped downward mutinously. "*Non*, I won't have it."

Leave it to Mother to kick up a dust.

Since Seonaid wasn't of age, they could prevent her from marrying. Unless she eloped or found an agreeable chap to compromise her.

Jacques's chiseled features sprang to mind.

She choked on a sad laugh. Ewan would force Jacques to marry her, and then he'd lose his beloved estate. Not the makings of a contented husband.

She mentally crossed him off the list of potential candidates. The remainder of the imaginary page remained starkly blank.

"I'm determined in this, although I'm sure you're opposed. Nonetheless, as much as it grieves me, I must insist." Attempting to lighten the moment, yet perfectly serious, a wry smile curved Seonaid's mouth. She'd have an affair if she couldn't quickly acquire a husband. "I'm so desperate, I might do something drastic, perhaps enter into an illicit liaison."

"Yer talkin' pure foolishness now, lass." Looking huge and helpless, Father implored Mother. "Tell her, Giselle. She nae ken what she be sayin'."

Mother flapped her hand at him. "Shh, I'm thinking, *ma chère.*"

Time to leave.

Mother proved dangerous when she possessed that determined countenance. No telling what manner of ridiculousness she might scheme.

"If you'll excuse me," Seonaid said, "I want to visit my menagerie. I've missed my pets."

"A house party," Mother announced, tapping her chin and slowly nodding, her blue-green eyes half-closed in deliberation. "Perhaps Hogmanay? *Non*, that's next week. Much too soon to plan a proper gathering."

"Pardon? A house party? Here?" Blast. Seonaid should have anticipated something of that nature.

"*Oui*. Travel might be challenging this time of year, but if I plan for early February, that might work. We rarely have much snow then."

Mother's face brightened, and she grinned, clapping her hands together once. "I have just the thing. A Valentine's celebration. I'll invite every eligible young gentleman we know in Scotland and England. Oh, and perhaps France too. It's perfect, *non*? You'll have your choice of a husband from amongst the most eligible men."

Heavens, no. A quiet, gentle Scot would do Seonaid perfectly fine.

"I would much rather not." With her luck, she'd have an episode in front of every potential beau, and they'd be kicking up their heels in haste, rushing to their chambers straightaway to pack. "It sounds too much like a High Society rout or assembly."

"Now, I must insist, *ma chère*." Deep in contemplation, Mother stood, a finger pressed to her lips. "A list. I must start planning at once so the invites can be mailed soon."

Arms folded, Father chuckled and shook his head, his longish hair scraping his leather vest's collar. "Och, see what ye've done, lass? We'll have coxcombs, twiddle poops, and jackanapes underfoot."

"Do be serious, Hugh," Mother admonished. "Seonaid wouldn't marry a twiddle poop. She's far too intelligent for that."

Laughing, he winked and picked up a piece of toast. "Aye, that she be."

"Are you going to mention on the invitations that I'm husband-hunting? So I can free myself from my second sight, and any unmarried men are potential candidates?" Seonaid had no idea what manner of wickedness prompted her to ask.

Consternation flickered across Mother's pretty face. "You think they wouldn't come if that were the case? You do yourself a disservice, and the gentlemen too. Besides, you're the one who insisted we find you a husband posthaste, *non*?"

Remorse pricked Seonaid, its pointed little talons jabbing deep. "That was uncalled for. Please forgive me."

"*Chérie*. Are you having second thoughts already?"

"No, no, I do want to marry." Not precisely true. She wished to abolish her second sight, and that entailed marriage.

Mother shrugged. "There's no other way to swiftly introduce you to a broad array of gentlemen from which to make your selection."

"It's a brilliant notion. Truly." Summoning a cheery smile, Seonaid tried to appear enthusiastic.

Mother hurried to the cherry wood secretary desk beside the door, her violet skirts swishing around her trim ankles.

After withdrawing a piece of foolscap and unstopping the silver inkwell, she dipped the quill. Feather poised above the paper, she swung around.

"Seonaid, please find Ewan and request he meet me in my solar at his earliest convenience. I believe he's in his study conversing with Monsieur le baron de Devaux-Rousset."

Seonaid scrunched her nose, then quickly smoothed her features lest Mother or Father ask her to explain her displeasure. She'd preferred Jacques not be about, causing her emotions confusion and upset as she sought to speedily acquire a husband.

Why had he continued on to Craiglocky? True, his mining operation was somewhere nearby, but he might have stayed at one of Craigcutty's inns.

She scratched her cheek before taking another sip of aromatic tea. Might as well take a look at his injured hand. The bandage hadn't been changed since yesterday.

Ewan probably had wished to speak to him regarding Reverend Fletcher's ugly accusations. Given their harried journey and the lack of privacy, it wouldn't surprise her if he hadn't insisted Jacques stay at the keep last night to discuss the matter with Ewan this morning.

"*Tut*, do inquire if Monsieur le baron is available too, *ché*rie." Scribbling away, Mother murmured the request without looking up.

Wary, Seonaid slowly rose. "Might I ask why?"

Glancing up, Mother beamed. "Surely, he'll know the finest French gentlemen I should invite."

What Frenchman possessed with an iota of common sense —*other than Jacques, that is*—journeyed to Scotland in the winter?

In any case, Seonaid preferred to marry a Scot. At least then, if her visions continued and she hied to a mountain hovel or cave, she might convince her family to visit her once in a while.

"I'm loath to impose upon Monsieur le baron since he has other, more urgent matters on his mind. I'm sure you're aware that he's in Scotland conducting business, and he's no doubt eager to be on his way."

"Nae in that weather, he isnae." Father interrupted his munching to point toward the window.

Confound it all, snow fell unceasingly—the most they'd experienced in years. Perfectly horrid. Jacques couldn't leave, and other suitors couldn't call. "Well, as soon as the weather permits, then."

A curious expression furrowed Mother's forehead. "*Chérie*, I was positive you were aware. He's residing at Craiglocky while in Scotland."

TWELVE

Two hours later, after having delivered the messages as Mother asked, changing Jacques's bandage, and spending an hour visiting with Yvette and playing with Broderick, Seonaid secured her thickest pelisse's clasps at her neck. Beneath the heavy double-layered wool, she wore a simple gown, far past its prime but acceptable for tending her animals.

She wandered to her chamber window. The picturesque view brought a reluctant smile to her lips. Cocooned in pristine white, the peaceful scenery appeared untouched. Virginal.

Something she didn't intend to remain much longer.

Raised around livestock and farm animals her entire life, she'd seen what copulation entailed. The actual act itself didn't trouble her overly much, though why the Good Lord couldn't have designed something a scant less noisy and awkward did perplex a mite.

Her choice of partner mattered a trifling more.

Fine then, more than a trifling.

He must be clean, both in person and clothing, with well-tended teeth, and not given to drunkenness. Wouldn't do to gag when he exercised his husbandly rights. For her family's sake, she'd try to marry first, albeit she might go mad in the meanwhile.

Dread drove her uncharacteristic rashness. How could she explain her desperation, the frantic need compelling her to take these extreme measures? How could she explain something she didn't fully understand herself?

She wouldn't intentionally bring disgrace upon her family but eliminate the second sight, she must. No matter the cost. Slipping her hand into a glove, Seonaid grimaced. When had she come to be so calculating? So selfish and self-centered?

Tears blurred her eyes, and she wiped the moisture away before donning the other glove.

She didn't like this woman she'd become, but she'd abhor the creature her visions would transform her into even more.

Why, a few minutes ago, while climbing the stairs to her chamber, she'd been assailed by yet another episode. The sudden increase in events boggled. What in God's blessed name went on?

This vision hadn't been terribly significant but still important enough to prompt her to don her outer garments and trudge through the calf-high snow to the outbuilding housing her beloved pets. She'd be needed there soon.

A man would find a starving cat about to give birth. Because of his hat and greatcoat, as well as the snow spiraling around him, she couldn't tell who. If her visions foretold things of this more pleasant nature, she wouldn't resent them again. She could help a cat and her kittens. Deaths or tragedies, she'd no power over.

Minutes later, her head lowered against a biting, angry wind, Seonaid tramped her way to her refuge. Pushing the door open, familiar scents—animals, dung, straw, and medicinal ointments—engulfed her. So did a bone-warming peace.

She was home.

Everything remained as she'd left it weeks before. Healing herbs hung from hooks overhead, and a shelf beside the door held her assortment of salves, ointments, and tinctures. Inhaling deeply, she set the bundle she carried atop a low table and stamped her feet to loosen the snow clinging to her boots.

Sorcha had given her liver and fish to feed the mother cat.

Seonaid spent so much time in here that Father had insisted the miniature barn be insulated since a stove was dangerous and impractical. Square windows on two sides of the cozy closure provided grayish light, but she lit a lantern all the same.

In her absence, her menagerie had been well cared for. Unless the weather prevented it, as it did today, her pets wandered the bailey or nearby fields during the day but always slept in here at night.

What would happen to them when she married? Or, barring finding a man willing to form a union with a peculiar woman who saw things before they occurred, she isolated herself in a reclusive hut?

No real reason she couldn't take them with her. At least she wouldn't be lonely.

Upon seeing Seonaid, an assortment of creatures, from doves to sheep, noisily greeted her.

"I missed you too."

And she had. More than she'd realized.

Laughing, she removed her pelisse, the hem of which was heavy with clinging snow, then hung it on a wall peg designed for that purpose. Her gloves and bonnet soon joined the wrap.

Yes, she most definitely would take the dears with her. Better ask her father to make that a marriage settlement stipulation. Her husband would receive a hefty dowry. She should be permitted her pets.

She squatted and then buried her face in her beloved deaf border collie, Chester's, rough coat. He wiggled and whined, happily attempting to lick every part of her face. His ungentle-manly penchant for rolling in cow or sheep dung earned him banishment from the keep, but no foulness clung to him today.

Agnes, a ewe missing one hind leg, tottered to her pen's opening and baaed softly. A dove flew to perch on Seonaid's shoulder while several cats, purring loudly, twined 'round her feet.

"We have a new friend coming soon." Examining the empty cages and pens, Seonaid tapped her mouth thought-fully. "Where shall we put her? She's weak, and she's having kittens."

Deciding on a cage in a quiet corner, Seonaid pulled a clean towel from a neat stack on another shelf. After arranging the soft cloth into a sort of nest, she set about preparing the cat's food. Once she'd finished and was satisfied everything was ready to receive her newest guest, she went about properly greeting her other pets.

Bent over Milly, a crippled goat sharing Agnes's pen, Seonaid scratched the doe's ears and brushed her thick coat. "There's a good lassie." Agnes nudged her arm. "No, Agnes, you don't need your wool combed. I'll scratch your ears though, jealous girl."

The door swung open, and the wind whipping into the warm enclosure lifted Seonaid's skirts and sent a frigid chill skating up her thighs to her bum. Startled, she dropped the grooming brush. Bent over, she peered between the slats. A man's shadowy figure blocked the entrance.

Chester barked a warning, the cats dashed to their usual hiding places beneath tables or shelves, and her pet doves flew to an overhead rafter.

Stretching over Milly to retrieve the brush, another blast of cold smacked her spine and bottom. "For pity's sake, please shut the door before you cause us to freeze."

"I cannot, *ma petite*. My arms are full."

Seonaid whirled around.

Jacques held the emaciated cat wrapped in his jacket.

"I didn't expect you'd be the one who found her."

Swiftly exiting the pen, she pointed to the table nearest Jacques. "You may lay her there, but don't let go. She's no doubt terrified, and she's liable to bolt. I'll shut the door."

"You expected me? Here?" He gently placed the trembling cat atop the gouged, discolored surface, really more of a tall bench than a table. "A vision, I presume?"

Seonaid nodded and secured the door. "Yes. Here, let me unwrap her, but please stay where you are in case I need your help."

This wasn't the time to worry about propriety.

She wedged herself between him and the table, her rear pressed to his thighs and, despite her misgivings, enjoyed his cozy closeness and subtle cologne.

Gingerly unfolding the expensive coat, she gasped. "Poor thing. She's nearly starved."

Sparse black hair covered clearly visible ribs above a distended belly. White frosted the cat's four paws and an oatcake-sized patch on her chest. Wary, tired citrine eyes blinked up at Seonaid above twitching white whiskers.

Seonaid fed the ravenous cat a bite of fish, then another.

"I couldn't leave her. I went for a walk, and I heard her pathetic meowing." He ran long fingers between her ears, and the cat closed her eyes in contentment. "I think she's in labor."

"She is." Touching his arm, she smiled up at him, momentarily surprised at the fleeting intensity in his gaze. She bent over the cat, cooing softly. "She likes you. That's good. She'll feel safer delivering her kittens with you near."

~

"*Non, ma petite*, I have no skill with animals." Seonaid's tight, rounded buttocks jostled against Jacques's groin, and he gritted his teeth against his manhood's immediate and predictable response.

The earlier sight of her bending over, her lush rear pointed upward, popped to mind again.

God help me. Please.

"There's no skill. Just kindness, gentleness, and love. All creatures respond to those three things." Making more soothing noises in her throat, which unfortunately for Jacques's swelling member sounded similar to a woman in the throes of ecstasy, she scooped the cat into her arms.

Seonaid's derrière bumped firmly against his penis, and he closed his eyes against a powerful surge of pleasurable pain.

What had he done to deserve this torture?

McTavish had warned him to stay away from Seonaid, and Jacques had fully intended to. But everyone he showed the pathetic cat to had directed him to this small building.

"Do you want to name her?" Seonaid scooted past him as she asked the question. "You rescued her. I think you should have the honor. Something special since she's been a brave darling."

"Freya. It's Norse." Naming the amber-eyed cat Freya after the cat-worshipping fertility goddess of love and beauty probably wasn't the wisest choice, especially considering his current aroused state, but he couldn't summon another noteworthy feline name.

He supposed it fitting, however. At present, his mind seemed stuck fast on sexual musings. Taking advantage of Seonaid's distraction with the cat, he discreetly rearranged himself beneath his greatcoat.

"Bring me what's left of the fish, will you, please? I fear she's too weak to give birth." She gave him another radiant smile over her shoulder. "You might want to remove your coat. Birthing can get a mite messy."

That wasn't all he'd like to remove. Every stitch of his clothing. Then hers. At the image, his cock jumped like a dog performing tricks for a treat.

If she kept smiling at him like that, he'd either go blind or toss caution and every ounce of common sense he still possessed to hell and tup her in the sheep's pen.

Or against the wall.

That fresh stack of hay piled in the corner would do too.

Mon Dieu. McTavish would slay him for his thoughts alone.

Jacques should leave. A prudent man would.

He'd done what he'd set out to do. Delivered the cat. Yet, he wanted this time. Wanted to savor every second with Seonaid. The two of them, sharing this special, intimate situation. He didn't dare desire more.

If the mine is profitable, perhaps—

He squelched the notion, grinding it beneath his boot heel. Too dangerous, that thread of thinking. Nevertheless, he removed his greatcoat and then rolled up his sleeves.

This warm, welcoming Seonaid, he couldn't resist.

An hour later, he peeked over her shoulder, breathing in her light perfume, as they watched four tiny, mottled, and still damp kittens nursing their purring mother. "I confess, I've not seen a cat give birth. I've never seen anything born before."

Seonaid lifted her face, close enough the silvery and emerald specks in her wondrous, rich brandy-colored eyes glittered at him. "Never? Truly?" Her focus dipped to his mouth for a fraction. "I've seen all sorts of animals born, even humans. It's quite an amazing experience."

Her sweet breath caressed his face.

Once again, her lovely eyes sank to his mouth, and the tip of her pink tongue darted out to moisten her plump lower lip.

Anticipation gripped him.

With a groan, Jacques cupped her face between both hands and claimed her mouth. Nothing about watching four bloody, squirming masses birthed had been the least erotic, but he'd never been more aware of a woman before in his life.

Every nuance, every glance, each time she bent or twisted and her gown stretched taut across her breasts or cradled her delectable bum, he fell further under her seductress's spell.

Standing perfectly still, one hand gripping his bare forearm, Seonaid didn't resist.

Turning her in his arms, he slanted his lips across hers, lightly teasing the corner of her mouth with his tongue. How could a woman taste so splendid?

She released a long, shuddering sigh and, twining her arms about his neck, opened to his probing.

Groaning low, he swept his tongue over the honeyed cavern and nearly exploded in his pantaloons when she tentatively met his bold strokes.

He cupped her buttocks—they fit his palms perfectly— and lifted her against his rigid length.

Rising onto her toes, she edged nearer, making soft, hungry noises in the back of her throat.

A shout outside, followed by laughter and a series of rapid thuds against the outer wall, reeled in his lust.

Mais que diable faisait-il donc?

What the hell *was* he doing?

If the snow fight hadn't brought him to his senses, how far would he have gone? Seonaid deserved better, and he couldn't offer her anything but admiration from afar.

Kissing her breathless isn't exactly drawing room decorum.

She wasn't a loose trollop whose skirts he could lift for a few blissful moments and be done. She was the gently bred sister of a man he admired and who had warned him away from her.

Fool.

Giving her another soft kiss, he set her from him. "Forgive me, *ma petite*. My behavior is inexcusable."

Cocking her head, her lips moist and reddened from his onslaught, she smiled shyly. "Don't apologize. I enjoyed it. Very much, as a matter of fact."

Dammit. Drawing upon Herculean strength, he managed to resist yanking her into his arms and taking advantage of the hay pile.

"As did I, but it cannot happen again. We must think of your reputation." Jacques tenderly brushed a stray curl from her flushed cheek.

He should have considered that before he agreed to stay and watch the birth, but he'd been a selfish *bâtard*. Anyone could've seen them kissing through the window, though doubtful since they stood in the farthest, darkest corner. Nevertheless, he'd been alone in here with her far too long.

She continued to stare at him, as if she could see his soul and read his thoughts.

Mayhap she could. Had she known what would happen between them? She'd known about Freya. What else had Seonaid perceived and kept to herself? Such an intriguing, mesmerizing woman. And she couldn't be his. Ever.

More laughter and shouting echoed outside, and again snowballs pelted the building.

Best put a respectable distance between them in the event someone entered. As he stepped away, she faced the cat family once more.

"Jacques, may I ask something of you?"

Unrolling one of his sleeves, he glanced up, his eyes hooded. "*Oui, ma petite.*"

She peered over her shoulder, an unfathomable light in her almond-shaped eyes. "I have need to rid myself of my maidenhead and wondered if, perhaps, you'd consider, ah, assisting me?"

Thirteen

S eonaid hadn't meant to blurt the request, hadn't known she'd chosen Jacques for the task until the words left her mouth. Holding her breath, she clamped her jaw until her teeth protested by sending jarring pain to her taut cheeks.

What a botched, inept proposition. Assisting her. As if she required a package carried from the milliner's or a book retrieved from an upper shelf.

Oh, by the by. I have a small task for you. Please relieve me of my virginity at your earliest convenience.

After his plundering kiss sent her mind and emotions toppling breast over bum, had she instinctively known he should be the man to end her visions? Must be the man she lay with?

Oh, how she wanted to.

Admitting her yearning warred with her astonishment and confusion. Mayhap the intense dislike she'd harbored had truly been nothing but vehement denial of her instant attraction.

For certain, what he'd agitated in her since the inn wasn't animosity or indignation.

His expression unreadable, Jacques slowly continued to right his clothing. Behind him, the lantern light reflected off the top of his ebony hair but didn't light his silhouette's bold planes.

Did the muscle of his jaw flex? Was the line of his mouth thinner? Sterner?

An uncomfortable, pregnant silence filled the outbuilding. Even the animals, except for Freya's contented rumble, grew quiet, as if they, too, awaited his response.

Much hinged upon his answer.

Squeezing the cloth she'd used to wipe the kittens, Seonaid inwardly cursed her impetuous impulse. Her outburst put them both in a deucedly difficult position.

Sensing her dismay, Chester sidled near and whimpered once, leaning into her legs. Amazing what animals sensed, one reason why she preferred their company to humans' obtuseness at times.

She tightened her grip upon the wadded cloth.

Why didn't Jacques say something?

He'd finished fastening his shirtsleeves and set his attention to buttoning his waistcoat, failing to lift his eyes even once.

Revelation struck with lightning's sudden force and speed.

He didn't want her.

Previously, she hadn't been concerned with her figure or looks. Possessing neither Isobel's exquisiteness, voluptuous shape, or brilliant intellect, nor Adaira's darker exotic beauty, daring, or uncanny gift for breeding horseflesh, Seonaid had been content to remain unnoticed and unremarkable.

Mother insisted she was nothing of the sort, but the looking-glasses didn't fib, and until this moment, Seonaid hadn't minded that much that she was simply ordinary and unexceptional.

A man's rejection quickly brought her inadequacies to light, however.

Most particularly when the rogue she'd approached for a dalliance boasted impossibly broad shoulders, narrow hips, and legs whose muscles were clearly visible through his pantaloons. Never mind his suaveness and sinfully striking looks.

Likely, he had his choice of beauties, much like delectable sweets presented on a china plate, and he indulged his taste whenever he pleased.

More fool she for not having considered rejection.

Humiliation like none she'd ever experienced surged from Seonaid's chilled toes to her burning hairline, searing every pore and nerve in between. She mustered a trembling smile and fiddled with the kittens lest she see his scorn or revulsion.

After he'd kissed her that third time, she'd been certain, had assumed he found her desirable and would accept her unconventional offer.

Desperately seeking a reason to keep her back to him, she picked up a kitten. Cuddling its wee form beneath her chin, she closed her eyes and tried to calm her uneven breathing.

"You needn't answer. Suggesting such a scandalous thing was rash and brazen." *And naïve and foolish.* Her brimming tears squeezed between her eyelids and spilled dual, scalding paths over her cheeks. Yet somehow, she succeeded in keeping her voice steady. "Please don't judge me or think me immoral."

How could he not? For God's sake, she'd proposed he take her virginity with the casualness of a *haut ton* peeress offering a guest a cup of tea and a biscuit.

Still, he didn't utter a syllable.

Could one die from mortification?

Death was preferable to this shame.

A penitent laugh escaped her, the stricken sound pathetic and tinny even to her ears as she returned the kitten to its mother. "I assure you, I don't make a habit of offering myself to men."

Large, warm hands cupped her shoulders, and Jacques kissed the crown of her head, his lips warming her scalp. "I swear, I've not received a request I honored more in my life, *chérie*, but we both know my answer must be *non*. I won't disgrace you so."

She wanted nothing more than the scuffed, straw-littered floor to swallow her and extinguish any sign she'd ever lived. How could she look him in the eye again?

Or her parents?

They'd be horrified if they discovered what she'd done. Who would tell them? Certainly, neither she nor Jacques would be that imprudent.

Given his reputation as a rake, she assumed—*hoped*—he'd consent. Oh, she wasn't naïve enough to believe anything more than physical attraction enticed either her or Jacques.

But losing her innocence to a man whose gaze sent her pulse frolicking ranked far above either surrendering her virtue in a loveless marriage or turning into a fusty old crone who children pointed and laughed at.

Or ran from in terror.

You could accept your exceptional talent.

A sob shook her, and she slapped her hand to her mouth. "Please go," she whispered against her fingers. The tenuous grasp she held upon her emotions wouldn't last much longer.

He sighed into her hair, then, after a tender squeeze, withdrew his hands and stepped away.

"I shall because I don't want a scandal or you compromised, but don't think, *ma petite*, I don't want you. I cannot offer you marriage. At least not at this time. Perhaps never, and I won't deceive you and pretend otherwise. I'm a poor man trying to restore my estate, as I've explained before."

"I know, and I do understand." And she did. He'd made his position clear from the onset. Chagrined to her bruised soul, she couldn't restrain her sobs any longer. "It's all right. Now, please go."

Their previous mutual disdain had been far easier to bear than his rejection or scorn.

He touched her bent neck, the softest of brief caresses. "I'm not sure of your reasons for offering your innocence, Seonaid, but the act cannot be undone. I pray you reconsider whatever has you so distressed that you'd make such a sacrifice, and if I can assist in any other way, you've simply to ask me, *oui*?"

A moment later, the latch clicked, the sound resonating in the small enclosure, and she buried her face in her hands, weeping for far more than shame and mortification.

"Assist in any other way? There isn't another way."

That she knew of.

How could she face Jacques after this? Surely, things would be awkward and strained between them going forward. She sniffled and, squaring her shoulders, dashed at her tears. Well, she'd caused this situation, and she must face the consequences with grace and poise.

Her loud, disdainful snort startled Freya, who leaped to her feet. The kittens weakly snuffled, issuing tiny mewing protests.

"Oh, forgive me, darling. Your bairns miss their mama already." Gently petting the leery cat, Seonaid coaxed her to lie down once more, and the distraught kittens nuzzled her teats. "There's a good lass."

Too bad Seonaid's circumstances weren't as easily remedied.

She must be patient, wait for the house party, and in the meanwhile, pray no more visions came upon her in public. She would focus on her blessings and stop bemoaning the episodes. And she'd avoid Jacques at every turn else she walk about continually red-faced.

Silly, self-pitying ninny.

Why get in a dudgeon about what might or mightn't be? She'd been so focused on her plight; she'd overlooked how much she had to be grateful for.

Chin up, stiffen your backbone, and stop behaving like a childish nincompoop.

Och, imagine if Jacques hadn't been a gentleman and agreed to her reckless suggestion. Misjudging him chafed her conscience. He didn't seem the same opportunistic scoundrel who'd snatched a kiss in Paris.

After giving Freya a final pat and tucking a towel around the kittens busy nursing once more, Seonaid secured the pen's latch. True, she couldn't deny that she wished for the ability to use her gift to foresee her future and others too.

Would she marry? If so, who? Would she have children? Suffer heartache? Would her family?

Had Jacques, in fact, been a spy?

His manner reminded her of Ewan's, and she couldn't prevent her mind from again making the comparison.

Would his mining venture be profitable, and would he succeed in renovating his estate?

How she wished she could see those details. No, not entirely true. She wanted to know if the outcomes were favorable, not the reverse.

And that made her a shallow coward.

In any event, it mightn't make a difference as far as Jacques was concerned. A kiss did not a proposal make, and her premature contemplations would surely lead to more heartache.

Still, it would be helpful to have a morsel of knowledge in advance.

Wrapping her pelisse about her shoulders, she released a sorrowful sigh. Her second sight never worked that way, and after nearly a decade, she didn't expect her gift to abruptly change.

Gift.

Odd that at this moment, she considered the sight of a seer a gift. This confounded doublemindedness had her at sixes and sevens. One moment, she loathed the second sight and would do anything to quell her visions, and a bit later, she bemoaned not having the ability to foretell the future.

She'd better make up her mind what she truly wanted and stop behaving like an indecisive, feckless halfwit.

Well then, until the Lord provided a means to remove it —or Seonaid forced the issue through marriage—she'd endure the visions with much more grace than she had in recent days.

She'd throw herself into preparations for the house party and start assembling a *trousseau*. That ought to keep her occupied. Busy hands and an occupied mind worked wonders to keep unwanted musings at bay.

Feeling more optimistic than she had in weeks, Seonaid bid her pets farewell and stepped from the outbuilding.

A snowball splatted against her shoulder.

"I saw that, Bruce McKenzie."

"Nae be me, Miss Seonaid." A broad grin wreathing his round-cheeked face, and the lad pointed to a strapping tartan-clad man. "Douglas McLean be guilty of hittin' ye."

"Ye be too much of a temptation, lass." A devilish smile creasing Douglas's chiseled face, he let loose with another miniature white cannonball. This one splattered below her chin, sending wet gobs trailing between her pelisse's collar and her neck.

"Try to hit me. I dare ye." Skipping about the bailey, he waved his arms, challenging her.

Overgrown child.

He'd teased her good-naturedly for as long as she could remember, and he made her laugh with his silly antics. His guffaw became a strangled choke when she hurled a hefty blob straight into his face.

Laughing, she scooped another handful of snow and then hurled that one at Douglas too.

Retaliating, he pelted her with three at once, and the shiny-nosed children exploded with laughter.

Others in the courtyard joined the fray, and she spent the next few minutes in a rousing snow fight.

Panting, teeth chattering, and wet to her soggy stockings, Seonaid waved farewell. A hot, oil-scented bath and a cup of piping hot whisky and honey-laced tea lured her indoors. "I've had enough. I'm freezing."

Douglas trotted over to her, his usual half-grin slanted across his kind face. His leaf-green eyes twinkling and droplets plopping onto his face from his saturated nutmeg-colored hair, he fell into step beside her. "It's happy I be to see ye home, lass. I feared ye'd marry a Sassenach dandy and break my heart."

INSTEAD OF RETURNING to the keep's warmth, Jacques detoured to the stables. Besides needing time for his raging erection to subside, Craiglocky boasted the finest, largest horses he'd ever seen. Truly magnificent giants.

Smiling in appreciation, he scratched a colossal gray's forehead. This one stood eighteen hands, maybe more.

A fly's sneeze could've knocked him over when Seonaid offered up her innocence. Dangerous, that. Another, less scrupulous man would've tossed up her skirts in the outbuilding without a second thought.

The gray blew against his shoulder, and Jacques scratched the beast's broad forehead again. The letter in his pocket crackled as he stretched his arm high overhead.

His curiosity demanded he probe to discover Seonaid's reasons for her boggling request, but what good would that have done? He couldn't exactly tattle to McTavish and explain how he came by such knowledge, and Jacques wasn't a close friend or family member she'd welcome advice from.

When had her hostility transformed to attraction? For he'd no doubt she felt the same undeniable, powerful draw he did for her. An allure he must—*must*—put from his mind.

What a turnabout in a week's time.

He couldn't help but think her request had something to do with her visions or Fletcher. Mayhap both.

Running a finger across his mustache, he scowled.

The thought of Fletcher cooled his ardor swifter than running barefoot and bare-arsed through the snow-covered pasture visible beyond the stable's partially open doors whilst being bombarded with rock-hard snow pellets.

Leaning against the stall's rough door, he withdrew the letter, then rotated it twice.

Ah well, might as well see what dark news Faucher sent.

What a fussy, gloomy fellow, always predicting the worst.

With a flick of his thumb, Jacques broke the seal, then swiftly perused the single page of scribbled writing.

Merde.

All but a few faithful staff had left the *château,* and though his creditors promised they'd wait until March to collect, they demanded a partial payment now.

Which brought Faucher to the true point of his letter.

Jacques could picture the sweat dripping from the nervous little man's face as he wrung his hands and spluttered the news.

An anonymous buyer had come forth offering a generous price for the estate. A very generous price, in fact.

Suspiciously generous.

FOURTEEN

Mentally checking off what she intended to accomplish today, Seonaid skipped down the last riser, her boots clacking noisily against the smooth stone. As a child, she jumped up and down the stairs, deliberately creating eerie echoes.

Giving in to impulse, she hopped up the riser, then bounced down again. The sound spiraled hollowly up the stairway, and she grinned.

The medieval castle, with its one-hundred-seventy-plus rooms, never frightened her. Well, the dungeon proved rather sinister. Many generations ago, people had died in the keep's bowels. Some tortured local legends claimed.

Despite the sun streaking through the mullioned window high above the keep's entry and splashing miniature rainbows onto the ancient walls and floor, she shuddered.

Enough morbid musings.

Except for an occasional glimpse, she'd managed to evade Jacques for nearly a week. It helped that the weather had cleared, melting the snow, and he'd made several trips to his mine.

On those days, he didn't return until well after the family dined. Likely, he avoided her too. Hopefully, his extended hours away meant the mining operations went well, and Jacques was pleased with his investment.

She *should* be pleased, for his absence spared her chagrin. Unless she reminisced about their toe-curling, stomach-toppling, pulse-skipping kiss and the ensuing humiliation afterward.

Not that she cared.

Fine, she cared, in a polite, distant sort of way, but she couldn't blame him. Though the notion pricked her tattered self-esteem—more like pounded it with a battering ram—she conceded his aloofness was for the best.

Dodging him for weeks, on the other hand, might prove blasted difficult. If he stayed the full three months, he'd be at Craiglocky until the end of March.

However, if everything went as her mother anticipated—she didn't quite share Mother's enthusiasm or optimism—wedding preparations might be underway by then.

Perfectly wonderful.

Even Seonaid's thoughts resonated with cynicism.

Freya, her kittens, and the other animals kept Seonaid busy, as did helping Mother with the house party arrangements. The activity eased her apprehension about Jacques, as well as her visions.

At this juncture, Seonaid might accept the first well-groomed man under the age of forty who asked for her hand. And she'd told her parents as much.

Father had frowned, loudly *harrumphing* his displeasure, and Mother had brushed Seonaid's declaration off as nonsensical twaddle.

"Flimflam, *chérie*." Clicking her tongue, Mother shook her head. "Of my children, you're the most romantic *and* sensible, *non*? You'll not marry without affection, Seonaid.

You're too caring and generous to be that cold-hearted and calculating."

Wonder what she'd do if I told her I brashly asked Jacques to deflower me?

Heat tracked up Seonaid's face, so she'd bent over her sewing to hide the telltale flush.

"Mother, I've explained my reasons for wanting to marry quite clearly, and sentiment doesn't factor into my decision." Although, liking her husband somewhat was preferable. Someone comfortable and good-natured. Someone like Douglas, for instance.

"*Zut.* I begin to lose tolerance with you." Mother impatiently swiped the air with her hand. "You wait and see. I'll wager, you fall in love at first sight, *non?*"

Non. Nae. *No.*

Seonaid didn't have time to wait for love to pay her a call.

Besides, how was falling in love at first sight sensible? No one in her family had done so, although Father insisted he adored Mother from the instant she set foot in the keep, married to his closest friend. Not that he'd acted on his love until she'd been widowed for quite some time.

Winking, he bobbed his shaggy head. "*Aye,* I am thinkin' that thing myself, Giselle. Our Seonaid be confused. She doesnae ken what she wants."

That miffed more than a trifling since his words held a jot of truth, but Seonaid kept her vexation to herself. To her immense relief, she hadn't had another unnerving vision, and her life had returned to a somewhat normal state.

That day in the shed, Jacques had left his coat on the outbuilding's table, but rather than returning it promptly, she'd taken the garment to her chamber intending to have it cleaned.

Only she hadn't.

Instead, twice now, she'd taken the garment from its

hiding place at the rear of her wardrobe and sniffed the fabric, relishing his scent lingering there.

Perhaps she'd already gone daft. How else could her peculiar behavior be explained?

What were the first signs of lunacy?

In the village, dotty Mrs. Tipperary mumbled to herself and saw things that weren't there. She hid from people too, dashing behind furniture, lurking behind trees, crouching in corners.

Splendid. I'm halfway to loony already.

Headed to the kitchen to meet Mother and discuss the menu for the party, Seonaid passed the music room. The pianoforte's lilting strains slowed her steps, and she cocked her head.

Yvette played with such inspiration that listening was a joy. Perhaps she had ideas of what to serve their guests for the Valentine gathering.

After all, she was the keep's true mistress. Come to think of it, had Mother consulted with her about the house party? Surely, she must have, for courtesy demanded they include Yvette in the preparations.

Well, that was remedied easily enough. Simply invite Yvette to join her in the kitchen. If she felt well enough. Her stomach had grown quite huge, and Ewan regularly speculated another strapping son rested in her womb.

Perhaps Seonaid ought to tell them about the twins. She pressed her lips together, wavering, Not yet. But soon. Very soon.

With a short rap, she heaved open the heavy double doors. "Excuse me for interrupt—" She stumbled to a halt, jaw slack and still clasping the door handle. "Oh. It's *you.*"

At her entrance, Jacques pivoted halfway on the bench, one hand yet upon the keyboard.

Spinning 'round and bolting from the room was the

height of bad form, but hiking her skirts and dashing away was tempting nonetheless.

Weariness lined his molded features, but his expressive eyes, such beautiful eyes, lit up upon seeing her.

Hadn't he been sleeping well?

She had an herbal sleeping draught for insomnia. She'd send a cup to his room tonight.

Even with purplish shadows beneath his eyes, the deep tobacco brown of his coat emphasized his swarthy features. Simply gazing at him caused a swell of something pleasant yet unnamable. Something she didn't dare examine closely.

He wasn't *her* destiny.

"I thought you were Yvette." Nothing like stating the obvious, for pity's sake.

Seonaid ought to go at once, but instead, her feet carried her farther into the room, rather than scurrying along the corridor to the kitchen as her common sense and bruised dignity advised. Silently shrieking in unison better described their indignation.

Jacques's mustache twitched. "I'm sorry to disappoint you."

"Oh, I'm not disappointed." For God's sake, did she have to sound breathless and wanton? "I... We're deciding the menu for the house party next month."

Do blather about more trivial nonsense and make a hash of that too.

She gestured toward the instrument. "I wasn't aware you played, Jacques."

A full-blown smile whisked across his face.

Was her brain functioning today, or had it ceased upon seeing him?

She glanced downward, hiding a wince.

Drat, she wore the same shabby affair he'd last seen her in, but after wheedling another treat from Sorcha for Freya,

Seonaid intended to walk to the village and call upon Mrs. Drummond and her new bairn. No one would see her gown beneath her cloak.

Nausea had plagued Mrs. Drummond her entire pregnancy, and Seonaid had provided her with an herbal tea to ease her discomfort. She'd also promised to visit when she returned from London.

Smoothing her hands down her front, more for something to do and to dry her suddenly damp palms than the need to erase the few wrinkles, she quashed her vanity.

What did she care if Jacques saw her in the same drab gown?

Once a lovely shade of deep green, rather like the Highland hills in high summer, the fabric had paled to a grayish-brown moss color resembling the slime that accumulated between the rocks on Loch Arkaig's far side.

Lovely comparison and one sure to bolster my confidence.

Taking a deep breath, Seonaid composed herself and then offered a polite smile. "You play brilliantly."

"Thank you. I couldn't resist the temptation." Gratitude lit his face. "Playing clears my head, and this is a spectacular instrument, tuned to perfection. That surprises me, given the castle's atmosphere."

Seonaid nodded, edging farther into the room. "Yvette is most meticulous about its care. She adores playing as much as you."

"I haven't indulged in months, truth to tell," he said. "Not since my *mère* died. She was gifted and had performed for royalty, such was her talent."

Jacques ran his long fingers over the ivory keys. Though he curved his mouth pleasantly, his scar stretching with the movement, he exuded despondency and discouragement.

Despite her determination to remain impervious,

Seonaid's heart constricted, and she almost gasped in empathy, so crushing was the insight that came upon her.

He's lonely. Terribly, long-sufferingly lonely.

With everything in her, as if this insight, too, was second sight induced, Seonaid had staggered upon his secret. Or one of them. He had more, and she itched to uncover the rest.

She knew he had no one in France to return home to.

There was nothing to hold him there except an estate that contained cherished memories of the family he'd lost. No wonder he was determined to return and restore her.

His home was all that he had left.

Crossing to him, her boots made no sound on the plush sage, russet, and ivory Aubusson rug Yvette recently purchased to give the room a degree of warmth. Except for Mother's solar, Craiglocky wasn't cozy or particularly inviting.

Embarrassment over her recent kiss with Jacques strained to raise its malevolent, misshapen head, but Seonaid redoubled her determination to act graciously. After pelting the emotion into the ash bin, she continued on to him.

Once beside the pianoforte, she clasped her hands behind her back lest she brush the lock of hair temptingly tumbled over his noble brow. "I trust everything at Oakberry goes well now that the snow is mostly gone?"

"Not quite as good as I'd hoped at this point," he confessed. "The weather, equipment mishaps, a minor cave-in, and a bout of stomach sickness amongst the miners has put us behind schedule." He shoved his hair off his forehead before slicing a quick glance to the open doors. "And the manager hasn't returned from a trip to Edinburgh yet—supposedly to talk to potential buyers."

His attention veered to the doors once more.

Did Jacques fear Seonaid would throw herself at him again?

Her stomach tumbled in that queer discomfort-mixed-with-chagrin way. He needn't worry. She wasn't an idiot or eager for another stinging round of mortification. Scots would relinquish their beloved plaids and go about naked as a needle to their knees before that ever happened again.

Skirting the instrument, she put a safe distance between her and Jacques. In his presence, she reacted most disconcertingly, and she didn't trust herself.

"How did you get your scar, Jacques?"

God's teeth!

How horridly rude. Of late, she spewed her thoughts.

No, the irritating, ill-mannered practice only occurred with him. No others.

He touched the fine, white line, tracing its length with his forefinger. "I had a rather unfortunate encounter with a knife-wielding fellow determined I should I not live a moment longer."

Resting her forearms atop the pianoforte's glossy surface, she winked. "When you were a spy?"

FIFTEEN

*M*erde.

Only years of training kept the surprise from registering on Jacques's face. What clues had he inadvertently given that led Seonaid to her accurate conclusion?

Mayhap none and nothing more unusual than a clever imagination contributed to her insight. Or, unbeknownst to her conscious mind, had her gift revealed the truth? Could confidences or secrets be kept from her? Ever?

Wouldn't that make for an interesting marriage?

You cannot marry her.

Think of *le Manoir des Jardins.*

And his maman and the rest of his family lying in the cemetery. But absolutely nothing else anchored him to France. Nothing.

Except for his blasted, eight-generations-past barony title.

"*Oui, ma petite*, when I was an agent." Raising a forefinger to his lips, he leaned forward and winked. "Shh. That must be kept our secret, *non*?"

"I knew it!"

A satisfaction-borne grin tipped Seonaid's mouth, and she bounced on her toes.

He could trust her with the truth, especially since the war ended, and in this remote corner of Scotland, she wasn't likely to engage in a conversation with anyone regarding the matter.

"Did you ever work with Ewan?" Bent over the pianoforte, her eyes sparkling with excitement, she canted her head.

How did she discern such things?

Had McTavish chattered about his escapades?

No more than Jacques would have done.

Her bent position thrust her full bosom forward, taut against her gown's modest neckline.

Jacques swallowed and tore his gaze from the pearly flesh barely an arm's length away, and her hardened tips deliciously outlined. Without effort, Seonaid seduced and enticed, luring him. How could a mere mortal resist such a tempting armful?

"Did you, Jacques, even once?"

"*Zut*! Too many questions which I cannot answer."

He laughed and gave her hand a short squeeze, forgetting for an instant what touching her did to him. Fire raced to his loins, and he instantly released his hold. Instead, he made a pretense of selecting another piece of music. Something melancholy to cool his ardor.

A funeral dirge ought to suffice rather nicely.

"I suppose that's a rule." Sighing, Seonaid pursed her lush lips. Slanting her gaze sideways, she whispered covertly, "Can you tell me if you met any women spies?"

"*C'est assez*." Would she never cease? Persistent minx. He threw his hands up, then shook a finger at her. "*Non*, I cannot."

She blinked at him innocently, yet mischief frolicked in the uncanny depths of her eyes. "I should like to have been a spy. Or an informant. Imagine if I could control my visions, what a help I might have been during the war."

At what age? Thirteen? Fourteen?

Contemplating what would happen to a girl that tender age, Jacques shuddered. And someone with Seonaid's abilities? If she could indeed master her second sight? A shiver did skitter from shoulder to waist. Both sides would've exploited her gifts without remorse or conscience.

What *le bon ton* wanted from her, nonsensical parlor tricks to entertain their bored, elite masses, was child's play compared to what unprincipled, hardened generals would've done. Not so different than what Fletcher suggested, though certainly motivated and justified by a wholly different cause.

No wonder Seonaid wanted to eradicate her fey.

"I will confess one thing, *ma petite.*" He smoothed his trim mustache. "That night in Paris, I was supposed to meet an informant in the alcove and found you hidden away there instead. I've always been curious, why?"

"You were? Really?" Seonaid's eyes and mouth rounded for an instant. "I was avoiding an over-zealous beau." Consternation flicked across her face, and she ran her fingertips over the base of the silver candelabra sitting atop the piano. "I presume your contact was the courtesan you mistook me for?"

"*Oui.*" Jacques gave her a smile, a small shamefaced turn of his mouth. "But I never mistook you for my contact, *ma petite.*"

"You make a habit of kissing strangers, then?" Tone drier than the cold ashes lying in the hearth, her brow swept upward.

Masculine vanity tried to persuade him jealousy colored Seonaid's voice. "*Non,* only when danger of exposure lurks nearby, and the woman is beyond tempting. In that case, an enemy of mine saw me enter the alcove. Most careless of me."

"*Hmph.*" Pensiveness replaced her excitement, and she tapped the fingertips of one hand atop the piano, her short, oval nails clicking a soft staccato. "I might've saved lives, shortened the war, if I could master my visions' occurrences."

"I, for one, am glad you cannot. There are those who would've used you for ill-gotten gain." He stood, then dared to touch her creamy cheek for a fleeting instant.

Her eyes widened, and her breath hitched.

"That would've been tragic," he murmured, more to himself than to her.

Seigneur Dieu, but she was lovely. Her parted lips beckoned, and he'd lowered his head to taste them—then decency kicked him ferociously in the arse.

A man of his experience recognized a woman well along the path to becoming enamored, and he'd made the situation worse, had encouraged her affections by nearly kissing her once more.

That must not happen again. Four times a fool, he was not.

Jacques needed to distance himself from Seonaid, at least emotionally. Wisdom decreed physically as well. When she'd been furious with him, couldn't stand his company, it had been better. Safer. For them both.

Straightening, he raked his fingers through his hair. "I beg your pardon. I vow, that won't happen again."

A bemused expression flitted across Seonaid's refined features, but she swiftly donned an unaffected mien. Rolling a shoulder, she dropped her gaze and pressed her lips into a firm line. "As you say."

Hell, he'd offended her. Again. Well, better she feel insulted than let her entertain notions that might break her heart. Wasn't she busy planning a grand house party, hoping to snare a husband? McTavish made mention of the event in passing, grumbling about fawning swains underfoot. McTavish didn't think Seonaid was ready to marry.

Why the rush then?

The notion sent a jagged, rusty blade twisting in Jacques's innards. He had no claim, no right to harbor feelings toward her. The best he could do would be to help her in her husband-hunting endeavor, though why she was quite so eager to wed, he couldn't fathom.

Unfortunately, things couldn't be different between them. Otherwise, he'd ask to court her. Although their mutual attraction undeniably remained, they each sought to marry others, albeit for entirely different reasons.

Though he hadn't pursued anyone just yet, if Oakberry didn't start producing soon, he'd be prowling parlors and soirées in pursuit of a purse-heavy bride. Or mayhap, he'd send Faucher to America to locate an heiress.

Pulling upright, Seonaid pointed to his head. "Your hair is standing up every which direction."

Sliding a hand over his hair, he attempted to smooth the tousled strands. "As a young man, I'd mess my hair on purpose to vex my most proper valet. It gave him fits."

A smile teased her mouth.

"Most wicked of you, the poor man. He's in France still?" She'd wandered to the window, and after edging aside the draperies, peered outside. "Doesn't he care to travel?"

"*Non*. He died from a fever three years ago, and I didn't replace him." Didn't have the funds to, but by God, Jacques had become damned accomplished at tying a cravat.

Turning, Seonaid placed her hands behind her back. She leaned against the window, the sunbeams haloing her head and shoulders. Her expression inscrutable, she stared at him.

"Do you already have an heiress selected?"

Jacques faltered in taming his wild hair. "*Pardonnez-moi?*"

Seonaid couldn't possibly know his intentions.

Had he slipped and revealed something? Wracking his memory, he mentally picked through their conversations.

Non, he hadn't, except for mentioning he hoped the mine would enable him to restore and refurbish the château.

McTavish might have told her, but not likely. Unless he feared she'd set her cap for Jacques, but she'd done nothing publicly that hinted she'd a *tendre* for him. Nonetheless, she might not recognize her feelings for what they were.

The second sight then?

Gaze cast to the floor, she rubbed a finger across an eyebrow.

"My gift has altered slightly. Now, it seems I sometimes discern personal things. I'm not quite sure what to make of it yet." Golden ribbons reflecting off her sable hair, her placid countenance didn't change a jot except for the minute, momentary narrowing of her eyes. "At least I distinguish things about you. It's more of an impression, actually, and your astonishment confirmed them."

"Confirmed them?" Legs spread, Jacques crossed his arms. *Hounds' teeth.* "How?"

He'd been a spy—even been tortured once—and he'd perfected masking his thoughts and feelings. His reactions too, except for the obstinate member in his pantaloons which, of late, had a bloody determined mind of its own.

Angling her head, Seonaid stared at him through sooty lashes. "Your eyes betray you."

The oddest sensation blossomed in his chest, as if she'd seen straight to the depths of his soul and touched him there. Should he be intrigued or alarmed?

Glancing ceilingward, she dragged in a deep breath. Her gaze roved the solemn-faced portraits hanging from golden velvet cords throughout the room.

She cannot bear to look at me.

Behind her, the sun illumed her pert silhouette, enhancing her ethereal appearance.

"I won't say I'm altogether thrilled by another sudden

change in my second sight, but that's how I deduced you'd been a spy." She cut him a brief glance. "And about the heiress too."

"*Non*. I haven't chosen anyone."

Lying to her wasn't an option.

In any event, how could Jacques deceive someone who discerned things before they happened? Neck bent, he rubbed his nape, suddenly wearier than he could ever recall. Rather disconcerting, her poking around in his conscience.

"I yet have hope that such a monumental"—*horrendous*—"step won't be necessary. I've still several weeks left for Oakberry to make good."

Not really.

He'd written Faucher, giving him a list of items he could sell to temporarily appease the creditors. They'd not be pacified for long. Like hounds intent on a fresh fox trail, they hungered for their prize.

Jacques also asked Faucher to uncover who'd made the offer. A doubt didn't exist Faucher already knew, but he'd likely been paid to pretend ignorance.

Which pointed straight to Carnot.

Gliding to the door, Seonaid summoned an unhappy smile. "I truly admire your dedication to your home."

Even in a gown far past the peak of fashion and with a mantle of despondency shrouding her, she outshone every woman he'd seen in their court finery. She possessed a rare, inner beauty that heightened her outer loveliness.

He stretched his injured hand, now bandage free, toward her, anxious to explain and yet keenly aware he shouldn't. Didn't have the right. "Seonaid?"

She stared at his extended palm, lingering on the healing cut, before her attention slowly gravitated to his face. She stood silently, unmoving, disappointment warring with regret in her moist eyes.

What could he say to soothe her offended feelings?

He could help her put her infatuation for him aside. She'd detested him once. It was past time for her to hate him again.

For her sake.

And his.

When she regarded him the way she did now, despite his being an unworthy nipfarthing determined to acquire a fortune, he was sorely tempted to follow his heart. Just this once, to selfishly consider *his* wants.

No one he cared for remained to condemn him for making a selfish choice.

Non, but his family, at least *Mère* and his sister's family, might yet be alive if he'd been at home, not spying for the English or smuggling in another vain attempt to raise funds.

Guilt and remorse proved powerful motivators to return to a country and an estate that no longer felt like home—hadn't for a long while, truth be known.

Jacques would play his hand, and then remove himself to an empty miner's hovel for the remainder of his Scotland stay. Staying at Craiglocky was inconceivable after what he meant to do.

I am indeed an utter, colossal arse.

He bestowed his most charming smile on her. "I suspect my actions, my kisses, have misled you, Seonaid, and you've developed a *tendre* for me."

God, he loathed himself right now.

Seonaid flinched, pink coloring cheeks as pale as the marble busts displayed behind her, but she bravely held his gaze, nonetheless.

Oui, he'd been right when he'd told McTavish she was the strongest of the sisters. "But, if I may be perfectly blunt, I'm afraid your dowry wouldn't begin to suffice."

Churl.

The color drained from her face as quickly as the blush

had appeared. Her eyes luminous, she swallowed and fisted her hands in her worn skirt.

What strength of character she possessed. Any other woman would either be weeping or railing hysterically. Or have swooned.

"I didn't take you for a cruel man, Jacques. I'm perfectly aware you require a fortune to renovate your home."

Each softly spoken word in her lilting brogue stabbed, rapier sharp.

Lower lip trembling and tears shimmering in her eyes, she serenely forged on. "You've also made it clear you don't desire me, and I'll confess, my inexperience with men led me to believe otherwise." Her small chin angled upward. "However, I assure you, I'm not crushed by the knowledge. I, too, plan on marrying for convenience, and I have you to thank for helping me make that decision."

Non!

It was Jacques's turn to gulp in a hefty breath and swallow against the tightness in his throat, making speech impossible.

Seonaid should—*must*—marry for love.

Because she was unique. And extraordinary. And wonderful. And gentle. And had the purest heart he'd ever encountered.

He clamped his jaw and stiffened his knees against the need to stride across the room, take her into his arms, and whisper those very things. And that he wanted nothing more in this world than to make her his, all else be damned.

What of *le Manoir des Jardins*? His family? His title. His self-respect? His promise to *Maman*?

Did they mean naught?

Non, not compared to Seonaid.

He'd give everything up for her, but a pauper had no business marrying, particularly a woman of refinement and breeding.

How would he support her?

As a gentlemen's secretary or man of business? Assuredly not in the fashion to which she was accustomed.

A way existed which preserved his pride.

Sell *le Manoir des Jardins.*

To Carnot?

Who else? For surely, he'd made the offer.

That Jacques couldn't do. Anything but sell his cherished home to his nemesis, the man responsible for his sister's death.

He couldn't abandon Jeanette again.

Selfishly, Jacques committed to memory every angle of Seonaid's face. Her upturned nose, her Cupid's bow lips, and expressive, deep pecan-brown eyes. Her long, ivory neck, trim waist, and curves perfect for cupping by a man's hands. The way she held herself, elegant and poised, a hint of mystery hovering about her. How her mouth contorted and nose crinkled when she was deep in reverie.

He'd never know her intimately, never touch her satiny flesh, would never see her smile at him in adoration, or hear her cries of ecstasy when he brought her to fulfillment.

And still, though he'd spoken brutally, he beheld kindness, and, perhaps even now, a degree of adulation on her beautiful, ravaged face.

He'd done that to her, and though Jacques would rather sever a limb, he must wound her more. Must make her turn away from him in complete disgust and loathing. Must destroy the last vestiges of affection she harbored for him. So she could be free to eventually give her heart to someone more deserving.

Shrugging nonchalantly, he yawned widely. Rudely. Let her think him an uncouth bore. "Marry for convenience? If you're able to snare a man who can tolerate your second sight, that is."

Unmitigated, unforgivable, calculated cruelty.

A tiny, strangled gasp escaped her. Wincing, one hand at her throat, she stepped backward like she'd suffered a tremendous blow. For a beat, she didn't respond and just stood stunned. Then she jutted her perfect oval chin in the air. An icy haughtiness worthy of a *beau monde* patroness rippled off her rigid form.

"You're sorely mistaken, Monsieur de Devaux-Rousset, if you presume that I ever considered marrying you. I'm neither desperate nor deranged."

Sixteen

Five hours later, Jacques paced Mr. Newton's office, rubbing his nape, where pebbles huddled together in solid, unrelenting clusters to torture him. Giving the nubby mass a final squeeze, he lifted his head. "How long since silver ore has been mined?"

Easing back in his squeaky chair, Oakberry Quarry's manager scratched his bristly chin. "We've found cobalt and lead aplenty, but nae silver ore or galena in..." Staring into space, he tapped his fingers atop the desk. "Och, maybe eight or nine weeks."

Weeks?

Hell's bells.

Not unusual for a mining operation, but Jacques didn't have weeks to spare. The digging and extracting were only part of the process. Assessing the ores' quality and finding a fair buyer took time too. Precious time he didn't have.

He'd rushed into this venture, and haste might mean the end for him. But even desperate, he refused to overwork his crew, treating them scant better than beasts of burden or slaves as other mine owners were wont to do.

"Monsieur, all's no' lost," Mr. Newton said. "There's a good market for cobalt and also lead. It dinna pay as much as silver ore, but it's usually enough to keep us in supplies an' equipment an' to pay the crew."

Mr. Newton stood and, after scooting his lanky frame around the shabby, scarred desk, pointed to a series of tunnels depicted on the roughly sketched map hanging askew on the crude wall behind Jacques.

"Here's where we've found a few small, rich silver ore veins, and there's also cobalt throughout." He drew a stained, callused finger along a chamber. "I think we're close to strikin' a giant lode. The signs are all there."

Scrunching his eyes and studying the map, Newton tugged at his earlobe.

What signs did he see that Jacques couldn't?

"How can you be sure?" Jacques also studied the markings, which meant nothing to him. He hadn't researched mining before jumping at the offer Mr. Needham made him in London. An upstanding banker, he'd trusted the man, but uncertainty still nipped.

Had Jacques thrown all his eggs into the proverbial basket, merely to lose everything?

Newton chuckled, a deep belly laugh as if Jacques had delivered a fabulous joke. "Ye canna ever be sure, Monsieur. Call it gut instinct. Or intuition." He poked the wrinkled map again and nodded confidently. "I've been minin' for over twenty years, and trust me, sir, there's silver ore in Oakberry. Have patience. We'll find it. Shouldna take more than two or three months to dig the new shaft."

Jacques closed his eyes for a second. "Two or three months with our current crew? What if we hired more men? Could it be done in half that time?"

It had to be.

Nodding slowly, Newton pursed his mouth. "Experienced miners could do it—with the right equipment. If'n ye had enough and offered them a worthy wage."

Where would Jacques get the funds for that?

McTavish.

So much for the morsel of pride he still possessed.

God help him if Seonaid breathed a word of their conversation in the music room. McTavish would call him out, and justly so, even if he had warned Jacques away from her.

"See to hiring additional men. Make sure they're the best." At the door, Jacques swung back around. "By the way, I'd prefer to be closer to the day-to-day operations. Is there an empty cabin, or do you know of a miner who might be willing to accommodate me?"

Newton raised a grizzled brow.

"Sir, with all due respect, the men wouldna be comfortable with an arrangement of that nature." His sudden absorption in his jacket's button revealed his apprehension. "And if'n ye mean for me to double the crew, quarters are goin' to get mighty crowded."

"I see." Damnation. Jacques would have to get a room at an inn. An expense he could ill afford.

"The recent sickness has me concerned too, Monsieur. Especially if we bring more men on." Newton ventured to the grimy window overlooking the mining camp. "There are still three men and their families ill." His perceptive gaze veered to Jacques for a second. "And I dinna ken if ye're aware, but the Gibsons lost their toddler yesterday mornin'. Ain't sure if it was the same sickness."

"Has a physician been to visit?" Paying for medical treatment wasn't Jacques's responsibility. Regardless these people barely had enough for their daily needs.

"Nae doctor. They canna afford his fees, but Miss Seonaid

sent her tonics, and the new vicar has visited. He performed the burial ceremony for wee Willie. If you dinna mind my sayin', sir, the rector's a queer one, he is."

"He is indeed."

Fletcher rode clear out here? Well, at least he took his responsibilities seriously.

Jacques would forgo the inn, stay on at Craiglocky Keep, and use his meager funds to pay for a doctor. Avoiding Seonaid after his unconscionable behavior might prove trickier. Mayhap he could stay in the clansmen's barracks. Except that might give rise to tattle that he didn't want to explain.

Well, the sooner he had a healthy workforce, the sooner he could expect to see a profit and take his leave of McTavish's hospitality.

Jacques tiredly wiped a hand over his heavy eyes.

Could anything else go wrong?

SEONAID TRAMPED along the pinewoods-shaded dogcart path to Craigcutty, her angry pace and gait anything but ladylike. Her raucous thoughts fell far short of that mark as well.

Wet soil and decaying leaves, combined with the scents of the stately pines and low-lying underbrush, riddled the air with an invigorating but earthy aroma as she trudged along.

With each stomping step, her basket banging against her hip, she imagined slapping Jacques's handsome, mocking face as she'd longed to do in the music room earlier.

How she managed to curtail her tears and prevent calling him a bloody tosspot, or cracking him over the head with a Greek god's marble bust, still astounded her.

Never had she experienced an urge to do someone bodily harm. Not even vile Reverend Fletcher. She hadn't believed herself capable of experiencing such fury.

What was it about that despicable Frenchman that wriggled beneath her skin? Caused her to behave and think in manners so foreign that she scarcely recognized herself?

He'd scorned her second sight.

She'd naïvely believed he understood her plight, the wretch, and he'd essentially suggested her visions made her undesirable to men. Even unfit to wed.

The bite of his calculated words had punctured deeply.

Seonaid shouldn't have trusted him. Shouldn't have fallen prey to his dark good looks and suaveness. Should never have responded to his knee-weakening kisses.

Gone was the cordial, caring man of recent days, and the sardonic, cold devil she'd met in Paris had returned.

But why?

What did it matter?

She was stupid to have imagined he'd changed. He cared for nothing but acquiring money by whatever means available. A fancy man, no better than a demi-rep. It shouldn't have surprised her, and that it had made her more furious with herself than him.

Gullible ninnyhammer.

Thank God, she hadn't surrendered her maidenhead to the conceited, mercenary cull.

She snorted, startling a mountain hare that tore from the clearing as if snarling, teeth-gnashing hounds of hell chased it. Smart creature.

Seonaid should've done the same the instant she'd seen Jacques at the Hare's Foot Inn. She should've dived headfirst into the snow and taken her chances in the storm. Perishing from the elements was preferable to dying from mortification.

Developed a tendre for him, indeed.

She stamped along, leaving deep footprints in the saturated soil and finding a perverse joy in the act.

Jacques had kissed *her*. Thrice. Not the reverse.

True, she'd responded like a wanton that last time, but his kissing skills were well-honed. No doubt he'd had a great deal of practice. A bloody monstrous amount.

At the memory, a not-unpleasant tremor shuddered her from knees to breasts. Her treacherous nipples had the audacity to pucker. Even after what he'd said to her?

Oooh, the irksome boor.

Seonaid gave a pinecone a vicious kick, sending it airborne to bounce off a tree. Gritting her teeth and sucking in a bracing drag of tangy air, she balled her fists until her fingers cramped.

She did not desire him.

The arrogant rake. *Stomp, stomp.* Smug wretch. *Stomp, stomp.* Inconsiderate rakehell. *Stomp, stomp.* Egotistical scoundrel—

"Miss Seonaid, please slow down. I canna keep up with ye." Maeve, clutching her plumpish side and panting heavily, trotted several lengths behind Seonaid on the muddy, rutted path.

"Do forgive me, Maeve." Slowing her gait to a more sedate speed, Seonaid replayed the music room scene. Again.

"*Won't suffice,*" Jacques had declared. "*Snare a man,*" he'd sneered. "*Tolerate your second sight.*" That had been the *coup de grâce*—the death blow to the last vestige of warm regard she held for him.

Did anything bite deeper or fiercer than rejection and humiliation?

Seonaid blinked away scalding tears. She would not cry over the likes of Monsieur le baron. Raising her face, she welcomed the brisk breeze cooling her cheeks and temper.

Maeve caught up and, despite her labored breathing, gave Seonaid a toothy smile. "Thank ye fer askin' me to accompany ye. I haven't seen me da, mum, or sisters fer nigh on a fortnight."

"You're the logical choice to take Una's place," Seonaid said. "Poor dear. When her rheumatism acts up, she's miserable and can scarcely hobble a few steps."

Seonaid might have taken the dogcart, but fewer than two miles separated the village from the keep, and she needed vigorous exercise. It helped dispel her wrath, and besides, Maeve's parents lived on the township outskirts. The servant could enjoy a nice visit while Seonaid called upon Mrs. Drummond and ran a couple of other errands.

Ten minutes later, Seonaid returned Mr. and Mrs. McDuff's and their other five daughters' waves as they noisily spilled from their cottage edging the woods upon hearing Maeve's exuberant greeting.

Grinning, Seonaid called, "Maeve, I shall collect you in about two hours."

Maeve managed a nod before her chattering family whisked her indoors.

Another half-mile and Seonaid passed the rectory, purposely keeping her head turned away.

As her fiendish luck would have it, Reverend Fletcher descended the steps as a half-dozen noisy village children that had been playing in the street crowded around her. Laughing and jostling, they politely waited for the shortbread she brought to town for them.

Was it a coincidence that he happened along at that precise moment? Or had the busybody peeked from the window, watching passersby, and made it his business to meddle when he'd seen her? Rather than continue on his way, as courtesy dictated, he screwed his eyes to narrow slits and boldly watched her quickly dispense the treats.

The children, cheeks rosy with excitement, tore into the pastries, thanking her with their mouths full and spewing crumbs.

Drawing close, he eyed the basket suspiciously.

She held her breath as his unpleasant odor wafted past.

His face flushed and pinched with disgust, he scowled at the children stuffing shortbread in their mouths. "What be ye bewitchin' the bairns with?"

"Our cook's famous shortbread. There's one left. Would you like it?" Seonaid offered him the one remaining biscuit, but he threw his hands up and stumbled back.

"Nae, I'll not be takin' anythin' from ye."

What? Didn't he possess a cross or garlic to ward off evil spirits?

Dragging a rather grayish handkerchief from his pocket, he pointed at the pastry before mopping his sweaty forehead. "Ye might be tryin' to poison me."

"Oh, for pity's sake. Nothing of the sort. You certainly are overly suspicious." Seonaid bit into the crisp, buttery biscuit. "See. Perfectly safe and quite scrumptious."

Her stomach gurgled, and she took another bite. The upset with Jacques had caused her to forgo luncheon, and now she was quite ravenous.

"A witch canna poison herself with her evil concoctions or harm herself with her wicked spells either."

A few onlookers slowed and exchanged alarmed glances upon hearing his harsh declaration. Even the children, crumbs upon their lips and fingers, paused in chomping their biscuits.

One wee lad ogled the half-eaten pastry, then glowered at the vicar. Lower lip protruding, his small face puckered in confusion. "Miss Seonaid nae be a witch."

"Assuredly, I'm not a witch, Jack." Seonaid tousled his mop of red hair. "The vicar knows not of what he speaks."

One fisted hand resting upon her jutted hip, she dared the rector to contradict her. She'd had enough of men maligning her and her ways.

Fletcher slanted his skeptical gaze to her basket again. He pointed a knobby finger, and her stomach contracted at the grime wedged underneath his fingernail. "What be in those bottles and jars then?"

Busybody. Who was he to question her?

"Tonics and salves made from herbs. Mrs. Drummond's babe has colic. Midwife McCreary has a lingering cough. And Mrs. Tipperary's arthritis pains her." Seonaid lifted each out in turn. "I have a natural remedy for foul-smelling breath too." She smiled sweetly. "I would be happy to make you some."

A few children giggled into their hands.

"Ye make them?" Cunning sharpened Fletcher's features and voice. "Yerself?"

What of it? Was he truly so ignorant?

"Yes. From herbs and plants, I either grow or find." Once she'd secured the cloth around the medicines, she looped the basket over her arm. "You're aware many remedies come from plants made by the Good Lord, Vicar, aren't you? And one would hardly dare accuse alchemists or physicians of dabbling in witchcraft or sorcery."

He opened his mouth but snapped it shut when two women walked past.

"Good day, Miss Seonaid, Vicar," the elder said, a cheery smile rounding her cheeks.

Seonaid nodded and returned her smile but kept her attention riveted upon Fletcher.

He folded his hands prayerfully and, bowing his head, mumbled a cursory greeting.

Charlatan.

The wind picked up, whirling Seonaid's pelisse about her ankles. Her bonnet ribbons flitted across her cheeks as she examined the sky. A few charcoal-tinted clouds littered the heavens, and a good many more darkened the horizon. "If you'll excuse me. I must be on my way if I'm to make the keep before dark or it begins to rain."

After rapidly perusing the street, he edged nearer, releasing another waft of stale, pungent odor. "I be watchin' ye, Miss Ferguson. I take my duty to protect God's citizens—"

The rest of what he threatened was lost to her as an image of him abusing a young girl plowed into her mind. The short-bread she'd devoured a moment before threatened to make a violent reappearance.

Oh God. Ewan must be made aware.

"Miss Seonaid?" Someone tugged at her pelisse. "Miss Seonaid?"

Jack grasped the garment, the remainder of his shortbread clutched in his other hand. "Why ye be starin' at the vicar like that? Yer eyes look funny, and yer all white."

Procuring a false smile, she patted his head. "A bout of dizziness, I fear. I didn't eat luncheon today. Come along, children. It's time you made your way home."

Fletcher's beady gaze danced from her to Jack and back to her again before he brazenly gripped her forearm. "Ye looked the same dazed way at the inn too. And in the coach. Mighty curious."

She jerked her arm, but his hold remained fast, a dangerous—or was it mad?—glint in his watery eyes.

Lifting her chin, Seonaid leveled him a wrathful glare but, mindful of the children, spoke calmly. "Unhand me at once, else I tell my brother of your untoward behavior."

"He canna always be comin' to yer rescue. There be things a powerful laird like the McTavish has nae say about." He licked his lower lip before sliding the onlookers a superior look.

Alarm, concern, and disbelief skittered across their countenances.

"Things that an anointed man of God, like myself, be empowered to know and do."

Fletcher might be anointed, but it wasn't with godly

power. More like stale sweat and oily hair. Seonaid gave another yank, and this time he released her, a feral smile contorting his mouth.

"Ye see unnatural things, dinna ye, lass?"

Seventeen

Bile surged to Seonaid's throat.

Fear's bitter taste.

Fletcher knew. God help her. He *knew*.

A small crowd had gathered and whispered quietly amongst themselves.

"You have a dangerous imagination, Vicar Fletcher, and you'd best watch *yourself*." Her pulse faster than an injured bird's, Seonaid dredged up her last remnant of fortitude. "Ewan won't take kindly to you manhandling me or stirring up discord. Or making rash and dangerous accusations."

Folding his arms, Fletcher jutted his chin toward the wide-eyed children. "Ye dinnae deny ye be bewitchin' the bairns."

"I didn't think such ludicrousness needed a denial. As these good citizens can attest." Waving her hand, Seonaid indicated the small crowd. "I've been doling out pastries each time I venture to the village for years. And I assure you, none of them have ever made a child ill or caused them to behave in a peculiar manner."

"That be true," a woman called.

"Miss Seonaid is a healer. She is pure and kind." Another in the crowd defended.

"I be knowin' wickedness when I see it." He glowered at her supporters before turning his irate gaze onto her. Fletcher pointed to the basket again. "Ye admitted to mixin' potions."

"Bah, I did no such thing." *Completely off his little pointed head.* "I said I'd made tonics and salves for medicinal purposes. Healers have done the same for generations."

"Aye, 'tis true," one of the onlookers agreed.

Another declared, "Nary a family in the village hasn't benefited from Miss Seonaid's healin' skills."

"The Good Lord made healin' plants too, Vicar. Ye'd do well to remember that," Mrs. Bowie chastised. "Miss Seonaid, please tell yer mother I'll have her bonnet done soon. I'm a wee bit behind."

"I'll be sure to tell her, Mrs. Bowie. We're having a grand house party in February, so I expect we'll pay a call soon to order gowns."

Fletcher snorted his disapproval.

The passersby dispersed, a few casting troubled glances over their shoulders, then bending their heads near. Not intentionally unkind, they'd nevertheless spread the tale throughout Craigcutty faster than the Highland's brisk winter winds.

"Go along home, boys. Molly, I'll walk with you." Her mind still reeling, Seonaid took Molly's small hand and, pointedly turning her back to the rector without bidding him farewell, she steered the children to the village's center.

More than three hours later, Seonaid hustled toward the McDuffs' cottage. More precisely, she tried hurrying, but with muck for a path, she progressed slowly.

The clouds earlier heralding rain made good their threat and fell in a continuous sheet. As Seonaid slogged through the mire, her boots squelching with each squishy step, she berated herself for lingering in Craigcutty.

But Mrs. Drummond had been charmingly proud of chubby wee Cailin, and Mrs. Tipperary had been so excited to have a visitor that she insisted Seonaid stay for tea. Which she drank from a cracked teacup of questionable cleanliness as a mouse watched from the corner, grooming its needle-thin white whiskers.

It was a good thing Seonaid claimed a stalwart constitution.

Her basket contained two jars of preserves from Mrs. Drummond, a new mortar and pestle, and three medicinal books Seonaid collected from the alchemist's.

The final delay had been the delicate task of warning Molly's mother about letting her daughter play near the church.

Seonaid had fibbed a mite and suggested Vicar Fletcher preferred to maintain the rectory's holiness and peace and asked that the children play elsewhere.

Utter balderdash and poppycock, of course.

She couldn't announce she'd seen him...

A shudder rippled through her.

Well in truth, she wasn't quite sure what she'd seen, but it had been enough to curdle her blood and put her off food. That man was evil to his debased heart, and worse, he used the Kirk as a guise to practice his corruption.

Couldn't Ewan send Fletcher packing now?

Must he wait for a response from the bishop?

The good people of Craigcutty would carry on perfectly fine until Reverend Wallace's return. The Lord only knew what mischief and damage Fletcher might stir in the meanwhile.

The crafty satisfaction in his eyes today didn't portend well for her. Best she stay clear of him until he departed. Or take a male escort with her when venturing to the village.

Douglas would volunteer, but she wouldn't take him from

his blacksmith apprentice duties. She'd let Ewan or Father decide who should accompany her.

Clasping her hood tightly at her throat, Seonaid ducked her chin to her chest in a vain attempt to prevent the lashing rain from pelting her face with ice-cold droplets. It would be fully dark by the time she and Maeve made the keep, and Mother would cluck and fuss. If she hadn't already sent someone to retrieve her.

A branch cracked not far behind her, and Seonaid jumped, her heart thumping wildly. Another hare bolted across the path, likely headed for its warm den. Lucky creature.

Teeth chattering, she faced forward. She'd been edgy and tense since entering the pinewoods. Likely, that ugly business with the rector had unnerved her more than she'd credited. She'd traveled these woods, this path, hundreds of times with nary a hint of peril, yet at the moment, she wished she'd brought her dagger with her.

Thunder grumbled and crashed, shaking the heavens as lightning cracked the firmament. She jumped, barely stifling a startled yelp.

Hound's teeth, what a ninny.

Half expecting to see a specter floating behind her, she casually cast a glance over her shoulder, and when she faced forward again, a cloaked man, his hood obscuring his face, blocked the road a few feet ahead.

Fletcher.

Did he truly think she wouldn't recognize him?

Shoulders squared and head held high, she stood her ground. Today of all days to have forgotten her blasted blade. "Step aside and permit me to pass, Vicar Fletcher."

He snickered, shoving off his hood and revealing a whip.

Sweet Jesus.

"I mean to see ye repent of yer wickedness. Confess and I be lenient with ye."

"I shan't do any such thing, and you have no right to detain me." Firming her grip on her basket, Seonaid vainly searched the path for other travelers. "I'm tardy returning to the keep, and I expect someone has already been sent to fetch me home."

"Then I'd best be hurryin', hadn't I?"

He lunged, but Seonaid had anticipated his movement. Swinging the basket with every ounce of strength she possessed, she aimed for his head.

He ducked and twisted, kicking at her knee. His shoulder deflected the basket, though he grunted in pain. "Evil witch."

"Perverted despot. I saw what you did to that little girl." Clutching her skirts, she whirled to run in the other direction.

The whip's crack echoed an instant before the stinging leather encircled her ankle. With a cry, Seonaid tripped and crashed to the ground, landing on her knees and palms.

Before she caught her breath, Fletcher was upon her, viscously yanking her hair and forcing her head back. "Ye'll no' escape so easily, Satan's daughter."

"Let me go," Seonaid screamed, still thrashing.

He poured an awful, bitter liquid down her throat.

Choking and sputtering, she jabbed her elbow backward.

The blow glanced off his ballocks, and Fletcher howled in pain. His grip relaxed a fraction, giving her enough time to jerk loose, then turn over.

Frantically clawing the ground, she tried to find a rock or anything to strike him with. "Help! Somebody he—"

Laughing, he pounced on her, his eyes a terrifying mixture of lust and hatred-filled slits. Panting, his fetid breath gagging her, he ground his pelvis into her stomach, encircling her throat with his hands.

"Witch. See what ye do to me?" he groaned, rocking his hardened manhood into her. "Ye've cast an evil spell on me."

Her vision blurred as she bucked and gasped.

Jacques. I need you.

~

HUNCHED LOW IN HIS SADDLE, Jacques cursed Scotland's perpetual rain, the unpredictable mine, his lack of coin, and Fate's fickleness. He'd rather chew glass or hot coals than continue to reside at the keep or ask McTavish to extend him a loan, but what choice had he?

The miners must come first.

Twilight hovered on the horizon, but within the pinewoods' shadowy gray-green coolness, dusk had already fallen.

Yanking his collar higher, he grimaced as rain trickled down his neck, further soaking him and blackening his already dismal mood. Every now and again, a gust of wind shook a branch and deluged him with an icy rainwater shower.

Head lowered, the mare plodded along the familiar road to Craiglocky. His impetuous decision to visit Oakberry today, after all, necessitated borrowing a horse rather than driving as he'd previously done.

After riding two hours to the mine, and the same number on the return journey, his arse ached. As did his throbbing ankle. He'd wrenched it exploring the new shaft with Newton —the one that was supposed to contain the silver lode.

A self-deprecating smile contorted Jacques's mouth. He was soft and pampered compared to the sinewy miners.

He flexed his injured hand but stopped when the scab drew the flesh taut. An image of Seonaid forced its way to the forefront of his mind—how she'd hovered over him, tending his wound, her bottom lip caught between her neat teeth and her brow puckered in concentration.

She'd smelled lovely: a delicate blend of her own scent and something light and flowery. A small mole on her nape enticed him unbearably, begging him to kiss the love mark and nibble his way along her silky shoulders.

He'd never enjoy the pleasure.

Merely thinking of her warmed him, and for a few moments, he indulged in a daydream with her as his baroness, their children cuddled upon their laps as they sat for a family portrait.

He wasn't a religious man, *per se,* but if the Almighty didn't intervene, and soon, not only would he have lost the one woman he'd ever come close to loving but literally everything else he held dear as well.

The last vestige of his self-respect had vanished this morning, the moment he'd uttered those hateful, untrue words to Seonaid.

At the precise moment, Jacques closed his eyes and lifted his face to the sky in silent prayer, a blast of wind shook the trees overhead, sending a cascade of water to soak his face.

I take it that's a no, Lord?

It was far too immediate and disappointing an answer, but not unexpected or undeserved.

Sputtering, he swiped his forearm across his face. Scant good it did. His caped greatcoat was nearly wet through and through. Sealskin would've been wiser, but he didn't own any.

Look at him. What he'd become.

Mud covered his boots and dirt smudges littered his calves and gloves. He hardly resembled an aristocrat. The knowledge didn't trouble him overly much.

Most Scots he'd met appeared a rough, rugged lot, and, yet, a more loyal and honest people he hadn't encountered. Hardworking and fiercely protective of that which they held most dear too.

If Jacques meant to work the mine, and he did, he would need other, more suitable clothing. *There's the rub, though.* He didn't have coinage for new garments.

Well then, his fine clothing would have to do, because he fully intended to lend his help in digging the new vein. Mayhap he could barter his fancier togs for more practical attire.

Able-bodied and bored, he might as well do something with his frustration, and chipping away at a mountain's innards would do as well as a bout in the ring. That he didn't know a midge's rump about the mining process didn't concern him. He'd learn, and if he failed at the picking, he would labor as a bandsman, putter, or barrowman.

Anything to keep his mind occupied and his flesh so exhausted that he wouldn't have the strength for sensual musings about a woman with soft topaz-flecked, pecan-brown eyes who couldn't be his.

Lost deep in his reverie and with the trees' gnarled branches thrashing and whipping overhead, thunder pealing in the distance, and an occasional crack of lightning rending the churning armor-gray sky, he didn't at first recognize the jarring noise sounding in the distance.

His horse did.

Rearing her head in alarm, the mare snorted and side-stepped.

"What did you hear, girl?" Bending forward, Jacques scratched her neck, making soothing noises.

The shrill cry came again. Not animal.

Human.

And a woman.

"*Hue!*" Kicking the mare's sides, he urged her into a run. Clods of mud spewed from her churning hooves as the mare flew down the stretch of road.

A choked shriek rent the damp air, lifting the hairs on his nape and curdling his blood.

Seonaid?

His beaver hat flew off, but Jacques didn't slow a whit. He simply bent lower over the horse's broad back.

Rounding a bend, he spied two people on the road's side. A man sitting atop a woman, holding her down. She struggled, kicking and thrashing, her stockinged legs visible to her slender thighs.

Mon Dieu. I will kill him.

Even in the gloomy half-light he recognized Seonaid's glossy sable hair and Fletcher's gaunt face. Damn his foul soul to the ninth layer of hell.

A bitter, coppery taste met Jacques's tongue. So great was his ire, he'd bitten the inside of his cheek.

Fletcher jerked his head up, and then renewed his efforts, to... To do whatever-the-hell he was trying to do to Seonaid.

"Allez. Hue." Pressing his heels into the horse, Jacques's vision narrowed, his entire focus aimed on her.

Writhing beneath the vicar, crying out in terror, Seonaid clawed at Fletcher's face.

A dogcart thundered from the opposite direction. Upon seeing the commotion, while the cart yet raced forward, a huge Highlander vaulted from his seat. He released a battle cry worthy of a medieval Celtic warrior, the likes of which sent a shudder to Jacques's toes.

God's blood. I wouldn't want to cross swords with that brute.

The mammoth Scot sprinted to Seonaid, and, cursing in Gaelic, hauled Fletcher off her. He tossed the rector across the road as effortlessly as heaving a child's ragdoll.

Screeching like a terrified old woman, Fletcher hit the ground with a weighty thud, then lay unmoving.

Seonaid awkwardly levered to her bottom, her mud-matted hair tumbling down her shoulders and back in filthy, saturated tendrils. Great, shuddering sobs shook her frame and echoed eerily as she pushed her skirts into place.

The man knelt beside her, murmuring quietly and tenderly brushing strands of hair from her cheek.

Flinging herself into his arms, she buried her face in his disgustingly wide shoulder.

Envy assailed Jacques, gushing into every pore as he helplessly watched the Scot soothe her. He should be the one comforting and reassuring Seonaid, easing her terror.

Encircling her with his cudgel-like arms, the Highlander spoke into her hair. "It be all right, lass. He canna hurt ye anymore."

The enormous Scot had been in the bailey playing with the children the day Jacques brought Freya to Seonaid.

Who was he? Kin?

God knew she had enough, living at the keep.

Bringing the mare to a halt, and after slinging a cursory glance at Fletcher to ensure he remained unconscious, Jacques slid from the saddle. He bit back a curse when his injured ankle threatened to buckle.

At his hobbling approach, the Highlander glanced up. "Monsieur le baron—"

Seonaid whipped her head upward, her eyes huge with shock and fear. And accusation.

At her tear-ravaged face, Jacques's gut clenched, coiling into a tangled knot.

A bruise had formed on her swollen left cheek, and crimson marred her split lower lip and smeared her chin.

Merde.

His breath hissed from between clamped teeth.

Fletcher had dared to strike her?

He was a dead man.

If McTavish didn't kill him, Jacques would. He couldn't be certain in the fading light, but he was damned near certain fingermarks encircled her throat as well.

Upon seeing him, her expression became shuttered, and she averted her gaze.

"Douglas," she rasped, her voice hoarse and raw. From screaming or strangulation? Likely both. "Please help me up."

At once the annoyingly broad-shouldered Scot carefully assisted her to her feet, where she wavered unsteadily. He wrapped a thick arm lovingly about her shoulders, his troubled gaze roving her injured face. "Easy, lass. Ye've had a tremendous shock."

He loves her.

Eighteen

Jacques wanted to shout his objection, yank Seonaid from Douglas's arms, but it wasn't his place or right to breathe a word of opposition.

He loves her. He loves her, played over and over in his head.

Nearly staggering under the revelation and finding it excruciating to witness the adoration emanating from Douglas's rugged face, Jacques cast his attention to the ground.

A cross, a whip, two small bottles, and their stoppers lay scattered beside where Seonaid had lain. A Bible, pieces of rope, and a tool satchel sat in a pile to the side.

What had the *bâtard* Fletcher intended? A damned exorcism?

At the morbid notion, boiling hot rage welled within Jacques, so powerful his vision blurred, and he couldn't draw a decent breath. If they hadn't come along— My God, what would Fletcher have done?

Jacques squatted and pain jabbed his ankle anew. His movement drew Seonaid's and Douglas's attention, and he held his breath until the spasm passed. Pointing to the two vials, he shifted his weight onto his good leg. "Holy water and holy oil, *oui*?"

Seonaid shook her head. "No. The round one contained holy oil. Fletcher dumped it all over my head to weaken the demons he claimed possessed me." Her haunted gaze sought his, and her lower lip quivered. "The other was ether. He tried to pour it down my throat."

"God rot his twisted soul." Jacques swung to glower at the prostrate cleric.

Douglas's thick brows swooped into a vee. "But why did he set upon ye, lass? Foolhardy at best. He canna think he'd get away with maulin' ye."

"A vision came upon me in the village today, and Fletcher was in it. He's a vile, evil man and abuser of girls." Tears streamed over Seonaid's pale cheeks, and she futilely swiped at them with her fingers. She dragged in a shuddery breath. "And he knows about my visions."

Dread clouded her eyes and stilted her words.

The more Jacques considered it, the more he became convinced Fletcher had intended a ritual purging. Surely, he must realize he couldn't have gotten away with it.

Unhinged lunatic.

Not trusting himself to speak without uttering the vulgar oaths parading through his mind, Jacques silently passed her his handkerchief, and then hobbled about, gathering the evidence of Fletcher's treachery. No doubt, McTavish would want to see everything.

Douglas had yet to release Seonaid from his embrace, and jealousy unlike Jacques had ever known taunted him. He hated this feeling, the powerlessness, the unreasonable, intense resentment toward Douglas.

This morning, Jacques had forfeited any right he might have to comfort Seonaid, but his heart yearned to mend her suffering. To tell her he'd been an unmitigated arse, and he didn't mean a single, vindictive word.

After drying her face and blowing her nose, Seonaid stepped away from Douglas. Retrieving her basket and damaged goods, she cocked her head. "Douglas, why are you here? Did Mother become worried and send you to fetch me?"

"Aye, lass. She sent me to collect ye, but not because ye are tardy returnin'." Pushing a strand of overly long auburn hair behind an ear, he sent Jacques a telling glance. "Lady McTavish be havin' pains, and they be afeared the babe comes too early. The doctor's been sent fer, and the midwife, but her ladyship be askin' for ye."

Seonaid paled further and swayed. Her skin nearly translucent, she pressed a hand to her chest. "No. No. It's too soon. They're not supposed to come until March. They won't survive."

"They?" Jacques and Douglas spoke at the same time.

Already headed to the cart, Seonaid nodded. "Yes. Twin girls. We must hurry. I have herbs and tinctures to help stop the contractions."

Jacques considered the man towering above him. "Does *that* ever get old?"

"I be wonderin' what she *kens* and doesna say. What secrets she might reveal." Douglas slid Seonaid a careful glance, then allowed a small upward turn of his lips. "It makes her mysterious, but she'd no' appreciate the comparison."

Non, she wouldn't. Smiling in return, Jacques permitted himself a lingering look at her. "*Oui*, precisely my line of thinking as well."

The rain lessened a degree, and Douglas adjusted his tam o' shanter, pushing it back to reveal more of his forehead. "I be Douglas McLean, sir."

Jacques extended his hand, and the Scot seized it in a firm grip.

"And I'm Jacques, Monsieur le baron de Devaux-Rousset, but I'm sure you were aware of that already."

"*Aye*. No' much stays unknown at Craiglocky, especially with Miss Seonaid about." He canted his head toward her as she marched to the cart a few feet away.

"I've no doubt," Jacques said.

"When she was a lass, no' more than eleven, my mither couldna find my sister. Senga were sixteen and bonnie. In recent weeks, two lasses had been abducted from farms by rogue Scots or Highland gypsies. Fearin' the worst, Mither bade me accompany her to the keep and ask Sir Hugh for help. The laird be at university at the time, ye ken.

"Sir Hugh promptly arranged a search party, and as we be prepared to leave the great hall, Miss Seonaid wandered in carryin' a scrawny cat. Homeliest wee rat of a kitten I ever did lay my eyes upon."

McLean bent his head and whispered, "She always be carin' for some creature or other."

His wistful gaze trailed to her.

Poor lovesick sot.

"Here, let me have the vicar's things, Monsieur. I can put them in the wagon."

After dutifully passing him Fletcher's possessions, Jacques gathered the mare's reins, then cleared his throat. "I assume there's more to the story?"

"Och, aye." Grinning, McLean adjusted his armful as he faced the dogcart. "Sir Hugh vowed, 'We will find Senga, I promise ye.' Miss Seonaid stopped pettin' her ugly as the devil kitten and blinked at us with her big eyes. 'Senga isn't lost. She's in the hayloft with Broden. Her skirts are rucked up. I think he's looking for a spider that crawled up her leg.' Then she skipped from the hall."

Jacques gave a short chuckle and wiped a rain droplet from his nose. "A spider? Surely not."

"Aye, and my sister now be married to Broden. Sir Hugh saw to that. She be expectin' her fourth bairn soon." McLean jerked his head in Fletcher's direction. "What do ye intend to do with him?"

Moaning, Fletcher still lay sprawled face down in the muck.

"I'd like to run him through," Jacques bit out. "The bloody bugger."

McLean spat, his face carved into fierce planes. "I'll help ye bury his rotten corpse after ye do."

Jacques wanted to hate the handsome, muscle bulging Scot, but he was too damned likeable. More was the pity.

They'd reached the cart, and Jacques rested an elbow on the side, taking the weight off his sore ankle. The other hand planted on his hip, he considered Seonaid.

She'd climbed into the seat and placed the pathetically mashed bonnet upon her sopped curls. More swelling distorted her lip and cheek. The doctor could tend her as well. Jacques would insist upon it.

"I suppose we let McTavish deal with Fletcher," Jacques said. "If he dares stay close after what he attempted. Should we tie him to a tree?"

"He's gone." Seonaid pointed behind them. "He ran in that direction."

Holy Christ.

Jacques and McLean spun around.

Jacques gritted his teeth to prevent his grunt of pain when his affronted ankle shrieked at his careless treatment. "I'll go after him. You take her home, Douglas. Make sure she's seen by the physician too."

"No, Jacques. He's dangerous. Let Ewan deal with him, please." Concern and something more potent shimmered in her eyes before she retreated behind her veil of indifference once more.

McLean regarded them, a slight frown marring his high, much too noble forehead. "It'll be dark soon. I'd do as Miss Seonaid asks, unless ye've the skill to track vermin in the dark as the laird does. He was a spy, ye ken."

Seonaid covered her startled gasp with a delicate cough, studiously avoiding Jacques's gaze. Shivering, she wrapped her arms around her shoulders. "We need to collect Maeve. She expected me over an hour ago. And we need to hurry. I must get home to Yvette."

Who the blazes was Maeve?

Seonaid would catch the ague if she didn't get warm and dry soon.

"Monsieur le baron, if I may be so bold." McLean regarded him keenly. Nothing about the Scot's demeanor suggested a jot of servility. "Ye take Miss Seonaid home, and I'll ride to the McDuffs' and tell them Maeve will be collected in the mornin'."

Huddled into a ball, obviously miserable to her toes, Seonaid managed through chattering teeth. "Aye, that would be best."

A moment later, McLean leapt onto the mare's back.

Bloody, talented show-off. Jacques hadn't ever been able to do that.

With a jaunty wave, McLean clicked his tongue and trotted his horse away.

Jacques unbuttoned his greatcoat, and after managing to climb into the squeaky cart without swearing in pain, he draped it over Seonaid's quaking shoulders.

She mustered a grateful, partial curve of her stiff lips while scooting as far from him as the small seat permitted.

Settling onto the narrow boards, he examined the leaden sky through the frolicking tree branches. They wouldn't make the keep before nightfall, and Seonaid was half frozen already.

Turning the cart in the direction whence it had come, he

kept his attention focused on the barely visible, miry path. Silence stretched before them, awkward and uncomfortable.

Hurt radiated from her in undulating, tangible waves, and he'd bet *le Manoir des Jardins* it was caused more by his actions and words this morning than the assault at Fletcher's hands minutes ago.

"You had a vision of Fletcher?"

"Yes." Seonaid shuddered. She put a hand to her throat and tentatively touched the bruises there. "It was awful. I cannot believe he's truly a cleric." A small sigh escaped her, and her shoulders slumped. "I should have told Yvette and Ewan of my vision about the twins."

"I'm sure you had good cause not to."

She faced him then, and for the first time since Jacques came upon her, she met his eyes, urgency in hers. "I did. I didn't want them fretting." Fiddling with his greatcoat's sleeve, she worried her lower lip. "I meant to tell them soon."

"Can I assume what you discovered isn't entirely welcome news?" He tooled the cart around a stump, careful not to venture where water had accumulated at the side. It was easy to get stuck in the thick sludge, and with Seonaid in her condition, he didn't relish slogging to the castle.

When she didn't answer, he covered her ice-cold hands with his. She didn't wrench away, which encouraged him. "Seonaid? You can tell me. Trust me, so you don't carry the burden alone."

He winced inwardly. She had valid reason not to trust him.

She stared straight ahead, her pert profile dark and tense against the twilight. "If the vision proves true, the birth will be difficult, and Yvette..." Her gaze dropped to her lap, and she drew in a shuddery breath. "She... She will nearly die."

Nineteen

Leaving Jacques's greatcoat upon the seat, Seonaid scrambled from the cart before he could help her alight. At the gatehouse she called, "Thank you for the use of your coat, Monsieur."

She didn't dare allow him to touch her again. When he'd covered her hands with his, she'd bitten her lip to keep from clasping his fingers and snuggling next to his delicious smelling warmth.

Well, she wasn't having any of that ever again. She'd been scorned twice. Thrice made her a daft nincompoop. Erecting a deliberate wall of indifference, she firmly banished her emotions and girlish behavior to a remote corner of her heart, kicked the door shut, and locked it.

Lifting her drenched skirt and pelisse, she ran into the keep.

Fairchild, their immensely tall butler, stood beside the entrance's open door. A guard must have alerted him to her approach. "Miss Seonaid, your mother awaits you in Lady McTavish's chamber."

He didn't as much as blink at her deplorable state.

"Thank you, Fairchild. Is the doctor here yet?"

"No, miss."

She lightly rested her hand atop his strong forearm. "How are you, Fairchild? I know Yvette's like a daughter to you."

His countenance wavered before he stoically schooled his noble features. "Lady McTavish is strong, and I trust you and the physician to care for her."

"I shall do my utmost to help. I promise," Seonaid said, unfastening her pelisse.

"I have no doubt, miss."

He assisted her from the sodden garment, and though she still shivered, it was a blessed relief to have the cumbersome weight gone. Her ruined bonnet followed, and his nostrils flared the minutest bit upon seeing her hair.

"Hot bathwater awaits you. I'll request cold water for your face at once too, Miss Seonaid." He accepted Jacques's sopping greatcoat, dripping rainwater and pooling onto the stone entry. "There's bathwater for you too, sir."

"Much appreciated," Jacques murmured, unusually subdued.

"I'm afraid mine will have to wait until I've seen Yvette." Seonaid shoved grimy hair from her face. "I would be grateful if you'd have someone fetch a high-necked spencer or a fichu from my chamber. Also, yam root and cramp bark from my store of herbs. And boiling water. Oh, and my pestle and mortar, along with a teacup."

She touched her damaged cheek. "I'll need my salve for cuts too."

"At once, miss." Gingerly holding the saturated garments before him, Fairchild marched from the entry.

She grabbed Jacques's arm, fairly dragging him toward the stairs. They left a trail of muddy footprints in their wake, but she must speak to him before her family realized they'd returned home.

Had it been this morning she'd acted like a child and jumped up and down these stairs? Only this morning when he'd crushed her heart with his merciless, callous words?

She'd dwell on that unpleasantness later. Right now, she must stop Yvette's contractions.

"I don't want Yvette to know what's happened to me. She mustn't be upset further." Rushing up the stairs, Seonaid cast a swift glance over her shoulder. "I think we should wait to tell Ewan too."

"Seonaid, one has merely to look at you to know something dreadful has occurred." He plucked a chunk of mud from her temple. "I suggest you take a few minutes to tidy up. If you walk into Lady McTavish's chamber looking like that, you're sure to cause more upset, *non*?"

Drat, Jacques was right, though it irritated her to her sore feet to admit it. She didn't want to give him that measure of credit.

"Very well, then." Still charging up the risers, she conceded. "Would you please have Fairchild send word to my family that I'm home but chilled and wet, and I need to change my clothing or I'll become ill? He can have hot water sent to my chamber immediately, and I'll also need Una to help me wash my hair."

"Seonaid?" Jacques touched her elbow, sending a jolt streaking to her chest. She shut her eyes against a rush of desire.

Blasted, traitorous body.

No. She wouldn't respond. She wasn't good enough for him. She paused at a bend in the stairs, snapping, "What?"

The question resounded, unyielding and unforgiving.

Angst sharpened the angles of his chiseled face. "I..."

He searched her eyes, and she swore remorse blazed in his before he dipped his head. Surely the light played tricks. A man didn't say the horrid, cutting things he had but hours ago and then have an abrupt change of conscience.

Once hurtful words were spoken, like milk from a cow's teat, they couldn't be returned.

"I'll see to the things you requested." His gait descending the stairs seemed slow and measured. Had he hurt himself?

First tend to Yvette, then worry about Jacques.

Seonaid let her shoulders slump as she trudged up the remaining stairs. Much had transpired today, and none of it good. She'd made her bedchamber door before Mother called her name.

"Seonaid. Thank goodness you're home. Come quickly, *chérie*. Yvette asks for you."

Slowly, dread clamping her lungs, Seonaid faced her mother.

"*Mon Dieu*," Mother gasped, clutching her throat, her gaze sweeping Seonaid's face and neck. She rushed forward. "What in the world has happened? Have you been attacked?"

She settled an arm around Seonaid's shoulder, but Seonaid stayed her with a raised hand. "I'm filthy, and if you hug me, you'll soil your gown."

"Do you think I care?"

"No, but you need to return to Yvette as soon as possible, and if you arrive in a different gown, someone is bound to question why."

"That might be true, but you will tell me how you came to be in such *dishabille*, Seonaid. I'm not moving an inch until you do." Her mother's tone brooked no argument. Giselle Ferguson might be a petite woman, but she was a formidable force when her temper was stirred.

Surveying the empty corridor, Seonaid relented. "Vicar Fletcher did this, Mother, but I don't want Yvette or Ewan to know yet. Monsieur le baron and Douglas arrived in time to save me."

"He accosted you?" Outrage snapped in Mother's sea-green eyes. "Your father and Ewan will see he is punished, *le démon*."

Seonaid clasped her mother's hands. "I'm going to take a quick bath, and then I'll be right in to see Yvette. In the meanwhile, have her slowly sip a glass of wine and lie on her left side."

Blinking back tears, Mother nodded once. "How will you explain your poor face?"

"I'll think of something." She kissed her mother's cheek. "I have news that will make you happy."

Mother raised a skeptical sable brow. "Oh?"

Seonaid produced a cheerful smile, though pain and worry tattered its edges. "Yvette carries twin girls."

A brilliant smile wreathed her mother's face, quickly followed by a worried frown. "But this early, she might lose them. Oh, how tragic to lose two *précieux bébés*."

Seonaid shook her head, wincing as tendrils of mucky hair slithered across her shoulders, like the fat, wiggly worms Ewan used to catch brown trout.

God, please let only mud be in my hair.

Fabulous. Now her head itched unbearably.

"I had a vision. The bairns and Yvette will be fine." Footmen bearing pails of water approached. She gave her mother a little shove. "Now go. I must hurry."

Twenty minutes later, her wet hair braided and twisted atop her head, Seonaid, wearing a high-necked, long-sleeved gown, stood beside Yvette's bed. She'd cleansed the blood from her face and applied a salve, but the bruising and cuts she hadn't been able to hide.

She gave Ewan and Yvette a contrite smile. "I'm sorry I didn't tell you about my vision sooner. I didn't want you to worry, and I have been wrong a few times."

Relaxing amidst a mound of jonquil and cream pillows,

and wearing a delicate blue rose embroidered robe, a slightly pale Yvette clasped Seonaid's hand.

"I feel much better knowing what's to come. I'm grateful for your gift, Seonaid." She sent a loving smile to Ewan, who perched beside her atop the bed. "And I'm sure Ewan is too."

He bent and kissed Yvette's creamy forehead. "Aye, that I am."

For the first time in a long while, Seonaid was also grateful. "Where's Mother? I expected to find her here clucking and fussing."

Ewan chuckled and pulled his earlobe. "She's escorting a belligerent Hugh to bed. Naturally, a servant let slip that Yvette was having contractions, and when no one took it upon themselves to inform him of the details, he assumed the worse. He hobbled here using two canes."

Yvette clasped Ewan's hand and giggled. "I feared Mother was going to throttle him. I've not heard her curse in French." Her deep blue eyes filled with amusement, she grinned. "I've never heard Gaelic cursing before either."

Ewan and Yvette wore delighted expressions.

"Who swore in Gaelic?" Seonaid asked.

Slapping his thigh, Ewan laughed outright. "Hugh. When, on Mother's orders, a half dozen of our largest clansmen picked him up and carted him to his room. She told him if he protested the minutest amount, he'd sleep alone for the next six months."

"That silenced him rather quickly." Yvette tittered again. "Except for the peculiar noises he made in his throat. Something between a growl and a smothered oath."

"I should like to have seen that, actually." Seonaid sat on the other side of Yvette. "Have the pains stopped or slowed?"

"Yes. They're coming irregularly now. Not like they did a few hours ago."

"Thank God." A white line rimmed Ewan's mouth, and his pallor was more wan than normal.

"I'm sorry you took a tumble from the dogcart," Yvette murmured sleepily. She yawned delicately behind her hand. "Pardon me. That bruise on your face looks quite painful, Seonaid. So does your poor mouth."

Guilt pricked Seonaid for lying, but surely her reasons for doing so outweighed the untruth. "As long as I don't smile, it doesn't hurt much."

Not so.

A maid bustled in with the tea Seonaid had requested. Thankful for an excuse to hide her face, she set about preparing a dose of tincture for Yvette. "Six drops in diluted tea, not more than once every two hours." She gave her sister-in-law a sympathetic smile as she passed her the teacup. "I'm afraid you'll have to stay abed until the bairns' birth."

"I don't mind if it means they're healthy." Yvette cradled her stomach lovingly and sipped the tincture, then grimaced slightly. "Not the tastiest brew I've ever sampled, rather like licking a damp tree."

"That's the cramp bark." Replacing the tincture's cap, Seonaid offered an apologetic smile. "It helps ease contractions and relaxes you."

A sweet smile curved Yvette's mouth. "I'll be quite the slugabed, sleeping my days away."

"It's best for you and the bairns. I'll speak to Mother about cancelling the house party." At least something good might come of Yvette's confinement. Seonaid would be spared the Valentine folderol. "Surely, the guests will understand given the circumstances."

"No, I won't hear of it." Yvette shook her honey blonde head, a determined set to her small chin. "Naturally, you must still host the party. It would upset me greatly if you canceled on my account. Mother has gone to such work already, and perhaps by then, I might be permitted to recline upon a couch and observe the merriments."

Bother and rot. There went that idea.

"I do hope you're that much improved." The agreeable smile Seonaid dredged up and managed to force her lips into would've done an actress proud.

Ewan rose and, after stretching, kissed Yvette's hand. "I need to speak with Seonaid, my love. If you'll excuse us?"

"Certainly, dearest." Another yawn escaped Yvette. "I'm feeling rather drowsy."

The maid took the cup, and then helped her mistress lie down once more.

"Ewan, I believe I should stay with—" Before Seonaid finished speaking, Doctor Paterson arrived.

"My lady." He winked and set his physician's bag upon the bed. "I heard a rumor your babe is eager to leave his warm nest. Exactly like an impatient McTavish."

Seonaid retreated into the shadows, turning her good cheek toward him.

By mutual agreement, no one mentioned her vision about the twins. Though Doctor Paterson was a forward-thinking fellow, he was a man of science, and informing him Yvette carried two girls might put him off a mite.

Still smiling, he addressed Ewan. "I need to examine her ladyship. If you will please wait outside?"

"I had her drink a small glass of wine and gave her a tincture of cramp bark and yam root." Indicating the small blue bottle atop the night table, Seonaid scooted past the doctor.

"Both of which I would've recommended. Excellent, Miss Seonaid." Opening his bag, he glanced at her as she passed, his keen gaze roving over her injuries. "I'll take a look at your face when I'm finished with her ladyship, though it appears you've done an admirable job of treating your injuries yourself. Might I ask how you came by them?"

His voice held no hint of suspicion, yet Seonaid couldn't help but suspect a man in his profession must know exactly what caused injuries like hers.

"I—er—had a mishap with the dogcart. It's quite slick outdoors, and I wasn't as careful as I might have been." Now she lied to Doctor Paterson, and from the skeptical slant of his white brows, he hadn't believed a word.

"*Hmph.*" He rummaged in his bag. "Well, I'll want to take a look anyway."

"Oh, and Doctor, a guest wrenched his ankle. If you wouldn't mind examining him as well?" That relieved Seonaid of the task. Trying to remain impervious to Jacques's animal-like, altogether too masculine attraction while touching his bare ankle and foot.

No, the good doctor could deal with Jacques.

"I'll see him after I examine your injuries." Doctor Paterson withdrew his pocket watch, then lifted Yvette's wrist.

The maid dipped a curtsy and, after she left, Ewan took Seonaid's elbow, guiding her from the room. He toed the door closed before spinning Seonaid to face him.

"You walked with Maeve to Craigcutty today. And Mother sent McLean to fetch you in the dogcart. Do you want to tell me what really happened to your face?"

<h1 style="text-align:center">TWENTY</h1>

other.

Leave it to Ewan to remember those details.

"Let's go to your study." Seonaid darted a glance behind her. "I don't want anyone to overhear."

He cocked a raven brow and extended his arm, indicting she should precede him. "By all means then."

Once settled in an armchair, Seonaid pursed her lips. *Ouch.* Her mouth hurt worse than she'd admitted. Fletcher had struck her several times while "casting out the devil," and she had cuts inside her cheeks too.

Only soft foods for her for the next few days.

The fire roaring in the hearth did nothing to heat the far corners of the study or her chilled flesh. Even the gown she'd chosen, as much to stay the drafts as to conceal the purplish finger marks marring her neck, didn't keep her warm.

Sitting opposite her, Ewan bent forward, his elbows resting atop his knees, his intense turquoise gaze demanding the truth.

"Your face?"

"Fletcher did this." She swept her hand over her face. "I

had a vision in the village about him. We'd been arguing because he accused me of bewitching the children and brewing potions."

Ire evident in his hands gripping his chair and the crinkling at his eyes' corners, Ewan straightened. "He dared to strike you?"

"And to choke me." Careful not to disturb the tender, bruised flesh, she pulled her neckline down a few inches. "He claimed I had the devil in me."

Ewan surged to his feet, hands balled, a feral snarl contorting his mouth. He stomped to the door, then back to tower over her. "That's why your voice is hoarse. I assumed you'd caught a chill from your soaking."

A single rap echoed at the study door.

"Come." Ewan raked a hand through his hair, issuing a near-growl of ill-concealed frustration. As he strode toward a brandy decanter atop the liquor cabinet, Fairchild ventured in.

"My lord, Monsieur le baron de Devaux-Rousset insists he must speak with you. He was loath to interrupt you when you were with her ladyship, but would like to inquire if you're available now?"

"He might as well come in, Ewan." Then perhaps Seonaid could finally be done with Jacques's presence. In her current state, maintaining the appearance of indifference taxed her beyond her reserves. She flopped back onto the comfortable, worn leather chair, stretching her cold feet toward the frolicking flames. "He and Douglas rescued me."

She'd never been so happy to see Douglas in her life. He, unlike Jacques, made her laugh and feel special. She wiggled her toes, welcoming the heat soothing her soles and ankles.

"I expect a detailed explanation of what occurred, including what you saw with your second sight, Seonaid." Ewan poured a finger's worth of brandy into the crystal tumbler. "A man, cleric or nae, putting his hands on my kin will suffer serious consequences."

She rubbed her arms, loathing the terror Fletcher stirred in her. "He's a despot, Ewan. A perverted, despicable blackguard."

Quaffing back the amber spirit, he motioned for Fairchild to bid Jacques enter.

Seonaid rested her head against the chair's back and closed her eyes. Sleep beckoned, and she welcomed the oblivion in order to forget this wretched day had happened. Her head ached, probably a combination of strain and the ether. Vile stuff, that.

Jacques's slightly uneven gait alerted her to his presence before Ewan greeted him.

Forcing her lodestone heavy eyelids open, Seonaid sighed and sat up, plopping her feet to the floor. She couldn't have her calves showing for Jacques's perusal.

He saw much more than that earlier today.

"Were you injured in the fray with Fletcher as well, Devaux?" Ewan remained by the spirits. "Sit. I cannot stand the pinched look on your face."

"*Non*, I but twisted my ankle at Oakberry." Jacques carried Fletcher's possessions, including the mud-speckled satchel. After placing them atop the desk, he sank into the chair Ewan vacated.

"I've asked the doctor to take a look at your ankle when he finishes with Lady McTavish." Trying to gauge the extent of his injury, Seonaid surreptitiously examined him.

He'd bathed, and he wore Hessians, so his ankle couldn't be that badly swollen, else he wouldn't have put the boot on again.

"That's not necessary," Jacques demurred. "But I thank you."

She gave him a sharp look. Maybe he worried he'd have to

pay the physician. Surely, he realized Ewan would cover the fee. It wasn't her place to insist, however.

Light from the tapers in the mantel's silver candleholders reflected off his inky black hair, still wet from his bath, and his buff pantaloons and berry-toned coat accented his manly physique. Must he be so blasted attractive?

Her face battered and bruised, Seonaid felt about as appealing as a bald, toothless crone.

Jacques's warm perusal traveled over her, and his mouth bent into that rakish curve that caused her to blink like a hen-eyed simpleton.

He touched the side of the mustache his scar disappeared into, and his lips slanted a trifle more.

Charming rakehell.

He knew exactly what he did to her.

How could Seonaid still be so gullible?

Who did he think he was, regarding her like that? And in front of her brother. Well, Ewan couldn't see Jacques's face from where he stood, but, still, the man overstepped the bounds.

A good dressing down was what he deserved.

Yes, he'd saved her from a horrid situation, deadly perhaps, but that didn't mean he could engage his masculine charm, flash his perfect teeth, gaze at her through those alluring, hooded eyes, and pretend this morning hadn't happened.

Beckoning every ounce of indignation she could muster—a pathetic sampling, to be sure—Seonaid chastised him with her affronted gaze, then lifted her nose and presented her profile. Who cared if Ewan deducted everything wasn't wonderful between her and Jacques? Perhaps he'd be inclined to ask the suave, cocky Monsieur le baron to leave.

"Brandy? Or whisky? Devaux, you look like you could use a dram." Lifting a tumbler, Ewan waited. "I ought to pour you a dab too, Seonaid, after what you've been through. You look done in."

Wrinkling her nose, she shook her head. "No, thank you. I'll have a spot of wine before I retire."

"I'm fine as well." Jacques's regard never left Seonaid. "May I inquire how Lady McTavish fares?"

Stop staring.

A blush crept up Seonaid's face, and she made a pretense of examining the ribbon edging her sleeve to hide her discomfit.

Ewan capped the decanter, the clink of the topper sliding home, but he didn't join her and Jacques. She shifted in her chair.

Glass in hand, Ewan swirled the umber liquid, a bemused gleam in his eye.

Oh, dear. Had she been so transparent in her gawping? She scrambled for something to distract him.

"What's in that?" Seonaid pointed to Fletcher's battered case.

"Yes, what is all this?" Ewan set his tumbler upon the desk, then scowled as he picked up the lengths of rope and cross. "Fletcher had these with him?"

That finally drew Jacques's attention away from her. He slapped his palms upon his thighs. "I believe the demented wretch intended to perform an exorcism."

JACQUES WOULD'VE LAUGHED as McTavish's jaw sagged in disbelief, except nothing about this situation was humorous. A madman ran free, and Jacques didn't think they'd seen the last of Fletcher.

Seonaid couldn't be permitted to leave the keep without

armed escorts. In fact, that was why he'd wanted to speak with McTavish. He hadn't known she was in the study as well.

The swelling and discoloration on her beautiful face had worsened, yet she was even more precious to him. She must be protected.

Dropping the rope, McTavish clapped his mouth shut. "My God, he's bloody insane."

Jacques loudly cleared his throat as the Scot flipped the latch on the satchel.

McTavish hesitated long enough for Jacques to forestall him with a minute head shake. Seonaid shouldn't see the contents.

"I think Miss Seonaid should tell you what transpired with Fletcher, and then she should retire. It's been a trying day, *non?*"

Starting with his unpardonable treatment, but given her frosty looks, he'd succeeded in alienating her. It was for the best, but he would see her safe from Fletcher.

"Aye, Seonaid, tell me all." McTavish rested his hip upon his desk, his arms folded.

Head bowed, and her hands clasped in her lap, she recounted the incident, her voice occasionally shaky around the edges. Raising tear-laden eyes to her brother, she whispered, "He would've killed me because of my *an dara sheal-ladh*. It's not a gift, Ewan. It's not. I don't want it anymore."

Her control broke then, covering her face and weeping quietly into her hands.

Only clenching his fists until his nails dug into his palms prevented Jacques from hurling caution, good sense, and everything that had ever meant anything to him, to the dung heap and claiming Seonaid as his.

And chances were, he'd face McTavish's sword in short order as a result.

McTavish gathered her in his arms, pulling her close.

"Listen to me, Seonaid. I don't know why you and your grandmother amongst all our family have ever had the second sight. But know this, I believe with all my heart that God gave you the ability. I confess, I didn't realize the burden you carried, but you've saved many a life. Don't forget the good you've done, and the good you will do."

She snuffled into her brother's coat, and Jacques passed her his handkerchief. The second one today. He had one left. Pressing the cloth to her eyes, she nodded and whispered a croaky, "Thank you."

Jacques should leave; he felt like an intruder, but he still needed to speak with McTavish. Alone.

Tilting her chin, McTavish gave Seonaid a tender smile. "Mother revealed that's why you wanted to marry." He wiped a tear from her nose with his thumb. "You might still have the second sight afterward. You understand that, don't you? Is it worth rushing into marriage?"

A blow from Goliath's cudgel wouldn't have pained Jacques more. *Non*, bludgeoning him to a pulp would hurt less. That was why she asked him to take her virginity. She was that desperate.

She cut Jacques an embarrassed peek. "I'd rather not talk about that, if you don't mind. It's been a traumatic day. I should like to retire now."

Her brother kissed the top of her head. "By all means. I don't want you leaving the keep, though, until Fletcher's caught. And make sure you let Doctor Paterson take a look at your face."

He gave her another affectionate squeeze before setting her from him.

"Yes, of course. Good evening, Monsieur." She dipped her head but avoided Jacques's gaze.

He bowed. "Sleep well, Miss Seonaid."

And God grant you pleasant dreams, mon amour. You deserve them.

Neither man spoke until the door closed quietly behind her.

Sighing, Jacques faced McTavish. "If you have a few moments more, there's something of import I'd like to discuss with you."

"There's something I'd like to discuss with you too." He'd sunk into his chair, but rather than relaxing, McTavish looked poised to pounce. A shrewd—or was it predatory?—glimmer shone in his eyes. "Do you intend to tell Seonaid you're in love with her?"

After lying awake most of the night, flopping this way and that, fluffing her pillows only to smash them flat a few minutes later, Seonaid finally heaved a sigh and rose.

It was amazing how many nocturnal noises crept into her chamber in the still, morning hours: a cat's irate yowl, a cow's low moo, the wind carelessly ruffling pine branches or rattling her window. In the distance, an owl hooted, and she swore tiny, clawed feet had scampered across the floor.

Better have Una thoroughly search my chamber for mice.

Equally astounding was how interminably protracted the night slogged on—the minutes slowed by an invisible force— when the monologue in her mind wouldn't hush. When she kept reliving yesterday's wretched events. When Jacques's striking face wouldn't stay under the pillow she plopped across, then pressed against her face.

And, truth to tell, her cheek and throat ached something fierce. However, she'd refused the laudanum Doctor Paterson had prescribed. The one time she'd taken a dose, wool had filled her head and cotton stuffed her mouth.

Wrapped in a thick tartan, she sat in a chair she dragged

before the freshly stoked fire and tried escaping into the pages of a book. After she read the same passage several times and had no idea whether the page contained a recipe for marmalade, advice about proper comportment, or how to treat carbuncles, she abandoned the frayed volume.

Another chilly hour passed with Seonaid curled in her third story window seat, her head pressed against the slightly blurry glass. The sky had cleared, and the stars and a full moon glowed brightly against night's ebony backdrop. A lone stag, his antlers and head lifted reverently to the heavens, stood in the meadow past the stables.

The moon's silvery radiance bathed the bailey and beyond in translucent beams. A light flared in a blacksmithy window, casting a slight glimmer on the building housing her pets. Someone else had awoken early too.

Paying a call on her pets might be just the distraction she needed. After swiftly donning a gown and twisting her hair into a simple knot, she crept from her chamber, a pair of clean half-boots in hand. She paused for a fraction outside Jacques's door.

Shoulders slumped, she bent her neck and hurried onward.

Dawn hadn't roused her drowsy head before Seonaid slipped into the outbuilding housing her menagerie.

Whining, Chester nudged her knee.

"Good morning. Let me light the lantern, and then I can give you a proper greeting." Opting to leave her pelisse on as barrier against the early morn's biting chill, she made quick work of the task, watched the whole while by sleepy-eyed animals.

Milly lifted her head, blinked groggily, and perhaps a mite accusatorily too, then went to sleep again. Freya lay curled around her litter and, other than partially opening one citrine eye, didn't stir.

"It was a trifle rude of me to awaken you so early, but I couldn't sleep and needed company to divert me from my wayward musings." As Seonaid went about preparing their feed, she continued speaking her thoughts. "You have no idea how fortunate you are to not have to fret about what others think of you."

An indecipherable scratching interrupted her cuddling the kittens. Probably Douglas. He often dropped in before he started his day at the smithy.

"Come in."

Despite his deafness, Chester's ears perked up, and he cocked his head.

Still cuddling the smallest kitten under her chin, Seonaid faced the door.

Jacques stood over the threshold, hat in hand, sadness and strain about his eyes and mouth.

A sensation much like falling from a great height assailed her. "You're leaving."

He didn't have to tell her. She could feel his absence in her soul, see goodbye in his eyes, read farewell on his face. And the crushing ache that stabbed her heart and stole her breath sent a wave of paralyzing dizziness over her, so forceful, she thought she might swoon.

Breathe.

Brushing her cheek against the kitten's soft fur, Seonaid hid her dismay. She ought to be glad, but despair's sharp talons sank deep into soft flesh, shredding hope and drawing blood.

Stupid, fickle emotions.

"*Oui.* Not Scotland yet, but Craiglocky, so I can be closer to the mine." Jacques's melodic baritone resounded hollowly, and his fingers played upon the hat's brim almost nervously.

"That's prudent, I suppose," she said.

But it didn't make his going easier.

Seonaid had become accustomed to seeing him, if only from afar. Even if there couldn't be anything between them. Yes, she'd known that he must leave someday. Just not today. Or tomorrow. Or next week. Not until she'd had time to put him from her heart. That desire—to be his—had been dashed to smithereens.

Returning the kitten to her mother, Seonaid parted her lips and sucked in a bracing breath. She must be strong and brave.

Absolutely no waterworks. Not a single tear.

"I intend to labor alongside my workers, and that is more easily done if I live nearer Oakberry Quarry, *non*?"

Yes. No. Yes, drat it all.

She marshalled her courage and faced him, hands folded before her, the picture of poised composure. "Will you attend the Valentine gathering?"

Despite her determination to remain unaffected, her voice quivered, as off balance as she, and Seonaid bit her lower lip.

Well, so much for poise and composure.

He shook his head, causing that stubborn, endearing lock to fall forward. His hungry gaze trailed over her face as if for the last time. Finally, he responded. "I think it best if I don't, *ma petite.*"

"I see." She couldn't see a blasted thing from the moisture blinding her, but nonetheless, she painted a bright smile onto her face and resolutely blinked her tears away. "I bid you farewell then, Jacques. I wish you good health and prosperity."

So polite. So formal.

When what she wanted to say, to beg, was stay.

Please, please stay. Forget about the mine. Forget about returning to France. Forget about le Manoir des Jardins and your dead family.

Stay here. With me.

"*Adieu*, Seonaid."

He smiled at her then, that bone-melting curve of his firm mouth that heated her in unmentionable places and made her want to lunge into his strong arms and be held forevermore.

"Be happy, *ma belle*." Tenderness and perhaps something more laced his voice. "And if you ever think of me, please know I wish with all my being that things could've been different between us."

God. How could Seonaid ever be happy? She loved him. And he was leaving. And she wouldn't ever see him again. And they'd both marry other people. And she would be utterly, wholly, forever miserable.

Not trusting herself to speak, she nodded as a single, plump droplet spilled onto her cheek.

He tracked the teardrop's slow descent, and Jacques opened his mouth.

"Devaux."

Ewan.

Blandness immediately replaced Jacques's fond expression, and he dropped his gaze, his jaw tightening.

Stern-faced, his hair mussed, and barely decent in only his shirt, pantaloons, and boots, Ewan loomed behind Jacques.

His manner wasn't altogether friendly either.

What? Had he sprung from his bed and sprinted after Jacques? Precisely *what* had occurred after she left the study last night?

"I was merely saying *adieu*, McTavish." With a final caressing look, a glance filled with all he hadn't said, Jacques ducked out the entrance.

Only her brother blocking the doorway prevented Seonaid from running after Jacques and professing her love. However, something in Ewan's bearing rooted her cold feet to the even colder floor.

Eyebrows scrunched, he watched Jacques leave, then stepped inside, shutting the door behind him. Chester trotted over and, after a cursory pat upon the dog's head, Ewan folded his arms and leaned a hip against the table.

"Is that all he said to you, Seonaid? Farewell?"

"Yes. What else would there be?"

Certainly no undying avowals of love.

Anger at Ewan's interference made her voice shrill. "I cannot say I think it your concern, and surely not urgent enough to have you rush outdoors partially dressed before the cock has even crowed."

"What are you doing out here this early?" Suppressing a yawn, Ewan's bleary gaze traveled around the building.

What would he do if she claimed she and Jacques had an early morning dalliance? That they'd been sneaking out for private *tête-a-têtes* since he'd arrived?

No, that would be unfair to Jacques. Ewan would force him to marry her, and he'd lose his estate if the mine didn't produce. Even if it did, how long would the ore last?

She harbored little mining knowledge—likely as much familiarity has Jacques had with birthing or blending herbal remedies, but she understood the industry was unpredictable at best.

"I thought you were exhausted," Ewan said. "And I didn't expect you to rise until late."

His persistence poked her vexation, and she pressed her lips tight, shrugging and closing Freya's pen.

"I couldn't sleep." *Because of the man you practically chased from here.* "My pets bring me comfort, so I sought them."

Carriage wheels clacked and horses' hooves clopped across the bailey's frozen ground. Of its own volition, Seonaid's attention strayed to the window. Jacques's conveyance lumbered past, his shadowy outline barely identifiable through the window in the half-light.

He carried her mangled heart with him.

Would she truly never see him again?

Her future loomed desolate and interminable before her.

"I'd rather you not leave the keep alone," Ewan said, stifling another wide yawn. "I believe I made that clear last night."

Dejection's vice-like grip riddling her, she sighed.

His head angled. A speculative expression lighting his face, Ewan regarded her.

Why must he intrude at this moment?

A few minutes to come to grips with Jacques's departure would've been welcome. An audience to her doldrums wasn't. She couldn't indulge in a good cry, and, at the moment, she truly needed to vent her heartbreak.

She repressed the harsh retort thrumming against her teeth. Lack of sleep and Jacques's parting had her short on patience. "Am I to understand I cannot venture here, to the stables, or anywhere outdoors without an escort?"

Scrubbing a hand over his whisker-shadowed jaw, Ewan nodded. "Fletcher could gain entrance to the bailey. I've asked the guards to be extra vigilant, but as they've never seen him, he could slip by."

She snorted, startling the doves overhead. They flapped their wings and cooed softly. "I don't think he's that daring or courageous. More of a craven, lurking behind bushes and buildings. Attacking unsuspecting children and sneaking about causing havoc. All the while, the coward makes sure he's out of harm's way."

"Nevertheless, I must insist." Ewan yawned again, and chagrin speared her. Mayhap, worried about Yvette, he'd also slept little.

Sighing, she relented. "For how long?"

Days? Weeks?

"Until Fletcher's caught." He scratched his chin, his expression guarded. Did he expect her to kick up a dust?

Closing her eyes, she swallowed her protest and gave one weak half-nod. "How is Yvette?"

"Well, thank you. She slept through the night." Relief laced his words. He'd been through much too.

"I'm glad." Hoping he'd take his leave, Seonaid puttered for a few minutes, annoyance tempering her movements.

But he continued to loiter, that same contemplative look sharpening his face each time she slid him a covert glance.

Finally, she could tolerate it no more. Arms akimbo, she slanted a brow askance. "Did you need something else?"

Lowering his head, he cupped his nape and sighed.

"Seonaid, I think you should know that I asked Devaux to leave."

"Why?"

My, I sound quite unruffled.

"I believed it best. For you." Ewan's gaze faltered for an instant. "He isn't free to marry, and I feared your affections might have become engaged. Have they?"

None of your business. Stop interfering in my life just because you're the laird.

Lifting his head, he met her eyes directly.

At the moment, remembering Ewan was her beloved brother proved a Herculean task when she wanted to hurl something at him. She eyed the refuse wheelbarrow, then a wooden bucket.

Yes, that would do quite nicely.

Taking another deep breath, she braced her hands on Agnes's and Milly's pen and, shoulders hunched, tucked her chin to her chest. Whacking him wouldn't solve anything, and she'd regret her actions later.

Perchance.

"Ewan, I'm striving to hold my tongue and control my temper, but you go too far. I'm perfectly aware Monsieur le baron de Devaux-Rousset has obligations in France. I'm also old enough to make my own decisions and guard my heart." Facing him, she made a frustrated gesture. "I don't need you to do either, and that you would take it upon yourself to demand he leave when he has scarcely two coins to rub together is both uncharacteristic and uncharitable of you."

How would Jacques live?

Did he have the means to let a room?

Perhaps Oakberry had accommodations. Not likely comfortable ones. For a man of his station, having a reverse in fortune must be humbling. "You do know he isn't flush in the pockets? That he invested heavily in the mine?"

Ewan replied with a sharp jerk of his head. "I extended him credit with the condition he take his leave this morning."

Seonaid gasped and dropped the grain scoop. "You *paid* him to leave?"

Why hadn't that occurred to her? That Jacques would accept a loan from Ewan and then bolt? Mayhap that had been his intent all along, to wheedle his way into Ewan's good graces because he needed financial backing.

More fool she, then.

At once Seonaid's conscience chastised her.

Threads of honor and decency ran deep in Jacques. Else he would've taken advantage of her chastity and wouldn't have been committed to saving his family's estate. He might have desperate need of money, but he hadn't accepted it as a bribe.

Her focus gravitated to the window again where it looked like giant fingers had feathered muted pink, lavender, and peach streaks that spanned a purplish-cobalt sky.

Jacques had left because he knew, or at least suspected, she loved him, and he couldn't love her in return.

And because he required Ewan's money.

The latter was indispensable. She wasn't.

Outside the window, Douglas strode to the blacksmithy.

Grinning, he gave Niall a hearty hug. Douglas would marry her, but a man so worthy deserved adoration in return.

A penetrating calmness descended upon Seonaid, and absolute certainty directed her. "Ewan, doesn't Yvette correspond with friends in America still?"

"Yes. Several in fact. One of Fairchild's sons operates her shipping business offices there while the other twin gallivants 'round the world delivering supplies on his ship." He straightened and opened the door for her. "Why?

With a renewed sense of purpose, she swept past. "Because I'm taking control of my life. I'm going to America."

Twenty-Two

Sore as hell from two and a half weeks of digging and hacking in Oakberry's bowels made Jacques much more appreciative of the miners' plight.

He rubbed the crook of his elbow across his sweating forehead, but almost as soon as he wiped the moisture away, more formed, running in sticky rivulets down his face and temples.

The first day, when he'd arrived ready to perform whatever task they set him to, the rugged lot raised their shaggy brows and exchanged skeptical looks. Truth be told, a few muttered, scornful oaths as well.

He wasn't surprised they'd set him to the brutal labor right off. A test of his mettle. One he meant to pass.

They no doubt had assumed the fancy French gentleman wouldn't soil his fine clothes or blister his hands. They'd been wrong on both accounts, and he'd earned their grudging respect.

After working side by side for a day, the men stopped whispering and slanting him wary looks. Now, they almost treated him as one of their own.

Except for his name.

Grinning, he lifted his pickaxe.

Hearing their thick Scots brogue butchering his name, Newton laughingly suggested they call him Laird Jock. And so he was dubbed.

There was something satisfying in working the mine, even more than spying, and certainly more than dallying with rum running as he'd dabbled in for a few months.

Newton had hired on the additional hands and procured a new roll, jib, and steam pump with McTavish's money, but so far, nothing more valuable than cobalt had been found.

Some days, Jacques cursed the mine for her stubbornness to produce an ounce of silver ore, like a virgin nun refusing a chaste peck on the cheek. And other days, he coaxed and cajoled, even prayed she'd share her coveted treasures.

At least mining for silver and cobalt proved far safer than collieries where the constant danger of dust, gases, and explosions lurked.

After seeing the men's acceptance of Jacques, Newton offered to let him share his cabin. *Le Manoir des Jardins* it was not, but Jacques had a pallet to sleep on, food in his belly, and freezing water each morning to bathe with.

Nights proved worse as his mind returned over and over again to Seonaid. Her exterior hid a woman much more complex than she'd first appeared.

His musings inevitably strayed to a sensual nature.

Were her nipples dusky and swollen or rosy and pert? Did she have more tempting moles hidden by her clothing? Would she be shy and quiet when bedded, or a wild temptress?

He laid a fierce blow to the rock he'd been working. The vibration radiated up his arms to his shoulders, the sound ringing in his ears in harmony to the other miners' rhythmic strikes.

What was it about a person that they inevitably yearned for what they couldn't have?

Revealing the truth to McTavish about loving Seonaid mightn't have been the wisest course, but why prevaricate? Nevertheless, McTavish's disapproval stung rather more than Jacques would have liked to admit.

Would McTavish feel differently if Jacques were flush with funds? His French heritage wasn't the issue, for McTavish was half French. Perchance his reputation as a man about town worried McTavish, and he didn't think Jacques capable of faithfulness.

If gifted a splendid woman like Seonaid, only an *imbécile* sought another woman's arms.

He hadn't expected McTavish's stipulation regarding the loan either.

Leave Craiglocky at first light and make no attempt to contact Seonaid again. And don't tell her of our agreement.

When Jacques had seen the light in the outbuilding, he could've no more resisted bidding her *adieu* than cut his heart from his chest. In the end, the pain had been much the same. So, he took his anger and frustration out on Oakberry's interior daily.

Soon, he and the others would quit for the evening, and tomorrow was Sunday—the one day the mine didn't operate.

He'd be up at dawn, headed to Craigcutty to look for signs of Fletcher's whereabouts. Jacques hadn't received word from McTavish that the vicar—or whoever the hell he actually was—had been apprehended, and until he did, Jacques would spend every Sunday hunting the rat.

That had been Jacques's one demand before he conceded to leaving Seonaid. McTavish was to keep him informed of the progress in capturing Fletcher.

Until the cur was imprisoned or dead, Jacques couldn't

rest. And he assuredly couldn't leave Scotland. Not when Fletcher posed such a peril to Seonaid. He could do that for her, make sure she never feared the wily, deranged cleric again.

A whistle's shriek pierced the air, carrying into the shaft.

Quitting time. And dinnertime.

Not having eaten since half-past five this morning, Jacques was ravenous.

Ham-fisted Laise pounded Jacques's shoulder, nearly knocking him flat. "I be so ravenous, I could eat a bull by meself."

"Only one?" Jacques quipped, gathering his tools.

Laise guffawed, revealing a missing front tooth. "Aye, empty enough to swallow two whole, that I be."

Considering the quantity of food the hulk downed at every meal, the exaggeration wasn't altogether farfetched.

Stepping into the line of miners filing from the shaft, Jacques fished his once pristine handkerchief from a pocket and wiped his face. Seonaid still retained the other two as well as his coat.

Would she keep them as tokens to remember him by? Or would she vent her anger and hurt by chucking them into the rubbish pile?

Thoughts of her tormented him, her marred face, the sorrow in her eyes as she bravely bid him goodbye.

Who would she marry?

McLean? Another clansman? Or perhaps a peer?

So nurturing and gentle, she'd make a wonderful mother and a thoughtful wife. How Jacques wished he were the man who would see his seed grow in her belly and welcome their children into this world.

He'd like to plant that seed too.

Tripping, he plowed into Laise's broad, sweaty back. "*Pardonnez-moi.*"

Laise grunted a guttural response.

Jacques best turn his thoughts away from Seonaid, at least until he was alone.

His stomach rumbled embarrassingly loud.

Most likely mutton stew for dinner again, along with oat bread and ale. The humble fare tasted delicious, but he did occasionally crave the delectable dishes his chef—*former chef*—prepared. Louis had departed with the other servants and now probably cooked *gratin dauphinois* or *coq au vin* for a fussy *demoiselle*.

Striding out the mine's entrance, Jacques inhaled deeply. He'd learned to appreciate simple things such as fresh air, cleanliness, and a hot meal.

The Highlands held a provincial, rugged beauty far different from France's intoxicating allure. The scenery and people enticed in a rustic, untamed way, nonetheless.

Varying shades and heights of gray, brown, and green trees rose against the craggy, boulder-strewn hill. Narrow paths, like a nest of gargantuan snakes, coiled through the trees, around the mountain's base, and led to the cabins and the mining camp perched serenely below.

Men scurried about the encampment, stacking powder kegs or watering and feeding the mule teams. A few unloaded supplies and rations from two wagons before the cookhouse.

A movement amongst the stout trunks drew his attention. Probably a red deer or a miner seeing to his personal needs. Not a lot of privacy in the shaft to attend to that sort of business.

That night, his belly overly full, Jacques reclined on his thin pallet, covered in coarse blankets and listened to Newton's sonorous snores. In his mind, he strolled through *le Manoir des Jardins's* rooms, one by one.

Jacques first entered the dark, richly paneled library dominated by a grand desk and chair. He vaguely recollected his father bouncing him upon his knee there.

Wandering the rose and jade plant-filled solarium *Mère* had adored, he heard her bevy of birds—long since dead—chirping and tweeting and inhaled the blossoms' sweet perfume.

And meandering the wide terrace at the *château's* rear, he conjured an image of him and Jeanette as small, indulged children playing with their dogs.

Closing his eyes tighter, he mentally ambled into another room. Only this one wasn't empty. He wasn't alone.

Seonaid lay upon his wide bed, her ivory skin glistening in a dozen candles' shimmering light. Her lustrous sable hair lay spread upon golden sheets, her eyes narrowed to slits as she opened her arms and legs to him.

Shouting and cursing roused Jacques sometime later.

Minutes or hours might have passed since his sensual musing seduced him into slumber's arms. The sky remained blanketed in pitch blackness, but loud pops, like gunshots repeatedly firing, rent the peaceful night.

"Bloody hell." Newton scrambled into his clothing as Jacques came fully awake. "Laird Jock. Wake up!"

"*Que se passe-t-il donc?*" The overseer didn't speak French. Jacques lurched upright, his focus riveted on the window. "What the hell has happened?"

"Somebody's lit the powder," Newton shouted, clomping down the stairs.

Only taking the time to yank on his shirt and pantaloons before stuffing his feet into his filthy boots, Jacques tore after Newton.

Men scrambled every which direction, pulling equipment and supplies away from the mine shafts or filling buckets with water to extinguish the fires set to wagons, carts, and a few of the cabins.

Breaking into a run, he charged toward the virgin shaft where the new roll and jig were. The steam pump hadn't been needed yet, and its placement a hundred yards away from the current peril was one less worry.

If something happened to the other two pieces of equipment, though, he could abolish any hope of making something of Oakberry.

And it wasn't simply about him anymore either. These men, their families, all depended upon the mine. Many had mined coal before, and not a man wanted to return to that treacherous profession.

Sprinting toward the equipment, Jacques yelled, "We have to move the roll and jig. Hitch the mules. Hurry."

He skidded to a halt upon spying a half-dozen or more kegs stacked within the shaft's entrance. Flames licked from the cribbing and the vertical support beams as well as snaked along a thick black powder trail leading directly to the equipment.

On the equipment.

Merde.

Squinting, he tried to see through the billowing smoke. Powder kegs also lay under the roll and jig.

Sabotage.

Someone had done this deliberately.

Wheeling around, he waved his arms at the oncoming men. "Stop! Go back. She's going to blow."

Lungs burning, he lengthened his strides into a full sprint, frantic to outrace the igniting powder's evil red streaks.

The explosion's deafening force tossed him high into the air, the scorching blast searing his spine and pelting him with debris and shrapnel. He plummeted to the earth several feet away, ribs cracking, shoulder wrenching, and his head slamming onto the frozen ground.

Blurry blackness swirled, weighing him down as he spiraled in and out of consciousness. Squinting, he blinked to clear his vision of the blood oozing down his forehead, to see the frenzied men talking above him. He couldn't hear them, merely felt searing, agonizing, paralyzing pain.

Everything had been destroyed.

Injured as Jacques was, the truth didn't escape him. He'd gambled and lost. He'd failed. Seonaid would never be his. He'd nothing to live for.

Forgive me, Seonaid. I shall always love you.

Far above him, the sky gradually parted, and a hazy, undulating image appeared.

BLAZING pain stabbed Seonaid in the shoulders and the back of her head. Moaning, she stretched, but her spine felt afire, and a crushing force squeezed her ribs.

Jacques's bleeding face floated across her dream, and in an instant, she awoke.

"Nooo! No! Please, God. No."

Leaping from her bed, she sprinted to her door, and after fumbling with the handle, yanked it open. Running the corridor, her bare feet slapping against the runner, she yelled at the top of her voice, her horrified cries carrying through the maze of corridors.

"Wake up! There's been an explosion. Ewan. Mother. Father. Jacques is hurt."

Doors flew open as her family spilled into the passages, pulling on banyans and night robes, or holding candles, their faces twisted with worry. Hurried footsteps echoed along passages as Dugall, Duncan, his wife Kitta and their twins, Alasdair and Gregor, ran from their wing of the castle. Kitta immediately set to lighting the hall sconces.

Weeping, Seonaid raced to Ewan, still seeing Jacques broken and prostrate on the ground, a hellish fire roaring in the background and the sky lit with flying debris. Gut-churning fear tearing at her middle, she grabbed Ewan's arm. "He's hurt, Ewan. Badly hurt."

Mother rushed to her. "Who is, *chérie*?"

"Jacques." Pride didn't matter anymore. Seonaid didn't care if everyone discovered she loved him. Drawing in a breath torn ragged around the edges from fear, she swiped at her tears. "We have to help him, Ewan. Please. I love him."

These past two weeks, she'd tried to tell herself she'd been infatuated with Jacques, nothing more. That once she arrived in America, she'd forget him. The self-deception hadn't worked.

Ewan finished tying his banyan, concern pinching his features taut. "You're sure the explosion has already happened?"

"Yes. I saw him." She put her fist to her mouth, nearly bent double in anguish. "God, he cannot die. He cannot."

Mother wrapped her arms around Seonaid, making muted, soothing noises. "Hush now. Naturally, we shall send help."

"No, he needs to come here. I think he's burned and..." Shutting her eyes, Seonaid's voice dropped to a whisper. "I don't know what else, but I must tend him."

She'd seen more, much more, but she couldn't voice the horror for that would make it true. Other men had died, their mangled bodies, some dismembered, strewn about the encampment. How could Jacques survive those kinds of injuries?

"I have to help him." Seonaid brushed at her tears. "Don't you see? It's what I'm meant to do."

"Ewan McTavish," Yvette called from their chamber. "You'd better be astride a horse in ten minutes or find yourself another place to sleep." Taking a cue from her mother-in-law, she added, "For the next six months."

Alasdair's initial chuckle stuttered into a strangled cough when Ewan hurled him a heated glare.

Father appeared in his doorway and exchanged a telling glance with Mother. However, she didn't scold him for leaving his bed.

"Father, please." Seonaid wasn't beyond begging. "Tell Ewan he must go." Whirling to Duncan, she implored, "You're his war chief. You've seen severe injuries. Surely you know how imperative it is the wounded are treated directly. Tell him he must leave straightaway."

No one told Ewan anything. He was laird, the McTavish chieftain. He ordered others about, not the reverse.

Nodding, Father rested his somber gaze on Ewan. "Ye need to go, for her sake, Son. She'll nae be able to live with herself if'n ye don't and Devaux dies."

He cannot die. I shan't permit it.

Ewan touched her bruised cheek. "Aye, for you, Seonaid. We'll go."

He swung his sea-blue gaze to the other men. "Be in the bailey in ten minutes. Rouse a dozen clansmen to accompany us. We'll need a wagon." Rubbing his chin between forefinger and thumb, he added, "Gregor knows what is needed."

"Aye, Ewan." Duncan gestured to Dugall and Alasdair. "Get dressed, and then alert the men. I'll meet ye in five minutes."

Gregor was a healer too and, truth to tell, his skills exceeded hers in many ways. But he'd been shot when Isobel had been abducted and hadn't yet fully mended.

Seonaid rounded on Ewan. "No, I have to go. Gregor's still recovering. He can help Mother prepare things here." Tension-induced shivers shook her, and she hugged her shoulders. "Oh, and someone needs to send for Doctor Paterson too."

"We can notify the doctor when we pass through the village."

"I'm nearly my old self, lass, and a ride in a wagon isn't goin' to harm me." Gregor's eyes filled with compassion.

Though truly Ewan's cousins by birthright, Seonaid, her sisters, and Dugall considered Alasdair and Gregor their cousins too.

"Nae lass, that I canna allow." Leaning against Mother, Father shook his shaggy head. "I be guessin' there be carnage I dinnae want ye seein'"

Mother nodded in agreement.

"Seonaid, put on a wrap, then meet Gregor in the salon. You can make a list of the injuries you think Monsieur le baron has, and Gregor can prepare accordingly." Mother shoved her long braid behind her. "I seriously doubt we can have all ready in ten minutes."

"I'll alert the kitchen staff," Kitta said, already dashing toward the stairs.

Mother cast a cautious glance to Yvette's bedchamber. "Yvette, *ma chère*, might Ewan be permitted thirty minutes before he mounts his horse?"

"Only if he rides like the devil once he does," Yvette called. "And I intend to question the others when they return to see if he did."

Ewan nodded. "Let's be about it then." Halfway to his chamber, he hesitated. "Seonaid, if Devaux dies..."

Tears welled, but Seonaid bravely held them at bay, though her heart disintegrated into a myriad of pieces and scattered like particles of dust blown by winter's wind. "Then bring him here. He has no family. No one to bury him. No one to mourn him."

He stared at her an elongated moment, indecision warring in his gaze. "You understand what the explosion means. For him? His future?"

Confusion tempered the others' countenances. She understood perfectly, even if they didn't.

"I bloody well dinna." Father scrunched his face and scratched his stubbly chin.

"It means," Seonaid said flatly, "if Jacques does survive, then the remotest hope I've naïvely harbored that he might marry me has been obliterated."

TWENTY-THREE

Later that morning, Seonaid paced the battlement as she had for the past two hours. Dense fog mantled the meadow and forest, and the sun hadn't risen high enough to burn the low-lying clouds away. Squinting, she searched the misty horizon and strained her ears for the slightest hint of riders.

How far was it to Oakberry Quarry exactly?

She hadn't thought to ask Ewan. Had Jacques mentioned the distance? He might have, but she paid meager attention to such trivialities when with him.

How could she when her very being became consumed with his presence? The timbre of his voice, his unique manly scent, the soft brush of his mustache on her lips?

Touching her fingertips to her mouth, Seonaid battled tears. Oh, if only she could kiss Jacques again.

One last time.

A chamber, medicines, and linens had been prepared for him, and Doctor Paterson had sent word he'd join Ewan's entourage on their way back to the keep. *If* Jacques yet lived.

That knowledge, along with frequent prayers sent heavenward, enabled her to eat a partial piece of toast and sip a cup of tea. She'd need her strength for the extended hours of care she anticipated Jacques would need.

He *was* alive. He must be, else she'd sense it, wouldn't she?

Surely, God hadn't permitted her to see him injured simply to allow him to die. No. He must have wanted her to help Jacques.

Her mantle and pelisse didn't prevent her teeth from chattering, though her fraught nerves and taut stomach, knotted tighter than tangled embroidery threads, might be as much to blame as the frigid weather. One needed a robust constitution to endure Scotland's winters.

Hunching deeper in her mantle, she strove to erase the horrendous vision from her memory. Tears pricked behind her eyelids, but as she'd stubbornly done each time they'd attempted to surge forth these past hours, she forced herself to think of something else.

Jacques playing the pianoforte.

Charging to her rescue.

Trailing his long, slightly calloused finger over her cheek.

Kissing her until they breathed as one and her knees came unpinned.

A disturbance in the distance sent several birds to wing. They circled high above the pinewoods, raucously scolding the intruders into their domain.

Seonaid rushed to the battlement's wall, and with one hand gripping the side, leaned between the coarse gaps in the parapets.

There, on Loch Arkaig's other side, did shadowy specters slowly emerge from the heavy mist?

Yes! Riders, a wagon, and a curricle.

A curricle?

Doctor Paterson.

Jacques lived.

Bolting to the stairs, Seonaid's heart lifted with joy.

He lives. Jacques lives.

As she tore down the flights of stairs, she yanked off her mantle and pelisse, then her bonnet and gloves. She didn't stop to put the garments in her chamber, no time to waste, but tossed them onto a stuffed bench in the corridor beneath Ewan's four times great-grandfather's ugly-as-the-devil portrait.

Breathless, she ran into the great hall to find her Mother and Kitta quietly sewing before the mammoth hearth, enormous enough that a man could stand upright in it with room to spare. A trio of charcoal boarhounds lay sprawled before the spirited flames.

"Mother. They're coming. I saw them, and Doctor Paterson is with them. That means Jacques is alive."

Seonaid ran to the mullioned window. Standing on her toes, her nose practically pressed against the glass, she searched the inner ward as she had as a child, waiting for Father or Ewan to come home.

"I'll tell Sorcha to prepare hot water for Monsieur le baron and food for the men." Kitta slipped from the hall.

Mother joined her at the window and, after wrapping an arm about Seonaid's waist, quietly asked, *"Ma chèrie,* are you up for this?" Her mother's pretty, troubled eyes searched Seonaid's. "If Monsieur le baron is as injured as you say—"

"Yes, Mother. I must do this for him. Surely you can understand." Leaning into her mother's comforting embrace, her familiar perfume a calming essence, Seonaid managed a weak upward turn of her lips. "Wouldn't you do the same for Father?"

"Oui. Without hesitation." Cupping Seonaid's cheeks with both hands, Mother kissed her forehead, then leaned away a mite. "You truly love him, *non?* Why didn't you tell me? Why do you insist on marrying someone else, then?"

Mother might as well have the whole of it.

"Because he cannot marry me, and I was foolishly determined to end my second sight. After last night, however, I've come to appreciate how selfish I've been." She paused as the truth of her words sank in. She *had* been selfish, unforgivably so. "Had I not had the vision about Jacques, I wouldn't have known he needed help. If someday my visions cease, then it will be because God deemed it time, not because of my scheming."

Standing on her toes once more, Seonaid scanned the courtyard.

What was taking them so long?

A hound yipped in its sleep, drawing her attention and a small smile as well. Great, lugging beasts.

She surveyed the hall with new awareness, taking in its stone walls adorned with pennants, ancient shields, and hunting trophies. The minstrels' gallery at the far end, the trestle table she'd dined at her entire life, and the dais where Ewan and Yvette sat for council.

What was *le Manoir des Jardins* like?

Certainly, it must be wholly different from Craiglocky.

She'd seen many magnificent *châteaux* in France, and to compare them to a Scottish castle was rather like comparing a silk wrap to a belted plaid. Only the owner truly appreciated the garment.

Truthfully, she hadn't much considered the history of Craiglocky or Ewan's pride in his castle. The place was drafty, dark, and lacked many of the niceties she'd enjoyed in Paris and London. Yet, she loved the keep and understood Jacques's dedication to his home.

"Why can't he marry you?" Scrunching her brow, Mother swept an elegant hand toward Seonaid. "You're part French and speak the language fluently. You're also gently-bred, intelligent, and would make a splendid baroness."

"Jacques's greatest desire is to save and restore his family home, and the only way he can do that now is to marry an heiress." And still, Seonaid had fallen completely, irrevocably, eternally in love with him. "He's been entirely forthright about his intentions and hasn't encouraged my affections. In fact, being an honorable man, he did his utmost to discourage them."

Frowning, Mother stepped away, her confusion evident. "But the mine?"

Seonaid lifted a shoulder. "Was a risk that didn't bear fruit."

"Ah." The single syllable revealed much more. "And if he recovers? What then, *chérie*?"

"He *will* recover." Seonaid forced herself to speak the other words. "And I'll let him go. Because I must, and because I've made the decision to go to America in the spring and stay with Yvette's friends."

"*Non.*" Mother shook her head as well as the finger she pointed at Seonaid. "I won't allow it. It's too far away."

Seonaid hugged her mother. "Only until my heart heals, and then I shall come home. I couldn't ever leave Scotland permanently."

She would if Jacques asked her.

A ruckus outdoors announced the clansmen's arrival. Seonaid hurried to the door, which Fairchild held wide open. Several tense-faced underfootmen and maids stood ready to lend their assistance.

Intending to meet the wagon carrying Jacques, Seonaid lifted her skirt and started out the door, but stalled in her tracks. Doctor Paterson trotted up the steps, his countenance grave.

He took her elbow and pivoted her indoors. Craning her neck at the plaid and leather-clad men clustered around the wagon, she reluctantly allowed him to tow her into the entry.

"Miss Seonaid, Monsieur le baron requires surgery, and I shall need both Gregor's and your help." He gave her a stern look. "Are you up to the task?"

Not trusting herself to speak, she nodded as Mother tutted in the background and the servants exchanged anxious glances.

He scraped a practiced gaze over her burgundy and cream striped morning gown. "Have you anything older? Something you won't mind ruining? And you'll need to cover your hair with a cap."

"Yes, I'll change at once." She grasped her mother's hand. "Help me, please. It will be faster."

Doctor Paterson accompanied them into the entry, their rushed footsteps resounding off the walls. "Lady Ferguson, we'll require several aprons, linens, as much light as you can provide in the chamber, basins, and a continuous supply of warm water."

Without missing a stride, Mother nodded. "Seonaid saw everything readied, and our cook has been instructed to keep heated water on the stove."

Fairchild stepped forward and gestured to a pair of under-footmen. "See to the candles and lamps at once."

Less than five minutes later, attired in her faded green gown and her hair neatly hidden beneath a lace cap, Seonaid tied an apron at her waist as she fairly ran the corridor to Jacques's room.

Nervous servants waited outside, ready to do as bidden, and Mother hurried to inform Father of Jacques's arrival before going below to oversee the men's meal.

Taking a steadying breath and steeling herself for what she might see, Seonaid rapped once before pressing the latch.

Still, she gasped at the sight before her.

Jacques, his raven hair matted with congealed blood, lay on his stomach, his shredded shirt and pantaloons exposing a myriad of gashes.

God above, *stuff* protruded from some of the wounds.

Doctor Paterson barely glanced up as he waved her forward. He stood to one side of the bed. Gregor, his face creased with concern, the other.

"Monsieur's back is the worst, though he has injuries to his front too. We set his dislocated shoulder at the camp but didn't wrap his ribs. I think at least two are broken. I need to clean and stitch the wounds before I can do that. I believe he is concussed as well, and truthfully, that worries me most." Doctor Paterson did look at her then, sympathy in his kind hazel eyes. "We will do what we can for him, and the rest is in God's hands and Monsieur's will to live."

Her feet leaden, Seonaid forced one in front of the other and slowly approaching the bed.

Only the slow rise and fall of Jacques's back reassured her he yet lived. When she reached him, she held her breath and continued to the headboard, biting her lip upon seeing his beloved, battered face against the mattress.

Dear God.

She whispered in his ear. "Jacques, you're going to be all right. You're at Craigcutty, and the doctor and Gregor are here. I shall stay with you every minute. I promise."

Gregor awkwardly patted her shoulder, and the doctor noisily cleared his throat.

Determined and resolute, she faced Doctor Paterson. "Tell me what to do. Where do I begin?"

"By cutting his clothing away." He handed her a pair of scissors.

~

FOUR NIGHTS LATER, Seonaid jerked awake and bolted upright in the overstuffed chair beside Jacques's bed. The lamp on the bedside table burned low, and a fading fire snapped and sizzled.

The instant confusion and panic upon abruptly waking still thrummed through her.

Morning must be near.

Inhaling a calming breath, she wiped the drool from the corner of her mouth with her kerchief. Gads, she'd really been out. That was what came of barely sleeping, afraid to close her eyes in case he needed something.

Lest he die while she slept.

Seonaid swore he'd mumbled her name. The soft sound had roused her, but except for his chest's rhythmic rise and fall, he lay unmoving.

Four days and nights, and he hadn't stirred a bit. Not even when Doctor Paterson removed a three-inch-long shrapnel piece from his lower back.

Thank God for that. She'd lost count of the number of stitches she'd sewn, the cloths she'd used to wipe Jacques's blood, the tears she cried when no one could see or hear her.

Torn and pummeled by debris, Jacques was damned lucky he'd suffered nothing more than three cracked ribs and the dislocated shoulder, according to Doctor Paterson. And the nasty gash where something hit him on top of his head.

Yawning, she stretched her arms overhead, then uncurled her stiff legs, wincing as pinpricks rushed to the cramped limbs.

Infection was the greatest danger now. Careful not to disturb the bandage encircling his head, she laid the back of her hand against his forehead.

No fever.

She released her pent-up breath, yet her worry didn't subside.

The longer he remained unresponsive, the greater the probability he'd sustained a serious head injury. Unable to help herself, she framed his uninjured jaw with her fingers and kissed his forehead. Rough stubble rasped beneath her hand as she tenderly caressed his gaunt face.

"You must wake up, Jacques. Please, wake up."

After she turned up the lamp and drank cold tea to rinse the foul taste from her mouth, she picked up *Rob Roy*. Wiggling her stockinged toes, she flipped through the pages, searching to where she'd left off earlier.

"I should have marked the page," she muttered. "Let's see, I read something about women having a heart of honor."

"You've such a heart," Jacques croaked.

Issuing a startled squeak, Seonaid dropped the book.

"Jacques," she breathed, unable to quell the rush of tears or the joy choking her. She clasped his scabbed hand. "Oh, thank God. I've been worried sick."

He coughed, then released a guttural groan. "I feel like I've been plowed by a coach and four. A dozen times." He licked his lips and brushed his tongue against his teeth. "And like a herd of swine has taken up residence in my mouth. After rolling in a sty."

"And no wonder. You've been insensate for four days."

Seonaid wanted to rain kisses over his face, to hug him and tell him how much she loved him, but instead she stood, welcoming the floor's sharp coolness.

Closing his eyes, he inhaled a ragged breath.

"Here, drink this. It will help with the pain." She lifted his head as she touched the glass to his lips.

He opened his eyes, and obediently took a deep swallow, his gaze riveted on her face.

When he laid flat again, as she arranged the bedclothes atop his naked chest—a chest lightly matted with fine, black hair and beautifully contoured muscles—he touched her cheek.

"Your cheek has healed."

Then he laid his hand across her heart, and she feared the palpating organ would erupt from her chest.

"I hope one day, *ma petite*"—his words slurred as he struggled to stay awake—"your heart will too."

Never.

"Jacques?"

He'd drifted to sleep, and she gave into impulse and kissed him again. And again.

So much needed saying, but this wasn't the time. When Jacques recovered, and before he left Craiglocky, she would tell him she loved him. Enough to become his paramour if that was the only way she could be his. The only way to have him in her life.

Such a scandal it would cause, but a most splendid one.

Twenty-Four

The next morning, much refreshed after a shave, cleansing his teeth, and a sponge bath, Jacques relaxed against fresh linens and gritted his teeth against the pain radiating from his toes to his hairline.

A servant had opened the heavy green and gold brocade draperies framing the window, and sun spilled into his chamber, casting zigzagged ribbons atop the stone floor and rugs. For propriety's sake, the chamber door remained partially open.

A few minutes ago, Seonaid had entered, bearing a breakfast tray. After setting out the food, she gracefully sank onto the edge of the bed beside him. Smiling, she lifted the spoon. "Open up."

Hiding a grimace, Jacques dutifully swallowed the thin oat porridge Seonaid fed him.

Despite the purplish shadows rimming her eyes—a testament to her constant vigil at his bedside that she'd shyly confessed when he'd awoken—she was a vision with the sun's rays glowing behind her.

Her lace-edged velvet gown, the rich ruby of a fine wine,

enhanced her gardenia-pale complexion, amber-flecked, molasses- brown eyes, and lips tinted the same shade as his favorite dessert—raspberry *flaugnarde*. And they'd tasted as sweet too.

If Jacques closed his eyes, he could still conjure her mouth's dewy lusciousness beneath his.

His stomach grumbled loudly, and she spooned another thin mouthful between his reluctant lips.

If the hunger gnawing at his backbone was any indication, he was hollow to his spine. He'd much prefer a hearty Scottish breakfast, complete with sausage, eggs, and tattie scones.

Throw in toast and bacon too. And strong coffee. Lots of it.

Perchance the brew would help with the relentless hammering against his skull that threatened to sever his head from his neck unless he moved with an ancient decrepitude's feeble slowness.

"I'm not as weak as all that." He was. "Nor in too much pain." *Liar.* "I can feed myself." *Mayhap.*

Scratching his neck, he winced when he encountered yet another row of neat stitches. Was there a part of him that didn't have sutures? Had they used him for a clan-wide sewing social, for God's sake? The threads itched to bloody high heaven.

"Seonaid, truly, I can manage a bowl and spoon."

Shaking her head, she arranged the serviette more securely beneath his chin like he was a drooling infant. "Doctor Paterson said you aren't to exert yourself, else your stitches rip or you disturb your shoulder or ribs."

Such a serious expression she wore, her fine brows bunched together, and her pert mouth contorting as it did when she was vexed or thinking. She scooped another spoonful of the gruel and lightly blew on it.

He hadn't the heart, nor the strength, truth to tell, to argue. Gratitude warred with chagrin until Jacques's misplaced pride silently yielded to her fussing. *Merde*, he throbbed everywhere, and what didn't throb either stung or ached.

Pain lanced his lower back, and he shifted slightly, trying to alleviate the soreness.

"I saw you, Seonaid. Before I lost consciousness, I saw you jumping from your bed and running to the door, calling for help." Arching, he pressed his palm against the ache, then suppressed an oath when he bumped a wad of bandages. "You'd seen the explosion."

Spoon halfway to his mouth, her glowing umber gaze flew to his, her thick-lashed eyes wide with astonishment. "*You* had a vision? Of me?"

"Yes."

She wiggled the full spoon, and he opened his mouth again. Like a damned nestling. What would she do if he chirped? "It's the last thing I remember."

That, and thinking he loved her. How Jacques longed to shout those words and see her beautiful face alight with happiness. But he couldn't. It wouldn't be fair. Especially not now.

Weariness encompassed him, stealing his appetite and the joy he'd experienced in knowing she'd remained at his side.

Everything he'd done had been in vain after all. It would've been better if he hadn't invested in the mine or traveled to Scotland. Hadn't indulged the impulse to stay at Craiglocky and see Seonaid. Hadn't tasted her lips, for she'd spoiled him for wanting other women.

No use impaling himself with self-recriminations. He'd enjoy this time with Seonaid, and once he'd recovered, he'd bid her *adieu*. When he left Scotland, he'd leave his heart behind in the possession of a sprite lass with fathomless coffee-colored eyes.

Stiff from inactivity and the abuse he'd endured, Jacques stretched his legs beneath the bedcovering. God, he needed to move, but it hurt like hell when he did; a conundrum similar to his finances. He needed to sell *le Manoir des Jardins* to pay his debt, but he expected doing so would be excruciating.

As if sensing his discomfort, Seonaid set the bowl aside. "Here, bend over." She leaned him forward, then propped another fluffy pillow behind him. "Is that better?"

"Um, yes. Thank you." Her breasts pressing into his shoulder as she adjusted the pillow, and her intoxicating scent enveloping Jacques, caused an entirely different surge of hunger.

She seemed physically aware of him too, for rose tinted her high cheekbones, and she chatted like a magpie.

"Ewan and a few of the others arrived home yesterday eve. They stayed to help the miners and bury the dead. Mother told me eight men died, and that many more are injured. Several quite severely. Ewan also wanted to investigate what happened."

She collected the serviette before offering Jacques his coffee. "Are you able to hold the cup yourself?"

The glimpse of her creamy bosom she'd inadvertently given him sent his mind straying into dangerous territory. Again.

"Jacques?" Seonaid's face a mask of confused puzzlement, she lifted the cup a couple of inches. "Do you want your coffee?"

"I believe I can manage." Wrapping his hand around the cup, he promptly burned his fingertips.

Before admitting it, he'd gargle with boiling oil, however.

She'd no doubt insist on helping him, and though he was weak as a newborn colt, his body—his groin, more on point— acted of its own accord when she came near.

"I know exactly what happened." He blew on the steaming liquid. "Someone used black powder to sabotage the mine and equipment."

"Sabotage?" Blanching, she fumbled and dropped the silverware onto the breakfast tray she'd been straightening. "Who would do such a thing? Why would they?"

Once he'd taken a sip of the coffee, sighing in pleasure at the pungent heat, he answered. "I don't know yet. I'm hopeful your brother might have discovered that."

"I haven't spoken with Ewan, but this morning I sent word that you'd awoken. I expect he'll be here shortly to inquire about your recovery and fill you in on the details. Doctor Paterson will be here soon too."

A knock echoed outside the partially open door, and she bade, "Come in."

Ewan strode into the chamber, a grin lighting his face. "Devaux, I'm glad you've awoken." He slid Seonaid a sideways glance. "Gave us quite a scare. You look damned awful, I must say."

"Hush, Ewan," Seonaid chastised softly. "Don't listen to him, Jacques. Considering what you endured, you look quite robust."

"*Robust?* Looks like he's been trampled by a Highland cattle herd," Ewan whispered *sotto voce* into her ear.

At her miffed scowl, he chuckled and briefly patted her shoulder as he passed. "Have a seat, Seonaid. I have news you'll want to know as well."

Jacques wasn't altogether sure he wanted to hear what McTavish had to say. He waved his hand at his bed. "I'd offer you a seat, but..."

"At least your humor hasn't deserted you." McTavish leaned against the canopied bedpost and folded his arms.

Seonaid perched primly on the chair's edge that had been her bed for four nights and folded her hands. "I don't mean to seem rude, Ewan, but Jacques needs his rest. He's been up too long already."

Yes, an entire forty-five minutes.

Her practiced gaze roved him, lingering a mite too long on the hair-covered vee exposed by his nightshirt. Jacques hoped to hell McTavish hadn't noticed, but little escaped the hawk-eyed Scot. One reason he'd made an exceptional spy.

Hauling his gaze from her, he met McTavish's censure-weighted expression.

He'd noticed.

Small wonder he'd agreed to allow Jacques to convalesce at Craigcutty given his determination to keep Seonaid away from Jacques. Well, at least he needn't worry about being called out.

Yet.

Scratching his forehead, McTavish's focus gravitated between Jacques and Seonaid. "There's no delicate way to say this. Fletcher was found dead at Oakberry Quarry. It appears he was hiding behind the steam pump, and the explosion tipped the engine, crushing him. I'd bet Craiglocky he's who set the explosions."

Seonaid gasped, covering her mouth with her hand and blinking away tears. Even after what Fletcher attempted, she could feel compassion for him?

Jacques wasn't so noble. He struggled not to shout, *Hallelujah*. He ought to have suspected Fletcher from the start, such was the man's hatred of him.

"I'm glad. That makes me horrid, but I'm glad." A defiant tilt to her chin, Seonaid wadded her skirt. "Good men died because of him. Wives lost their husbands and children their fathers. And Jacques..." Her voice wavered, and she cast her attention to her lap. "He could've died too, and his dreams for the mine have been ruined because of that evil man. I hope even now, he'd burning in the lowest level of hell."

"It also saved me from running him through for touching you." No hint of mercy tinged McTavish's tone. He withdrew a letter from his pocket, and after unfolding it, stared at the fancy parchment for a lengthy moment. "This letter arrived while I was at Oakberry. It's from Bishop Archibald. Give me a moment while I find the passages I want to share."

Seonaid's wide, curious eyes met Jacques's, and he gave a slight shake of his head. He hadn't a clue what the letter contained either.

McTavish ran a finger down the page. "Ah, here it is."

~

I regret to inform you that Reverend Arthur Fletcher was found stuffed down the well on the small farm where he'd gone to call on a former cleric. Always an optimist, Mr. Fletcher still held hope Ralph Huxley would mend his corrupt ways.

After receiving your correspondence, Lord Sethwick, I became alarmed and sent two of my most trusted advisors to Huxley's.

Upon arrival, it was apparent to them, from the disarray and blood within the cottage, that a fierce struggle had taken place. I can only assume Fletcher told Huxley about his temporary assignment to Craigcutty.

Huxley was defrocked a year ago for participating in cruel and unsanctioned practices. Furthermore, I have cause to believe he has a perverse appetite for young girls, though I've never acquired the proof I required to see charges brought against him.

The man is dangerous and unhinged, and I strongly urge you to use utmost caution and to notify the authorities at once so that he might be apprehended.

"WELL, THAT CERTAINLY EXPLAINS A LOT, *NON*?" Jacques tried to stifle his yawn. "I say we're well rid of the lickspittle. Terribly unfortunate for the real Vicar Fletcher."

And the miners and their families. He would deed his share of Oakberry to them to work as a cooperative effort, but the mine was worthless.

"Ewan, Jacques is fatigued." Seonaid hopped up from her chair. "Let's allow him to rest, shall we?"

The struggle to keep his eyes open became colossal, and whatever draught she'd dosed Jacques's coffee with, the precocious minx, made lifting his eyelids virtually impossible.

After drawing the hunter green velvet bed curtains on one side, Seonaid collected the food tray, then waited at the door for her brother.

Was she aware she'd continually used Jacques's given name? Or perhaps she didn't care about the impropriety.

He'd detected a rebelliousness in her he hadn't previously observed. He quite liked it. The spirit he'd suspected lay dormant within her at last had surged to life. Sadly, he wouldn't be around to see Seonaid's transformation.

That McTavish wanted a word with Jacques was apparent from his hesitation, but Seonaid wouldn't budge from the doorway. A rather mulish glint in her eye, she tapped her foot. "Ewan. Aren't you coming? Jacques must rest. Doctor Paterson is expected soon, and I wouldn't want Jacques fatigued. What would the doctor think of my care?"

She was protecting him, and Jacques wanted to laugh and kiss her until she begged him to stop.

"Yes, what I want to discuss with Devaux can wait." McTavish separated himself from the post, and for the first time, real warmth shone in his eyes. "I'm heartily glad you were spared. I'll return this afternoon if you're feeling quite the thing."

"I shall look forward to it." As much as Jacques would enjoy having a tooth yanked. McTavish no doubt wanted to discuss the loan he'd extended to Jacques and the terms of repayment.

"I'll check in on you in a while, Jacques." Seonaid pointed to the bedside table. "There's a bell atop the nightstand, and I'll leave the door slightly ajar. You've only to ring or call, and someone will be in to assist you at once."

At Seonaid's gentle smile, his heart welled. He didn't deserve her love, but by God, he reveled in it, nonetheless. She probably meant to creep in later and continue her watch.

"*Merci.*"

He closed his eyes, welcoming the fatigue engulfing him. At least while he slept, he didn't have to think about returning to France and selling his *château*. Or what he'd do afterward with no home or prospects.

Maybe he'd go to America.

He'd almost fallen asleep when McTavish's hushed but firm voice roused him to wakefulness.

Clenching his teeth against the pain lancing him, Jacques maneuvered onto his side to peer out the doorway. Sweat broke out upon his brow, and he took several shallow, measured breaths. Not the wisest thing to have done. He'd never be able to turn over, and Seonaid would scold him soundly.

She and McTavish stood a few feet farther along the corridor, talking in muted tones.

Jacques strained to decipher their hushed conversation.

"Seonaid, I wish to speak with you about the propriety of you continuing to nurse Devaux." McTavish stood near her, his neck bent.

She smiled sweetly. "Ewan, I'm positive you mean well.

but I intend to spend every moment I can with Jacques until he returns to France, decorum be damned."

"Now see here—" Sternness riddled McTavish's low voice.

She flapped her hand in his startled face. "Don't take that lairdish tone with me."

"Seonaid," he warned. Many a man had cowered beneath the formidable visage now scowling at her, but she plowed on, unruffled.

"I shan't be deterred." Though her voice remained calm, there was no mistaking her steely determination. "I'm not a child, and I understand Jacques's plans don't include me—cannot include me. Still, I shall build a storeroom of remembrances. They won't be what you and Yvette have, but I'll take what I'm able. Would you begrudge me that?"

He touched her shoulder. "I wouldn't see you hurt and cannot think it is in your best interest."

She sighed and bowed her head. "I know, but how do I tell my heart to stop loving him?"

Jacques shut his eyes against her forlorn figure.

How did he tell *his* to stop loving her?

A FORTNIGHT LATER, Jacques stepped from his bath and was in the process of tying his banyan when someone rapped at his chamber door.

Not quite one hundred percent yet, he'd healed sufficiently to dine below this evening in celebration of Lady Ferguson's birthday.

He quite anticipated leaving his miniature prison, although his injuries, rather than a jailer, held him captive there. He scrubbed his palm over his freshly shaven jaw, his attention falling on the book Seonaid had been reading to him.

His warden had been a distinct delight, and every hour in Seonaid's company had been the sweetest of torments.

She'd forgotten her shawl, and he lifted the silk and sniffed, inhaling her unique essence. He battled the temptation to fold the wrap and stow it amongst his things. Sighing, he returned the fabric to her chair. He wasn't a thief.

Jacques had also recuperated enough to depart Craiglocky, but how he could leave Seonaid, even to do what he must in France, he didn't know.

McTavish generously offered to forgive the loan, but Jacques politely declined. He possessed his honor if naught else.

Another rap rattled the door.

"Enter," Jacques called, toweling his hair.

Fairchild opened the door, bearing a salver upon which a letter lay. "Forgive me for the interruption, sir. A letter arrived for you two days ago. However, Cummins, a second footmen, suddenly took ill after accepting its delivery. I'm afraid he quite forgot he'd placed it atop the basket of cheese delivered that same day. Cook just found the missive."

Holding the paper between his white clad thumb and forefinger, Fairchild extended the wrinkled and soiled rectangle. "Again, my apologies, and Cummins begs your forgiveness as well."

"No harm done." Nodding distractedly, Jacques tossed the towel atop the bed as he examined the scrawling penmanship. Not Faucher's precise pen strokes. Curiosity stirred, he broke the seal. He perused the scribbling, his grin growing more pronounced the longer he read.

"Well, I'll be hellfired."

Twenty-Five

"Jacques, what on Earth are you doing out of bed?" Clutching a jar of salve in one hand, Seonaid slapped her other palm to her hip. "It's been but two weeks. Doctor Patterson clearly advised—"

"I cannot challenge you to a game of chess lying abed, can I, *ma petite*?" A sheepish grin curved one side of Jacques's mouth as he sat at a table, a chess set arranged before him. His appreciative gaze roved her a mite longer than entirely proper.

Black, curly chest hairs peeked naughtily above the folds of his banyan.

Her senses hummed in anticipation, as they did whenever she was with him. Still, he might pull his stitches loose, and he should have asked for help walking to the table. She firmed her lips and procured a gimlet stare, earning her another charming smile and a rakish wink.

"Thirty minutes, and then I'll let you tuck me in again, *oui*?" Theatrically clasping a hand over his heart, he cocked his head and batted his eyes at her. "Maybe you can join me, rub my forehead, and sing me a lullaby?"

She burst out laughing. "I'll do no such thing, fool."

Not that she hadn't considered climbing into bed with him more than once while he slept. It probably wasn't altogether healthy the number of hours she'd spent watching him slumber, occasionally daring to hold his hand for a few minutes.

Flexing his shoulders, Jacques half-groaned, half-sighed. "Honestly, I needed to exercise my muscles. They ache from inactivity, and I grew bored too."

He did look much improved this morning. His color appeared normal, except for the array of yellow and green mottled bruises.

"If you show any signs of fatigue whatsoever, it's promptly back in bed for you." As she set the jar down, she checked the clock on the bedside table. "Thirty minutes, and not a moment more. That's plenty long enough. Understood?"

"Thirty minutes would never be enough, *ma belle*."

Sinking into the chair opposite him, his scorching gaze snared Seonaid's, causing her breath to hang suspended and a not uncomfortable heat to envelop her.

Yes, Jacques's recovery progressed quite well.

Sitting at her dressing table and humming a ballad, Seonaid dabbed perfume to her wrists, then between her breasts. As she replaced the crystal topper and eyed her bodice, a secretive smile bent her mouth. A mite more revealing than was typical for her. This gown had been created for her time in London and was amongst her favorites.

For the first time since the mine explosion, Jacques would join the family for dinner tonight, and she wanted to look her best.

Una raised a heavy, gray-tinted brow but kept silent as she

twisted Seonaid's hair into an intricate knot before weaving a gold-threaded, hunter-green ribbon throughout her curls.

The candles' glow caught the luster of Seonaid's freshly shampooed hair. She scarcely recognized the sophisticated woman with sparkling russet eyes staring at her from the oval mirror.

"You needn't frown so, Una. I usually wear perfume."

Every day for the past two weeks.

Seonaid also wore her finest gowns and jewels and took extra care with her appearance. Not once had she visited Jacques with her hair half tumbling down or her garments covered in pet hair and with dirt beneath her nails from tending her herb garden.

"Aye, miss, ye do, but it be the glow in yer eyes and yer constant flittin' about hummin' like an addlepated canary that gives me a crick in my bum." In the dressing table mirror, Una met Seonaid's gaze. "He be completely recovered, ye *ken*."

Una needn't say who *he* was.

Seonaid clasped Una's hand, giving it a reassuring squeeze. "I know. And that means Jacques shall leave soon."

These past two weeks, she'd kept hoping, praying that something would happen to change the inevitable, but nothing had. So, Seonaid braced herself for the day when Jacques announced he intended to depart.

He'd made no false promises, never mentioned either leaving or staying, and she hadn't probed, afraid to disrupt the wonderful accord that had developed between them.

Despite their many hours together, with the door open and a servant nearby to add to the propriety, he'd acted the perfect gentleman, not once trying to touch or kiss Seonaid.

Several times, she'd been tempted to send Maeve to fetch some frivolity or another for a few treasured moments alone with him.

While the dutiful maid applied herself to her mending or

darning, Jacques's eyes caressed Seonaid as surely as if his fingers had. They'd kissed her lips, brushed her cheeks, her neck and breasts, and in his continued silence, she was certain she heard what he dared not voice.

If he had another option—any at all—he'd not leave.

For surely, Jacques had become as enraptured as she. Hadn't he? How could she ever have believed this warm, intelligent man insensitive and arrogant?

But Jacques *didn't* have another choice.

So, as she'd told Ewan she would, Seonaid spent hours with Jacques each day, reading, playing chess or cards, talking, watching him sleep. The time spent with him was neither foolish nor wasted, and these moments were all she'd ever have.

It was better to snatch each memory and lock it in recollection's storehouse to take out and examine later when she felt lonely or despondent than heed prudence and avoid greater heartbreak by staying away.

With each passing day, Seonaid had fallen deeper, firmer, more irrevocably in love. That was why, when the time came, if he wouldn't agree to let her become his mistress, she would let him go without kicking up a fuss.

For if he forfeited his title and family home to live a mediocre life of questionable comfort and status in the rustic, and what many considered uncivilized Highlands, he couldn't be fully content. His happiness took precedence above everything. Even hers.

These memories would have to suffice a lifetime, for she doubted she'd ever marry. Unless she met a man who'd lost his first love as well and was satisfied to wed for companionship and someday, perhaps, have bairns together. She'd love to have children, Jacques's children. But Fate or Providence or God had callously deemed otherwise.

Giving herself a mental shake, she pinched her suddenly

wan cheeks. Time enough to dwell on dour thoughts *after* he left.

An irony borne smile twitched her lips. If she failed to wed, most likely the sight of a seer would remain for the rest of her life. Since the vision that saved Jacques's life, she reversed her stance on the matter. No more had come upon her during the past fortnight either. But should they, she would focus on the benefits.

She stood and shook her ivory silk gauze skirts. The deep green leaf design perfectly matched her hair ribbon, satin slippers, and emeralds glittering at her ears and throat. "Thank you, Una. I like what you did with my hair tonight."

"Ye'll do, I suppose." Despite her gruff tone, Una beamed as she handed Seonaid her gloves.

Seonaid hugged her. "I'm aware you worry for me, but don't. I'm happy, and I know what I'm doing."

"*Hmph*, I dinnae ken about that." Nevertheless, Una returned her hug, then gave Seonaid's cheek an affectionate peck.

Later, on her way to America, tucked in her ship's cabin, Seonaid would mourn her loss and add her tears to the ocean's salty depths. But for now, Jacques—and the possibility of making a new memory or two—waited below.

Eager to see him, she hurried down the steps. His recovery had been quite remarkable, if a jot swifter than she'd have preferred. Oh, it wasn't that she didn't want him well, but that meant he'd be leaving, and his joining the family tonight suggested he was fit enough for travel.

Another few days at most, and then she must face bidding him goodbye.

Seonaid shook her head to dislodge the rueful thoughts.

Reaching the lower floor, she smiled. Laughter resonated from the great hall, and Jacques's harmonious baritone rang loudly. She hadn't asked him if he also sang. Given his talent on the pianoforte, and his melodious speaking voice, she shouldn't be surprised if he did.

"Ah, there you are." His humor and leg restored, Father winked and beckoned her forward. Other than a mild, lingering stiffness that Doctor Paterson assured them would end the more Father exercised the limb, he walked almost as if there'd been no break. "Ye are exceptionally lovely tonight, lass." He winked and waggled his eyebrows. His expression acquired a more serious mien. "Our guest looks fit as a fiddle too."

Surrounded by Alasdair, Gregor, Dugall, and a couple of clansmen, Jacques raised his head. His gaze melded with Seonaid's across the hall. When the others shifted to see what he scrutinized, he flashed her a rakish smile. That smile that crinkled his eyes with a man's hunger and stripped her bare the same instant.

She ought to be affronted, but the heady warmth suffusing her simply made crossness impossible. When had she become utterly lost in him?

His weight had suffered during his convalescence, and the angular lines of his face had become more pronounced. The deep cobalt of his black velvet-trimmed cutaway accented his glossy hair, severe brows, and roguish mustache, the color of a midnight sky hovering above the ocean.

Her heart and stomach quivered. More aptly, bumped around against her ribcage like marbles in a tin. It was unfair, but still delightful, how he upended her composure each time she saw him.

Excusing himself, Jacques strode her way, his elongated strides swallowing the distance across the floor. He swept her a courtly bow, and she suppressed a giggle at his exaggerated politesse. "Sir Hugh, Lady Ferguson, might I steal your lovely daughter away?"

Her demeanor uncharacteristically starchy, Mother arched

a winged brow and looped her hand through Seonaid's elbow. "We're to dine momentarily, Monsieur le baron, but since it's my birthday, we've dancing planned afterward. You may claim her for one dance. If she's agreeable."

Seonaid gawped and blinked as if her mother had turned cabbage green with purple splotches upon her cheeks.

For certain, I'm agreeable. Most agreeable.

"I shall look forward to it." Assuming a nonchalant expression, Jacques inclined his head, but not before Seonaid glimpsed his confusion.

As he walked away and joined the others taking their places at the table, Seonaid mustered a polite upward turn of her lips.

No doubt he was seated at one end and she at the other.

Mother had decided to keep Seonaid and Jacques apart now?

A wonder she'd agreed he might dance with Seonaid.

"What was that about, Mother? You offended him."

"Nonsense." A false smile upon her mouth, her mother steered Seonaid toward the massive trestle table. The end farthest from Jacques.

Something was afoot.

"Whatever goes on?" Slowing her steps, Seonaid waited for those near them to move away, then drew up short. "You're acting most odd, and if I might be so bold, Mother, ungracious."

To a fellow countryman too.

Her mother was famous far and wide for her hospitality and cordiality. Why the impoliteness, then?

Mother's smile became brittle, and Seonaid feared her face might crack if she bumped her too hard. Something had sent Giselle Ferguson into a rare dudgeon.

Stepping closer, her mother whispered furiously in Seonaid's ear, "Monsieur is leaving. After you cared for him day and night, your affection as obvious as a... a... ram wearing a silk bonnet."

The ludicrous comparison stung. Quite fiercely, truth to tell. Still, Seonaid held her tongue. She had confessed her love for Jacques, and she wouldn't deny it now.

"His leaving isn't a surprise." Though the words stuck to Seonaid's tongue, she strove to appear unruffled. "I expected him to when he recovered fully. Returning to France has always been Jacques's intent."

Lips pursed, her mother cut him an unforgiving glower.

Why was she in a dither? She fairly shook with indignation.

"I was foolish, mistaken, to allow you to spend time with Monsieur le baron. But I hoped when he saw how much you loved him." Her grip tightened on Seonaid's elbow. "That he'd make an offer for you. But he hasn't spoken a word to either Ewan or your father about..."

Seonaid barely stifled her humiliated groan.

"Did you say that to him?"

Father and Ewan claimed their seats. Nowhere near Jacques. He'd been banished to the table's far end, surrounded by rough clansmen.

"Good God, Mother. Tell me Father or Ewan didn't mention their expectations. I'll never forgive them."

"Well, of course not," Mother huffed. "We're not *vulgaires*. But we expected it. *You* should have expected it. And now he is leaving."

Icy suspicion slithered up Seonaid's calves, then twined around her thighs before creeping ever higher to coil around her heart and squeeze unmercifully.

"When? How do you know?"

Acknowledging Father's inquisitive look with a slight tilt of her dark head, Mother finished in a rush. "A correspondence came for him this afternoon, and afterward, he promptly sent word to the stables to have his chaise readied at first light tomorrow."

~*~

Jacques sipped his wine, not tasting the scarlet liquid.

Likely, it was superb stuff, but it held no more appeal than the flavorless food he'd attempted to chew and swallow. After the first three courses, and everything acquired the taste and texture of sawdust, he'd scarcely touched the meal.

The wine he continued to down to dull his irritation, the twinges of his mostly healed body, and the searing ache in the vicinity of his heart.

One thing consumed his attention, and *she* sat at the table's far end. So great did the chasm loom between them, she might as well be on the Earth's other side.

From the darkling glares and accusatory looks hurled in his direction every few minutes by her family, and Seonaid's complete failure to look anywhere near his end of the table, it was apparent they'd learned of tomorrow's departure.

That explained why he'd been seated as far away from Seonaid as they could manage without feeding him in the kitchen.

Or with the livestock.

Even the wall-mounted trophies condemned him with their sightless eyes.

Jacques had planned to tell Seonaid, to explain, but there'd been no time before dinner, and that was why he'd tried to speak with her as soon as she'd entered the hall.

Blast and damn. Bribing a second footman to carry a message to the stables mightn't have been the wisest idea.

McTavish's servant's loyalty might be admired under other circumstances, but the diligent footman robbed Jacques of the opportunity to clarify his sudden departure to Seonaid.

Her hurt and bewilderment lay between them, and she'd retreated behind her bastion of silence and distance, locking Jacques out once more. By God, before he left, he'd have a few minutes with her, even if he had to steal into her chamber to have his say.

Dinner passed in agonizing slowness, and after he continually answered the banal questions put to him with grunts or terse responses, the Scots ignored him.

Finally, Lady Ferguson announced the interminable meal at an end. "Ladies and gentlemen, bear with us a few moments while the hall is made ready."

With skillful and practiced efficiency, she directed the servants. A half-dozen bustled about clearing the table, and others rearranged chairs and benches to the room's parameters, creating a makeshift dance floor.

Rustling and whispering in the minstrel's gallery, followed by the cacophony of instruments being tuned, announced the musicians' arrival. Several men disappeared, no doubt to indulge in a tumbler of brandy, providing Jacques the opportunity he sought.

Seonaid slipped from the hall, and in the commotion, no one paid him any mind as he followed. Head lowered and wiping her eyes, she darted into a chamber beyond the stairs he'd never entered.

Slowly opening the door, he peered inside.

A library.

On three walls, cumbersome, heavily laden bookshelves with sliding ladders rose to the ceiling. The fourth wall boasted an unlit fireplace centered between bay window seats, their drapes drawn wide open, allowing the moonlight to illuminate the room.

The smell of musty, old leather and linseed oil met his nostrils as he quietly shut the door before leaning against its solidness.

Seonaid stood before a window staring into the night, dejection clear in her sloped shoulders and folded arms.

He'd have spared her this hurt, had meant for her to hear from him that he intended to leave.

"Seonaid?"

She stiffened but didn't turn. "You shouldn't be here. It's not appropriate."

Her wavering voice revealed her turmoil. So strong yet vulnerable.

"*Oui*, I know, and I won't stay long, *ma petite*." Jacques joined her at the window, taking in the pristine, star-scattered sky. The Highlands felt closer to the heavens than France ever had. He touched her arm. "I received a letter today—"

Abruptly facing him, she held up her palm. "It doesn't matter. You must do what you must do, as must I. I shall cherish the past fortnight and the time we've spent together, and I'm truly glad you're fit enough to travel this soon."

She shifted to move past, but he wrapped his fingers around her slender arm. "We cannot part like this. You don't understand."

He saw his own anguish reflected in the beleaguered gaze she raised to his before she closed her eyes, the fan of her lashes dark against her pale cheeks.

"I do understand," she murmured, scarcely more than a pained whisper. "And I promise you, I truly wish for your happiness. I do."

"And I yours." He brushed his thumb over her cheek, wiping away a telltale tear. "*Mon Dieu*, Seonaid, surely you must know by now that I love you. I want to marry you. If you'll have me."

She gasped and clutched his arm, her eyes round and confused in the nebulous light. "But you must marry an heiress. To save your home."

Lightly pressing his lips to hers, Jacques drew her into his arms, then leaned his forehead against hers.

"Wherever you are, Seonaid, *is* home. These past weeks, I've come to realize *le Manoir des Jardins* is but an elegant house. I loved the place because my family had lived there for generations, and it held many precious memories." *Dark ones too.* "I felt guilty for wanting to put aside the responsibility. For wanting to have a family with you here in Scotland."

"Jacques, there's nothing I want more, but are you positive? You're a baron. You'd be sacrificing so much. Everything, in fact." Seonaid wrapped her arms around his waist and rested her head against his chest. She fit neatly beneath his chin, as if created for him. "Even though I love you, I cannot ask you to give that up. Still, I'd go with you. As your mistress."

"*Non.*" He tilted Seonaid's chin up as he lowered his lips to hers. "Nothing is too much to sacrifice for you, and I'll gladly relinquish everything as long as you say you'll be my baroness."

A slight nudge of his tongue and her mouth parted. He plunged deep into her sweetness, savored her taste, her scent, his passion burgeoning. Their tongues entangling, he grasped her derrière and lifted her to his hardness.

Moaning, she writhed against him, sliding her hands through his hair.

"How can I bear to leave you?" Trailing kisses from her mouth to her neck, Jacques gently bit her earlobe.

"Why are you then, Jacques?" Leaning away, she shoved against his chest. "Mother mentioned the letter too. Is that why?"

"I'm leaving to sell my *château, ma petite.*" He dipped in for another quick taste of her mouth. "My man of business has found a buyer. And there are a few sentimental possessions I wish to collect."

"But Jacques—"

"Shh." Placing a finger over her lips, he cocked his head, listening. They'd been gone from the great hall too long. Someone was bound to become suspicious at their prolonged absence.

Casting a wary glance to the door, she whispered, "Did you hear something?"

He nodded. "I thought I heard a noise in the corridor, but I must have been mistaken."

"The letter you received contained the offer?" Still slightly breathless, she patted her hair as he combed a hand through his, calming the strands she'd mussed at his nape.

"*Non,* the offer to buy *le Manoir des Jardins* came in a letter weeks ago." He hunched a shoulder. "I don't know who the buyer is, though I have a pretty strong inkling. It matters naught, however."

Not anymore. He might not be able to wish Carnot happy of the place, but making a new life with Seonaid in Scotland mattered far more.

She stopped fussing with her wayward tendrils and stared at him, doing that cute thing with her mouth. In the dim light, reading her expression proved difficult. "I don't understand. You received an offer weeks ago but have now decided to accept it? Because you've realized you love me?"

"*Non, ma petite.*" He drew a finger across her collarbone, and she shuddered. "I've known I loved you since Paris. It is the real reason why I came to Scotland and was so desperate the mine be profitable."

Seonaid laughed and stood on her toes to smooth his hair. "Now you're telling mammoth taradiddles."

"I don't tell tales." Growling in mock anger, he grabbed her, tickling her ribcage. "One kiss, and I was wholly captivated, *mon amour.*"

"Stop." Giggling and twisting, she struggled to free herself. "Someone will hear, Jacques."

"Let them." He kissed her nose and hugged her close. "I want to announce to everyone tonight that we're to marry."

Applause sounded before the door swung open, revealing the Fergusons and McTavishes, each sporting idiotic grins.

"Took yer sweet time. I be afeared I might have to help ye along." Holding a candelabrum, Sir Hugh marched into the room, his gait only slightly lopsided.

The rest of the eavesdroppers surged in after him.

Mon Dieu.

Precisely how long had they been listening at the door?

Jacques eyed McTavish warily. He didn't relish being called out by the superior swordsman, simply because McTavish harbored a misplaced notion that he needed to defend his sister's honor.

Nothing in the Scot's manner suggested he was eager to run him through, and Jacques relaxed a mite.

Seonaid clutched his hand. "Father, Mother, please say we have your blessing."

"*Oui, chérie.*" Mother rushed to embrace her. "I shall like having a countryman as a son-in-law, and we can announce your betrothal at the Valentine party."

Dugall crossed his massive arms and grinned. "What was in today's letter that made ye rush to leave if'n ye want to wed Seonaid?"

Jacques boldly encircled Seonaid's waist, pulling her to his side. "The letter was from Oakberry Quarry's overseer. The explosion exposed a rich vein of pure silver. I'm a wealthy man, and I intend to make Scotland my permanent home."

Seonaid smiled up at him, a knowing glint in her eye.

"Exactly as the vision I had of you in Paris predicted."

EPILOGUE

One year later

Languidly waking, Seonaid smiled into her pillow as delicious sensations swept her. Jacques lay pressed against her back, nibbling her neck as his practiced hands explored her breasts and the oh-so-sensitive area at her woman's core.

Arching into his stiffness nudging her buttocks, she fairly purred in contentment. Wifely duties were quite one of her most favorite activities.

And since they'd moved into Heather Garden House—a miniature version of *le Manoir des Jardins*—last month, they'd sought their pleasure in quite a number of unusual places.

Likely scandalized a servant or two unbeknownst to them too.

"*Bonjour, mon amour.*" His stubble and mustache rasping against her neck sent a shudder rippling from shoulder to hip. "Did you sleep well?"

Yes, an exhausted, satiated sleep after a solid hour of vigorous bed sport last night.

"Good morning," she gasped as Jacques entered her.

Coherent thought scattered as he took her to heaven once more.

Later, as she lay sprawled across his chest and ran her fingers through the crisp black hair, she sighed.

He brushed her hair from her forehead. "What is it, *ma petite?*"

"For years, I wanted the second sight gone, and now that it is, I find I miss it." Even if the visions hadn't always been exactly accurate. Yvette had indeed given birth to twin girls three weeks early, but she'd breezed through the birth and suffered no complications.

"What do you miss about it?" Jacques's fingers played upon her flesh, stirring recently satiated hunger once more.

Seonaid kissed his dark nipple and grinned when he shuddered. "I didn't realize how much I depended on the things I saw beforehand."

Jacques hauled her upward until they lay chest to chest and thigh to thigh, his body hair rubbing deliciously against her wherever they touched. He kissed her, a mind-rattling, reason-shattering melding of mouths, making her squirm with want. "Having regrets already?"

"No. I'd not give up one minute as your wife for another vision." She gave him a naughty look. "But you'd best keep me satisfied, else I become discontent."

He lifted her to straddle his hips, gently lowering her over his shaft.

"Trust me, *mon amour*. I shall never leave you unsatisfied."

~

I hope you enjoyed
SCANDAL'S SPLENDOR
If you'd like to leave a review, I would be grateful.

Keep reading for a free preview of
PASSION AND PLUNDER
Book 8
Highland Heather Romancing a Scott: Castle Brides
Series...

~

PASSION AND PLUNDER
Highland Heather Romancing a Scot: Castle Brides
Book 8

Tornbury Fortress, Scottish Highlands

January 1819

Life's never predictable.

Lydia Farnsworth forced her stiff lips into a sunny smile and, smoothing the heavy russet counterpane across her father's once muscular chest, refused to acknowledge the sorrow clawing at her ribs.

For his sake, and the clan's too, venting her grief would have to wait until she sought her chamber. Future lairds, especially female chiefs, controlled their weaker emotions.

She inhaled deeply, longing for the crisp outdoor air rather than the stuffy sickroom's fug.

Wasting disease. Heart failure.

My God.

She'd lost Mum scarcely three months ago. Her brothers a mere six months before that. And the man she loved too, though he hadn't died. He might as well have for the grief she'd suffered. And if that wasn't chaos enough, mere weeks ago, her orphaned, American second cousin had arrived.

Unannounced.

And now this awful prognosis?

Wretched, bloody unfair.

Like something from one of Mum's gothic novels she'd kept stashed behind her half-boots within her wardrobe.

Lydia had devoured several as well. In utmost secrecy, of course. Chiefs didn't read risqué novels. Rather, they didn't get caught reading them.

"I'll see Doctor Wedderburn out, Da." She brushed a lock of gray-threaded, bright red hair from her father's pale, slightly damp forehead before kissing him.

Her hair, secured at her nape with a lavender ribbon a shade lighter than her gown, billowed forward.

Da's lips tipped up at the corners, and love glinted in his still brilliant hazel eyes, so like hers. He playfully tugged a tendril of her almost black hair.

"Nae need to look so solemn, lass." He winked. "I dinna plan on cockin' up me toes just yet, ye ken. I still intend to see ye wed and to bounce yer bairns on me knees."

A coughing fit interrupted his raspy chuckle.

Sorrow squeezing her lungs, Lydia passed him a fresh handkerchief.

Doctor Wedderburn waggled his grizzled eyebrows at his longtime friend. "Aye, Bailoch, ye're too stubborn and contrary to point yer knobby toes heavenward without a fight."

Da grunted and scowled, but his feet wiggling the bedding belied any actual annoyance.

Would he live long enough to play with her children?

Doubtful.

Besides, she wasn't even betrothed. Hadn't any prospects either.

Anymore.

Stop it!

Dredging up *that* heartache was pointless and just plain stupid, particularly with Da's looming health crisis. If she also ruminated on her broken heart, she might splinter—fracture into a thousand jagged, miserable pieces.

Lydia had neither the time nor the strength to lose her composure and indulge the pain she'd resolutely suppressed since last spring. Besides, she quite detested moping females, and sulking about in a fit of the blue devils benefited no one.

If hell had a season, she'd just borne several long, unrelenting months, and her torment didn't look to be over soon.

How much more could she endure?

Da stirred again and, though he winced, managed a puny smile.

For him?

I'll endure as much as I have to.

She and Da only had each other now. But God help her, at nineteen, though educated right alongside her brothers and often surpassing them in academics, Lydia wasn't prepared to be the clan's chieftain yet.

Would she ever be?

Did she want to be?

Not now. Not like this.

Even before Colin's and Leath's deaths, Da had trained her, took her into his confidence, asked her opinions, and insisted she speak the King's English with a cultured lady of the realm's accent.

So why did feelings of inadequacy still plague, sharp and frequent?

The harsh, even scathing, whispers about a female chief. That's why.

But proving a woman worthy of such a lofty roll as laird?

Well, that intrigued her mightily.

She'd love to prove the naysayers wrong.

Of course, Da had assumed she'd marry a high-ranking Scot to help her lead, not fall in love with a titled Sassenach. Nevertheless, to honor Da and her brothers' memories, she would accept the role.

If Da did, indeed, name her his successor.

Lydia had made no provision for otherwise, and that included any notion of nuptials.

By God, she'd do well by the position. She would.

She'd have a purpose then, a focus, something to work toward since her dream of marriage—at least a love match— had been ground to dust and the specks blown across the moors by the Highland winter's wild gales.

As she'd sobbed in his embrace after confessing Flynn had married another, Da had gently advised, "Only after a tree's weathered a fierce storm can it claim strength, Liddie lass. Dinna give up on love yet. Ye're too young. Given time, a wounded soul can heal and learn to trust again."

Not hers.

Grief's cumbersome weight pressed cripplingly, and she rotated her stiff shoulders, then kneaded her sore nape.

However, humoring Da couldn't hurt.

"Of course, you'll play with my children." Lydia drew one velvet bed curtain closed against the room's piercing chill, despite the hearty fire snapping a few feet from the bed's footboard.

She grinned and skewed a brow upward playfully. "All eight of them."

"Och, eight, ye say?" Da laughed and then slapped his gaunt chest when he started coughing again. "We'd best find ye a husband soon, and get started then. Ye've nae time to waste. A big, strappin' Scot, like one of those McTavish twins. That Alasdair McTavish, now he be a braw fellow. Keen too."

Flynn hadn't been Scottish.

Mayhap destiny had played a part in his marrying another since Lydia could no more have abandoned Tornbury after her brothers' deaths than Flynn could've forsaken his marquisate.

"A fine, honorable man," Da rattled on, oblivious to her ruminations. "A warrior who can protect ye and Tornbury when I be gone."

She didn't need a man to protect her. Far past time for Da to accept that a woman could, and should, be allowed to do what men had presumed were their exclusive rights for centuries.

The doctor canted his head toward the Italian baroque nightstand. "Take the medicines I left ye, follow me orders, and Tornbury may yet have the pleasure of their cantankerous laird for a goodly while." He rolled his eyes heavenward. "The guid Lord preserve us all."

"Wheesht." Da wagged his hand at Doctor Wedderburn, a faint smile pulling at his mouth. "Stop flappin' yer tongue, and get on with ye. I'll outlive ye by a decade."

An absurd exaggeration, if Lydia had ever heard one. Still, she summoned another valiant smile. "Da, I'll be back in a few minutes, and I'll bring you a tray. Cook made you cock-a-leekie soup and custard. Also, fresh oat rolls."

"I'd rather have a dram or two of whisky, beef collops, and mutton chops," Da grumbled, a scowl contorting his ginger brows. "Me pipe too."

She could use a tot of whisky-laced tea herself.

On second thought, never mind the tea and the teacup.

"No tobacco or whisky," Doctor Wedderburn admonished, shaking his finger before snapping his worn-about-the-seams bag shut. "But each evening, ye may have a half glass of red wine before ye retire."

"I'm no' a confounded half-wit or a droolin' invalid." Da made a disgusted noise, sounding very much like his familiar, disgruntled, bearish self.

Bernard, a rather spoilt tabby and one of the mansion's best ratters, cracked an amber eye open at having his nap disturbed at the bed's foot. He stretched his lanky form and sank his claws into the coverlet before leaping to the floor.

Perhaps her father did feel better. His temper, as fiery as the thatch atop his head, hadn't waned a jot.

Da pounded the counterpane. "I be Bailoch Farnsworth, laird of Tornbury Fortress. And I'll tell ye right now, I winna be stayin' in this confounded bed."

In the process of adding wood to the fire, Lydia dropped a log, launching a cascade of angry sparks. "But Da, you must—"

"My tribe needs their chieftain, daughter. Tornbury canna be seen as weak. I canna be seen as weak.

"Neither of ye breathes a word about me heart, ye ken? Not even to yer Uncle Gordon or cousin Esme, Liddie. I'll be up and about in a day or two. Ye tell anyone askin' ye, I've naught but a wicked bout of influenza."

As she swept ashes from the hearth, Lydia pressed her lips into a grim line. He asked much of her.

His eyes sunken and circled by purplish shadows, Da wilted further into his pillows, yet his commanding gaze held their attention, demanding their compliance. "I mean it."

"Yes, Da," Lydia half-heartedly agreed as Doctor Wedderburn gave a reluctant nod.

Not that keeping silent would do much good.

Concerned murmurs and worried glances had followed the laird these past few months already. A few of the more daring servants and clan members had asked probing questions she'd answered with platitudes and half-truths.

And, by George, she didn't like lying. Even for a compelling reason, as if that excused dishonesty.

Auburn brows pulled tight, Da jutted his square jaw in proud defiance. "I'm no' as feeble as ye think I be."

Yes. He was.

"That's wonderful to hear." His bravado nearly undid her, and she blinked away hot moisture as she escorted Doctor Wedderburn from the chamber.

"I'll be back tomorrow, ye cross old boar. Get some rest." Doctor Wedderburn's gentle insult earned him a rude gesture.

Shutting the heavy door, Lydia drew in a steadying breath. Drawing every ounce of mettle she possessed, she squared her shoulders and faced the doctor.

Hopefully, she appeared collected. Weeping and histrionics wouldn't earn the clan's admiration. Scots honored strength and forbearance almost as much as loyalty.

As they neared the stairs, she slowed her steps, and Doctor Wedderburn raised a bushy gray eyebrow expectantly.

"How long does Da actually have, Doctor?" Swiftly scanning the corridor and stairway, she lowered her voice. "You must understand the gravity of our situation and the clan's precarious position right now. We've no war chief since Lundy drowned."

He'd been on the same ill-fated boat that sank, snuffing her strapping brothers' lives far, far too early.

Doctor Wedderburn's half nod confirmed his agreement.

"And Da hasn't chosen another, nor named his successor as laird. None of us dreamed both his sons would die before him, or that he'd fall ill so early on. And though he's all but told me I'll be the next laird . . ."

The doctor rubbed his nose and puffed out his florid

cheeks. "A year at most, lass. Likely less. Six months would be me best guess."

Anguish lanced Lydia, and for an endless moment, she couldn't speak or draw even a spoonful of air into her lungs.

Her entire family—gone in less than twelve months.

Either she'd been cursed, or she had the most confounded lousy luck. She'd better never wager a shilling at the gaming tables.

Tornbury might be lost with the toss of a die.

Stop feeling sorry for yourself.

"And?" She blinked against the hot tears stinging behind her eyelids. "Yer sure? There truly be nothin'—" She sucked in a shuddery breath. "Nothin' at all that can be done?"

Misery thickened her brogue and stilted her speech.

Da would scold her until her ears glowed red if he overheard. Why must her speech mimic a lofty lady's when his brogue was thicker than congealed porridge?

"Nae." Doctor Wedderburn shook his head. "I'm afraid nothin', except to reduce yer father's stress. Keep him calm and try to prevent upsettin' him."

Far easier said than done.

He suddenly chuckled softly, covering his lips with a forefinger. "I ken Bailoch, though, and he winna be a biddable patient. Ye should be prepared fer him worsenin', perhaps rapidly, if he refuses to follow me directives."

He'll follow them, all right. Even if I have to tie him to his bed, the ornery dear.

Nodding, she swallowed the lump mounting in her throat.

Neither spoke as they descended the stairs and made their way across the parquet floor to the grand entrance.

Gordon Ross, Lydia's maternal uncle, emerged from the study, carrying a short stack of thin books in his gangly arms. He stopped, appearing startled upon seeing her. He cut a troubled glance to the stairs. "How fares Uncle?"

Straight to the point, as always. No "Hello," or "How is your day," or "Such lovely spring weather we're having."

"Da's resting and should be up and about in a day or two," Lydia said. Not precisely the truth, but not an outright lie either.

"Nothing serious, then? He'll recover?" A frown wrinkling his forehead and crunching his black eyebrows, his pewter gaze swung between Lydia and the doctor. He slid the ledgers under an arm, holding them close to his chest. "There's nae need fer concern?"

"Rest assured, laddie, the laird isna ready to topple into his grave just yet." Firming his grip on his medicine bag, Doctor Wedderburn exchanged a conspiratorial look with Lydia. "I'll see ye on the morrow, lass."

He took his leave, and Uncle Gordon's scowl deepened, but whether from the doctor calling him laddie, or because he'd detected the nuance of untruth in Doctor Wedderburn's words, she didn't know.

At the moment, she didn't care, truth to tell.

Not a thing new about Gordon's darkling temper, and, today, she wasn't in the mood, nor did she have the patience to cajole him out of his pout.

"Please excuse me, Uncle Gordon. I promised Da I'd fetch his midday meal. He didn't eat much breakfast and is quite famished."

Slight exaggeration there, but he must eat. He'd grown far too thin in recent months.

"Lydia, ye do ken I want to help ye in any way I can, dinna ye?" Uncle Gordon touched her shoulder, his eyes filled with compassion.

His concern moved her, and she softened minutely.

"Ye've born much, and a woman be fragile. Your delicate constitution isna made to carry such heavy burdens."

And there went her pathetically short-lived empathy. "I assure you, I'm neither fragile nor delicate, Uncle."

He bristled, and quickly masked irritation flickered in his eyes before he schooled his angular features. "I'm nae a fool, Lydia. I ken Uncle be ailin', has been fer a wee while. Time he named a successor, but with yer brothers dead . . ."

~

I hope you enjoyed this free preview of
PASSION AND PLUNDER
Book 8
Highland Heather Romancing a Scott: Castle Brides
Series.

From the Desk of Collette Cameron®

Dearest Reader,

Seonaid and Jacques's story has always been one of my favorites, and I think you'll find this second edition slightly more tantalizing than the first. After all, hard-won love and happy ever afters are so satisfying.

Though I always pronounce Seonaid's name See-Oh-Nade in my head when I'm writing it, the Scot's pronunciation is Shawn-Aide. She's an intelligent, kind lady who isn't sure where she fits in her family or the world. Jacques is a man who is willing to sacrifice everything to save his home—even love.

Those of you familiar with Scottish lore will undoubtedly have heard of the second sight. Some legends claim only virgins can see the future, and I incorporated that folklore into the story. Unfortunately, even in the 1800s, ignorant people believed anyone with such a gift was a witch. Though it wasn't common, there were instances of women accused of witchcraft being burned at the stake.

For those who read French, I had a professional translator review the French text. As I don't read or speak the language, I can only hope it is accurate, and if there are any inconsistencies, I am forgiven. After all, it's the story that counts, right?

Many of the characters in Highland Heather Romancing a Scot: Castle Brides series also appear in The Honorable Rogues® series. You can read the first chapters of all my books for free at **collettecameronbooks.com**.

Hugs,
Collette Cameron®

If you haven't joined Collette's exclusive mailing list click on QR image to sign up! You'll get access to exclusive content, sneak peeks, contests, giveaways, and more...
(P.S. No spam!)

https://collettecameronbooks.com/freegift

Collette loves to hear from readers.
You can contact her via her website: collettecameron-books.com.
Or email her directly at collette@collettecameron-books.com.

You can also follow Collette on social media:
Facebook: https://www.-facebook.com/ColletteCameronNovels/
Instagram: https://instagram.com/collettecameronauthor/
Goodreads: https://www.goodreads.com/collettecameron
Book Bub: https://www.bookbub.com/authors/collette-cameron

Pinterest: http://www.pinterest.com/colletteauthor/
YouTube: https://www.youtube.com/@ColletteCameronAuthor

Giggles are Guaranteed
Collette's Cheris Reader Group

If you love to chat about all things romance-book related and enjoy taking part in fun and engaging live events, contests, and giveaways join **Collette's Chèris VIP Reader Group, https://www.facebook.com/groups/CollettesCheris/,** my exclusive private book group on Facebook.

Giggles are guaranteed!

Hope to see you there,
Collette Cameron®

About the Author

COLLETTE CAMERON®

USA Today Bestselling author Collette Cameron® is renowned for her captivating, humorous, and heartwarming Scottish and Regency historical romance novels. With over 65 published titles, over 1.6 million books sold around the world, and multiple writing awards to her credit, Collette is a well-known author in the world of historical romance.

Readers love her witty and relatable characters including daring rogues, dashing scoundrels, and the strong and spirited heroines who capture their hearts. From the rugged highlands to the refined drawing rooms of Regency England, Collette's novels will transport you to another time and place, where love and adventure are just a page away.

Collette's Sweet-to-Spicy Timeless Romances® are the perfect escape for readers looking for romantic escape, poignant inspiration, engaging humor, and entertaining stories.

Based in the Pacific Northwest, Collette is surrounded by the lush greenery and rainy skies that inspire her writing. She dreams of one day splitting her time between the Pacific Northwest and Scotland. In the meantime, she indulges in her love of all things cobalt blue, dachshunds, chocolate, and of course, crafting her next historical romance.

Blue Rose Romance® LLC
collette@collettecameronbooks.com
collettecameronbooks.com

SEDUCTIVE SCOUNDRELS
A Sensual Marriage of Convenience
Regency Historical Romance

A Diamond for a Duke — Book 1

Only a Duke Would Dare — Book 2

A December with a Duke — Book 3

What Would a Duke Do? — Book 4

Wooed by a Wicked Duke — Book 5

Duchess of His Heart — Book 6

Never Dance with a Duke — Book 7

Wedding Her Christmas Duke — Book 8

The Debutante and the Duke — Book 9

Loved by a Dangerous Duke — Book 10

How to Win a Duke's Heart — Book 11

When a Duke Desires a Lass — Book 12

My Dearest Duke — Book 13

∼

FOR THE LOVE OF AN EARL (Wicked Earls' Club)
A Humorous Aristocrat and Wallflower
Regency Romance Adventure

Earl of Wainthorpe — Book 1

Earl of Scarborough — Book 2

Earl of Keyworth — Book 3

Earl of Renshaw — Book 4

∼

HEART OF A SCOT

A Passionate Enemies to Lovers

Scottish Highlander Historical Mystery

Romance Adventure

To Love a Highland Laird — Book 1

To Redeem a Highland Rogue — Book 2

To Seduce a Highland Scoundrel — Book 3

To Woo a Highland Warrior — Book 4

To Enchant a Highland Earl — Book 5

To Defy a Highland Duke — Book 6

To Marry a Highland Marauder — Book 7

To Bargain with a Highland Buccaneer — Book 8

A Christmas Kiss for the Highlander — Book 9

~

HIGHLAND HEATHER ROMANCING A SCOT: CASTLE BRIDES

A Passionate Enemies to Lovers Second Chance

Scottish Highlander Mystery Romance

Heart of a Highlander — Prequel

The Viscount's Vow — Book 1

The Highlander's Heiress — Book 2

The Earl's Enticement — Book 3

Triumph and Treasure — Book 4

Virtue and Valor — Book 5

Heartbreak and Honor — Book

Scandal's Splendor — Book 7

Passion and Plunder — Book 8

Wishes and Wonder — Book 9

A Yuletide Highlander — Book 10

~

DAUGHTERS OF DESIRE (SCANDALOUS LADIES)
A Romantic Class Difference Forced Proximity
Regency Romance with Aristocrats

A Lady's Scandalous Kiss — Book 1

No Lady for the Lord — Book 2

Love Lessons for a Lady — Book 3

His One and Only Lady — Book 4

Never a Proper Lady — Book 5

Lady Tempts a Rogue — Book 6

~

THE CULPEPPER MISSES
A Humorous Wallflower Family Saga
Regency Romantic Comedy

The Earl and the Spinster — Book 1

The Marquis and the Vixen — Book 2

The Lord and the Wallflower — Book 3

The Buccaneer and the Bluestocking — Book 4

The Lieutenant and the Lady — Book 5

~

THE HONORABLE ROGUES®